FriesenPress

Suite 300 - 990 Fort St
Victoria, BC, V8V 3K2
Canada

www.friesenpress.com

ISBN
978-1-03-910166-1 (Hardcover)
978-1-03-910165-4 (Paperback)
978-1-03-910167-8 (eBook)

1. FICTION, MYSTERY & DETECTIVE, AMATEUR SLEUTH

Distributed to the trade by The Ingram Book Company

THE
COUNTRY
OF THE
BLIND

ELIZABETH
GARLAND

え·l·え

*"In the country of the blind,
the one-eyed man is king—or is he?"*
(Old proverb, modified)

CHAPTER 1

"You bloody rapist! You're getting out of here and now!"

Paul Anstel was shocked into waking. His university roommate, Richard Prius, stood over Paul's bed, face contorted, shouting. As Richard's hands came down to grab Paul's shoulders, Paul sat up and pushed himself away toward the bed's headboard.

"What? What are you talking about? Have you gone nuts?"

Missing his first grasp at Paul, Richard stood up straight.

"I'm not staying in this unit with you. You're going to get out. I'm shutting myself in my room until you leave."

As Richard turned, Paul called after him, "What are you talking about? What rape? Who …?"

Richard turned back. "Sarah. You raped Sarah—as you know, you hypocrite. I've just come from taking her to Health Services. We also called Campus Security. Now get out." Richard left the room, and Paul heard the door to the second bedroom slam shut.

Partly tangled in the sheets and blankets, Paul struggled to his feet. For a moment, he stood with his bare feet on the worn carpeting and ran his hands over his brown hair, shaking his head to dispel the shock. He was wearing only his undershorts, his usual sleepwear. His jeans were hanging over the foot of the bed. He pulled them off the bedstead and stumbled into them, dragging them on with trembling hands. He lurched from his room into the small common room that separated the two bedrooms and, from there, into the bathroom that opened off the opposite side. Shortly, he emerged, crossed back to the bedroom side, and began to bang on his roommate's closed door.

"Richard, I have to speak to you. You've got to tell me what's going on!"

But there was no reply. Paul leaned his forehead against the closed door. "For God's sake, Richard, I never raped anyone." Still, there was no reply.

Instead, Paul heard a loud knock on the unit's main door. A woman's voice called out, "Paul! Paul Anstel! It's Melanie Amahdi here, Residence Manager. I need to speak to you urgently. Please open the door, or I will use my passkey. I have Campus Security officers with me."

Paul made a lunge to the main door and threw it open. "What is going on?" he asked sharply.

The larger of the two men, the one not wearing a uniform, stepped forward and put his foot inside the doorway. "Take it easy. We're just here to talk. You're Paul Anstel?"

"Yes, I am, but I have no idea what's going on."

The woman, Melanie Amahdi, spoke next. "There's been a serious complaint of sexualized violence made against you, Paul. We need to speak to you about it. This is Campus Security Director Blatt, and the uniformed officer is Officer Peradi. I need to explain the campus policy that covers this situation, and the security officers will handle the issue of the complaint. Please let us in."

Paul stood to the side. "Yes, come in." The three walked past him into the common area. Paul turned from the door to face them.

Martin Blatt put his hands into his jacket pocket, more relaxed. He noted that Paul appeared to be no immediate threat, and he was used to dealing with students. This young man, he thought, is either very cool or, more likely, has forgotten all about what happened last night.

"Paul," Melanie began, "you understand that a complaint has been made?"

"My roommate just woke me up. He said something about … about a rape? I can't understand what this has to do with me."

Martin Blatt spoke up. "The complainant …"

"Survivor," Melanie corrected him instantly.

"Right. The survivor is Sarah Yung. She has informed Campus Security that very early this morning—around 2:00 a.m., she thinks—you had intercourse with her without her consent while she was so intoxicated that she was unable to resist or give a meaningful consent."

Paul sat down on the futon that served as a sofa for the common space. "But I was here at 2:00 a.m. I got home about 1:00 and went right to bed."

"The complainant—sorry, Melanie, the survivor—is not certain of the time. It could have been earlier or later. That's not important."

"But I didn't do anything. We didn't have sex at all."

"But you were out with her, drinking," Martin continued.

"Well, she was drinking, but I didn't have much—a couple of beer before we left for the club and one cocktail there."

"So you were sober, but she was not?"

"She was drinking a lot. I helped her home. I tucked her up on her couch, and I left her. She was pretty wasted all right."

"So you saw your chance and took it."

"No, I did no such thing. Look, are the police coming?"

Melanie intervened. "The survivor has not yet decided whether to report your actions to the police. In the meantime, our campus policy requires me to tell you that you must leave residence housing immediately and must not come onto campus until the matter has been investigated."

"But my classes … and I don't have anywhere else to stay. I'm from out of town. I hardly know anyone here."

"We have an arrangement with a local motel. The university will pay for a week's stay; in the meantime, you can find somewhere to live. As far as your classes go, you cannot attend without special permission until the investigation is complete. In most cases, you will not be allowed on campus at all. You can contact your professors by email or phone and see if you can make arrangements for any necessary deferrals. Once the investigation happens and the Sexualized Violence Tribunal makes a recommendation about your case to the President, your situation will be finalized."

"But I did nothing. How can you throw me off campus when I did nothing?"

"We must protect the physical and psychological safety of our community," Melanie continued. "The policy is very clear that in the case of a serious sexualized violence complaint, the perpetrator cannot remain in residence and is normally not allowed on campus."

"But I am telling you that I am not the perpetrator!"

Paul stood up suddenly; Martin immediately stepped between him and Melanie. "Just take it easy, Paul. There's no need to get upset. Why don't you pack a bag, and I'll take you to the motel? Then you can tell me what happened last night, your side of the story."

Paul remained standing. "Look, I'm a graduate student in the law school. I've done nothing wrong. Maybe you do have the right to put me off campus, but I'm pretty sure I don't have to discuss this with you. I want to speak to someone who can give me advice."

"Lawyers are not permitted in the campus process, Paul," Melanie said. "We cannot have survivors revictimized by procedural wrangling and legal technicalities."

"What about my graduate supervisor? She's a faculty member."

Melanie hesitated, but Martin immediately replied, "That would be fine. I know this is all very upsetting. Take your time."

"If you fail to cooperate in the investigation," Melanie stated, "you will be expelled without further procedures. We cannot afford to have the university look like it's protecting perpetrators of violence against women."

"Melanie," Martin intervened, "the young man has had the first step explained to him—that he has to leave campus now. Give him a chance to get some advice before you talk about him not cooperating." He turned back to Paul. "Now, pack that bag quickly. We will call your supervisor. What's her name?"

"And please hand over your residence keys now," Melanie interrupted.

Paul went to the door and picked up a key ring from a wicker basket sitting on a small table beside the door. He removed two keys. He passed them to Melanie. "There's the front door and the unit keys," he said. Then he added in response to Martin, "My supervisor's name is Professor Alice Gordon. Her campus local is 5068, and she's usually in her office by 8:30."

"Fine," Martin replied, "I know Alice. I'll see she gets a call as soon as I drop you off."

I have chosen to start here because this accusation seemed to begin the drama that was to evolve over the next two weeks and shape the lives of many in our community for long to come. "Community!" What a false picture that presents of who we were in those days, ten years ago. The year was 2017, and the word "community" was popular. "University community; residence community; law school community" —oh, we were very free with the word. But unless you take "community" to mean imposing conformity to protect self-righteousness, privileges, and reputations, you have no idea what we meant by it.

But what really is the beginning? Which makes me reconsider. I suppose if I were trying to give you readers the whole truth, I might try to set my opening scenes in some past time when, shaped by culture and fuelled by dreams of revolution, our "community" evolved into that struggling mess. But that would not make a true story either. Rather, it would reshape the truth of events by imposing upon them one ideology or another. I have no wish to do that. We had plenty of those efforts then. When these events began, I was part of this community, which embraced a life that we were certain was far, far superior to the prejudices and bigotry of the past. How we got there is not a story I am able to tell.

Readers—if you ever exist—should not take my statements in the last paragraph to mean I am not speaking the truth in these pages, but most of it is, inevitably, the truth of the blind. Let me explain: Some of what I report here is my own experience; some, the experience of others who have told me details of what they did and knew in those days; and some only surmised and imagined as I try to understand how what happened could have come to be. But, as the reader will see, we lived in the country of the blind, and it is no wonder that I struggled—still struggle—to understand. So I will not attempt any historical or theoretical analysis that could only distort. I will tell the story of what happened as plainly as I can, and at the end, perhaps, readers will understand why.

But I now think I must take you back a day earlier, to the day on which the application for promotion and tenure of Dr. Elizabeth Maryfield, then an Assistant Professor in the Marjorie Ataskin School of Law, was being discussed in Alice Gordon's office.

THE DAY BEFORE.
WEDNESDAY, OCTOBER 19, 3:30 P.M.

Dean Haverman sat in Alice Gordon's faculty office on the office floor of the building that housed the Marjorie Ataskin Faculty of Law. Alice, reading glasses perched half-way down her nose, sat behind her desk and put down the piece of paper she had just read.

"You want me to chair this year's Promotion and Tenure Committee?" she asked.

"Yes, yes indeed. Absolutely." Hartman Haverman, known generally to his friends and colleagues as "Hart," cleared his throat and fidgeted.

"I feel that your experience and your solid scholarly credentials are just what we need, especially this year. Now, I know you always have a heavy committee load—it's a problem for our senior women faculty—but I am prepared to give you a unit's teaching release next term if you can undertake this job now. The deadline for submission of materials comes up next week."

"And the only case we have this year is Elizabeth Maryfield, her tenure application?"

"Tenure and promotion," Hart corrected. "But that's right, so it isn't a heavy caseload, but it is one that has to be handled very carefully. We simply can't lose Elizabeth. Her cutting-edge work absolutely could not be replaced."

"From what I see of her CV and of her, that cutting-edge work over the last couple of years has mainly been the production of a show of collages created by her students under the titles 'Law's Violence' and 'Law's Oppression' set up in the school's hallway."

"Ah," replied Hart, "but her creativity and originality are very popular with her students. She's won the students' choice teaching award for the last two years. And I understand she has a book in press."

"Really?"

"Oh, yes, a book of photographs of the exhibits together with theoretical text that discusses the significance of each piece. It's quite impressive."

"Hmm," Alice responded. "And you're quite sure I am the person to chair her committee?"

"Very much so. Absolutely."

Alice sighed, "Well, Hart, you know I make it a rule not to refuse committee assignments. But I'm not really sure why you think I'm the right person."

Hart stood up. "No doubt about it. Thank you so much, Alice. Now, I have another meeting, so I must fly, but do not ever doubt how absolutely I value your help."

"Sure," Alice replied.

Ten minutes later, Alice left her office and walked four doors down the hall to the office of her colleague, George Bush (no relation, as he was quick to tell everyone). She saw the door was open and George bending over his computer. She gave a quick knock. George turned around. He smiled as he saw Alice. At sixty, George was still slim and looked fit and younger than his years. Alice, on the other hand, tended to look her age, which was sixty-three, and she might politely be described as "rounded" rather than fit. Alice had joined the faculty two years before George and had been his mentor. They had, as he liked to say, aged together and weathered over thirty years of faculty politics and decanal insanities.

They were united in thinking the latest addition to the decanal ranks, Hart Haverman, was one of the weaker ones. But then, both Alice and George valued the technical aspects of the law and considered that there was much law could not do and should not attempt. Both believed, as Abraham Lincoln had said, that when courts were used to dictate government policies about questions affecting the whole of the country, democracy was traded for rule by oligarchy. That was no longer the opinion of most of their colleagues or of their Dean. It gave them a common source of both resentment and resistance that had become a basis for a professional alliance.

"Come in," George offered, pushing his chair back from his computer. "What's up?"

"I've just had a visit from our favourite Dean," Alice replied, easing her full figure into the remaining chair. Alice loved to cook and to bake and, unhappily, to eat. While she managed to keep the extra pounds down to about twenty, she could never shed those. In the last ten years, she had become resigned to it.

"Really?"

"Absolutely." Alice smiled, repeating a word Hart used in most sentences, to the amusement of both her and George. "But can you believe this? He wants me to chair the Promotion and Tenure Committee for Elizabeth! Why on earth has he picked me?"

"Well, my dear," George answered, "I think he's made a stunning political move. You know, even though the President is usually bamboozled by the Law Faculty, even he may choke a bit at Elizabeth's file. I mean, law? Maybe if she were in the Faculty of Visual Arts—although, no, her work's much too tame for them. Anyway, if you chair the committee, he wins, whatever happens."

"Wins?"

"Indeed. Wins. Look at it this way. You're a legal scholar of high repute—you've got four books, and you publish in the best journals. If our colleagues on the committee recommend Elizabeth, and they most certainly will, your reputation may be enough to carry the day. If not, and if the President balks at the tenure or the promotion, then Hart can blame you and those who cannot understand the 'cutting edge' of new legal scholarship; those arch enemies of equality and social justice."

"Oh," said Alice. "So I'm either the Judas goat or the scapegoat. What a great career opportunity. Say, George, have you still got any of your scotch left in your bottom drawer?"

"New bottle, bought yesterday. Close the door; I certainly could do with an early drink!"

Alice got up and closed the door. She noticed that George looked tired. "Problems?" she asked.

George smiled slightly. "Andrew's left me," he said.

"Oh George, I'm so, so sorry. What happened?"

"It's the sad old song: what I wanted, he didn't."

"But you were getting married."

"Apparently not," George responded as he poured them each a generous two fingers of scotch. "God, sex is hell. I think I'll try celibacy for a while."

"Oh George, you must be devastated."

"No, only crushed. Look, Andrew pointed out very clearly on his way out the door that marriage simply reinforces the heterosexual world view: monogamy, the family structure, and that, in turn, betrays what he called the 'queer ethos' of revolution. Unfortunately, what I want, what I've always wanted, is just normalcy. Someone to come home to, to cook dinner with, to watch TV with in the evenings, to complain to about my work. I want to matter to someone. I can't see why I didn't know that Andrew was drifting away. It was obvious that he never wanted any of that, but he put up with it for a while until he found someone better to move on with. I didn't matter to him one bit. But it hurts." He took a large swig of his scotch.

Alice sipped hers. "I know what it's like to be trashed. When Adam left me, he said, 'But I just don't love you any more.' Love? Thirty years of marriage, fidelity, and raising two children—isn't that love? But not to him."

"Cheers, Alice. To better days. Although with Hart as Dean, we're not likely to see them!"

"So true," Alice replied.

"You know, I likely wouldn't have gotten tenure with my politics if I hadn't been gay. Now I wonder if even that would save me."

"You're a fine scholar, George, and an excellent teacher."

"True, but no one cares any more about that either. How many students sign up for Elizabeth's course in feminist legal thought to make her collages? I hear she's got a waiting list. Now my seminar in Contract Drafting—well, Hart tells me if I don't get another three students, they're going to cancel it on me. Then I'll have to teach another of the big enrolment classes with all that marking. Look, enough of this. Let's finish our drinks and have dinner together."

"I have to feed my cat and …"

"God, is 'feed my cat' like 'I have to wash my hair'?"

"No, you silly man. I really do have to feed my cat. But what I was going to say is that I've got a big pot of Bolognese sauce simmering in my Crock-Pot at home. Come over and help me eat it. Save my freezer from another jar—I always cook too much. And I've got vegetables for a salad and cookies for dessert."

"Sounds lovely. I'll bring a great bottle of Chianti."

WEDNESDAY, OCTOBER 19, 7:30 P.M.

"What on earth were you thinking of, putting Alice Gordon in charge of my committee?" Elizabeth Maryfield set her beer bottle down hard on the kitchen table.

Hart looked up from mixing the salad. "Don't be upset. It's brilliant. She's a well-respected scholar, even though from another generation, with all the problems that entails."

"Right. And most of those problems lead to her hateful attitudes to women, gays, minorities—and to me and my work. If you think that she won't use this chance to stick the knife in, you're mad."

"But listen, Lizzie …"

"And don't call me Lizzie. It makes me sound like an axe murderer. Although, right now, if you were my father, Hart, I'd take an axe to you. I can't believe you would be so stupid."

"Elizabeth. Listen. The committee writes a single report. You know it will be in your favour because we've made sure that all the other members are absolutely committed to social justice and equality. She may disagree, but as chair, she will have to faithfully transmit the committee's—I repeat, the COMMITTEE'S—recommendation to the President. And the President will know it came from a committee chaired by someone he thinks is sound. I've thought a lot about this. I don't think Alice will even try to scuttle your application. Why should she? She's part of the old guard that's leaving. So maybe she doesn't want to retire just yet. But she doesn't want to be shunned by her colleagues either. She'll keep her mouth shut and let the committee do what they do."

Slightly mollified, Elizabeth picked up her beer again. "I still think it was a stupid risk. You could have put Sheehy Donovan on as chair. She supported my manuscript with Academy Press right down the line, gave it a fantastic review. 'Brilliant resistance to the hegemonic patriarchy and the sexist, homophobic bigotry of our system,' she said."

"But Sheehy is still only an Associate Professor, sweetie. Her voice won't count as much with the President. No, trust me, this is absolutely the best way to handle the situation. Alice will have to support the work of the committee she chairs. And the President will listen to her."

"And what if she whispers in his ear that the committee was wrong? What if she privately contradicts the committee's findings? Or what if she insists on some referee who shares her outdated thinking? Even a single negative letter could hurt me."

"Alice won't go behind the committee's back. She'd think that was dishonourable." Elizabeth snorted. "No, I mean it. She thinks of herself as a good university citizen. She'll play the game. That's something we can count on. And as for referees for your case, the thing to do is to make sure you line up your supporters and get a full list before the committee as soon as possible. Most of the committee members will be happy to take your suggestions. If Alice can come up with some oldsters who might see things differently, she won't have the chance."

Elizabeth took another sip from her beer. "I'm still not happy. But I do see that you think you've got a good solution here to the narrow-minded administration's reluctance to engage radical and progressive work.

"Hart," she continued, "I know you think I'm obsessed with this, but my work is what matters. I look at the mess we white settlers have made of everything—our society, the oppression, the cruelty, and the hate. We've built nothing but forms of power designed to keep people powerless. And until we break this—until we can hold up the mirror to this privilege-bearing, repressive university and all it has stood for in the past, our world can never be free. We can never achieve our deepest needs for equality. My work shows the obscenity of power, and the university hates it because it sees itself reflected in that obscenity."

Hart set down the salad tongs and put his arm around her shoulders. "I know, sweetie. And we'll do it. You'll get tenure and your promotion, and work like yours will be the future of our profession."

THURSDAY, OCTOBER 20, 8:15 A.M.

Sarah Yung sat in the examining room shivering, partly with cold, as the paper robe she was wearing gaped open at the back, and partly as the aftermath of her tears. She had stopped crying for the moment, and she was now sitting up, her legs dangling over the edge of the raised examination table. The woman doctor in jeans and a green T-shirt, with a picture of Che Guevara on the front, was making notes on paper held to a clipboard. Anne Mason, the university Personal Safety Coordinator, sat on a chair nearby.

"What birth control are you using?" the doctor asked.

"I didn't … I don't … I'm not on the pill. We just use condoms. I mean, I'm not seeing anyone regularly, so I don't …"

"So none," the doctor noted, writing. "Well, this guy didn't bother with a condom, so I'm noting here that you should be given Plan B on the way out. We have a stock, and it's pretty effective. You know what that is, don't you?'

"The morning-after pill?"

"Right."

"I don't know. I mean, it's not likely I'm pregnant, and couldn't I wait and see?'

"If you wait and see, then it will be too late for this to work. And if you are pregnant, it would mean an abortion, which will be tougher than this. Take the pill."

Sarah began to cry again. Anne got up from her chair and provided another Kleenex.

"All right, if you think I should."

"You definitely should," the doctor continued. "And you should report this to the police."

"I don't know. I need to talk about it first. I'm a law student. I know what happens to women who report rape. I don't want to go through that."

"Sarah," Anne began, "the university will give you support. You can be assured that the man who did this is already on his way off campus. I've got an appointment for you at Counselling once you're finished here. You're safe, and you will be looked after. You should think about the police, but you don't need to do anything right now."

"I need to speak to one of my professors. I'm supposed to be doing a presentation in her class tomorrow. I just don't think I can, but it counts for my mark, and I can't miss it."

Anne continued, "In this case, the university will grant you an academic concession. You won't lose the mark. We'll speak to the faculty member involved and arrange either for you to do it later or for the requirement to be waived. Who is it?"

"Dr. Elizabeth Maryfield, in the Faculty of Law. I'm also her research assistant this year, and I was supposed to meet her this morning at 10:00."

THURSDAY, OCTOBER 20, 8:35 A.M.

Alice unlocked her office door just as the phone stopped ringing. Her message light immediately began to flash.

She put down her bag and the stack of books she was carrying on the desk and undid her coat. She noticed the time. Five minutes behind schedule, but she and George had stayed up talking and finished off both his bottle of wine and some of her best brandy. He had left his car in her driveway and taken a cab home. By that time, she had felt in no shape to prepare for her ten o'clock class, so she had been more rushed than usual this morning. Fortunately, the class was a first-year Property class, and the material was basic. She had risen a half-hour early and reviewed the reading assignment and her notes before leaving for her office.

She hung up the serviceable navy raincoat and picked up the phone, pressing the voice mail button.

"Alice, it's Martin Blatt, Campus Security, here," she heard. "I'm calling at—oh, 8:35 about—about a matter involving one of your graduate students. It's important. Give me a call when you get this message. 6324. Bye."

Alice had known Martin for almost twelve years. He had come to the university from a big city police force to take up the post of Assistant Director and eight years later had been promoted to Director. There was not much they did not know about the university and its more unpleasant secrets. Alice remembered gratefully Martin's help and companionship after her divorce and after her ex-husband's death. It had been a terrible time. Although their relationship had not endured, it had been a steadying influence, and she still recalled their parting with some wistful regret. She immediately dialled his office number.

"Hi, Alice," he answered.

"Hi, Martin. I must have just missed your call. What's happened?"

"I think you're the graduate supervisor for Paul Anstel?"

"I am. He's in his second year of his doctoral program. Doing very well."

"Not now, he isn't. I just dropped him at the Dogwood Blooms Motel on Pemberton."

Alice knew what that meant: trouble. "Oh no. What's he supposed to have done?"

"Sexual assault, it looks like. We have a complaint from another law student, Sarah Yung, who says he raped her in the early hours of the morning. She's at Health Services at the moment, and Anne's with her. Once she's been seen medically, we have a counselling appointment for her, and then we'll get her full statement. But the basics are that this guy was out drinking with her—claims he didn't drink much, but she did. He brought her home, and it seems she passed out. She came to with him on top of her, but she was too sick and bleary to fight much. She passed out again when it was over.

"When she woke up this morning, she confirmed that there had been intercourse. I gather whoever it was didn't use a condom. Paul's

15

roommate picked her up and drove her to Health Services. They called us. Paul has refused to give us a statement until he has advice, and he's asked for you. You know how the university feels about lawyers in this process. But I told Melanie she should hold off until the boy has at least a chance to think."

"He wants to see me?"

"Yes. Says he won't cooperate until he's spoken to you. Of course, he's not on campus and not allowed to be, so, at the least, he needs some academic help to cover course work while the investigation proceeds. Although, as you know, Alice, in this kind of a case …"

"He's likely to be expelled. I know. Did he say anything? I really find it hard to believe he would rape a girl."

"He says he didn't do it, didn't even have sex with her. So that's a little different. Usually what I hear in this kind of case is that the woman consented."

"Are the police involved?"

"Not yet. Of course, we advise reporting sexual assault to the police, but you know how it is. And it's cleaner and quicker for the victim—excuse me, survivor—to have the whole thing handled by us."

"Okay. Well, this is dreadful news. I'll go and see Paul as soon as I can, but I've got a ten o'clock class, and I can't be there much before noon today. Can you tell him I'll come then?"

"Will do. Just so you know, he's in Room 15A. Sorry to start your day off like this! Good to talk to you, though. You doing well?"

"Well enough. Or I was a few minutes ago."

"I know. These kids … it's such a problem."

"Drink, drink, and drink; sex, sex, and sex. And no idea why their lives aren't working."

"So true."

THURSDAY, OCTOBER 20, 9:45 A.M.

"Sarah, what an appalling thing to happen. This is how our sexist culture destroys people. No woman ever completely recovers from this. The memories will be with you forever. Believe me, I know. That man has destroyed your life."

Elizabeth had received a call from Health Services that one of her students had experienced a health issue and required academic concessions for a presentation she was to do the next morning. It had not taken Elizabeth more than five minutes to extract from the Health Services clerk the basic facts of the case and that Sarah was now on her way to Counselling Services. And Elizabeth had dropped everything from her morning prior to her 11:00 a.m. class to meet Sarah there.

Seeing Elizabeth arrive in the waiting room, Sarah had begun another round of sobs. This time, Elizabeth provided the Kleenex and expressed her shock.

"He's ruined my life," Sarah sobbed. "You're right. Women don't recover from this violence."

"You must write it out," Elizabeth said. "Over the next week, put down everything you feel, every thought of what has happened and how it has affected you. Don't worry about your presentation for tomorrow. Do this instead for your class assignment. This is real, true research into the vulnerability and oppression of women."

"They want me to report it to the police," Sarah said, looking at Anne, who had stepped back to make room for Elizabeth.

"Well," Elizabeth commented, glancing briefly at Anne, "they would advise that. But you know from our work what happens then: you'll be reliving every moment; you'll have to face interrogation; and then if … if … there's a trial, you'll be cross-examined. Of course rape should be reported, but the process allows society to go on ruining your life while, in a lot of cases, nothing happens to the man. Remember, there is no rule about believing survivors. In fact, because of the stereotypes about women's sexual availability, research shows that most judges and juries are inclined not to believe them."

Speaking directly to Anne, Elizabeth asked, "And what's the university doing about this horror?"

"We are following our Sexualized Violence Policy, Dr. Maryfield. The suspect has been removed from residence and prohibited from coming on to campus. The investigation will begin in the next day or two, as soon as we can free up an investigator from their current cases. And a report will be made to the Sexualized Violence Tribunal."

"Yes, yes. I'm very familiar with the policy. So the man who did this is sitting cozy in some nice motel while Sarah endures all these questions."

"Sarah has not yet been asked to give her full statement. As you know, Dr. Maryfield, the policy mandates that the university's first role is to support the survivor."

"Support? What kind of support is it that lets this criminal sit in his motel room and work on his school work for weeks while you do an investigation? Sarah, make sure you take full notes of any questions you are asked. Note the details of how you are treated. We'll hold the university fully accountable for any further distress. And we'll make sure that this rapist never comes near this campus again.

"And, Sarah, remember that I'm here for you. In fact, the whole seminar group will be here for you. We'll focus on your experience as real-life learning. If you haven't done your graduation major paper yet, you should consider making this the topic. I would certainly be happy to supervise you, and it could be hugely influential in reforming how this campus treats survivors like you. And don't worry about the deadline for the research you're doing for me. Your experience here is far more useful. We should talk about doing something together, but all that can wait for now."

Sarah crumpled the Kleenex in her hands. "Thank you so much, Dr. Maryfield. I really, really appreciate your help. I know your advice is the right way to go. I don't want to talk to the police. The university can expel him, and I want to make sure this doesn't happen to anyone else. I promise that I will document everything. I just can't thank you enough for coming down here to help me."

Elizabeth nodded, acknowledging the gratitude. "Who did this, Sarah?"

Anne stepped forward. "Dr. Maryfield, as I said, the university is taking action. I don't think the name of the accused would be helpful right now, and it might be better for Sarah not to give a name."

"Secrecy?" Elizabeth spoke loudly. "This is all a part of blame and shame the survivor. She needs to talk about it; she doesn't need to hide."

"I'm not suggesting 'hiding,' but we haven't yet got all the facts, and …"

"Sarah," Elizabeth interrupted, "do you want to tell me?"

"Yes, I do. I won't be silenced by the administration. It was Paul Anstel. He raped me. He—oh my God! He has the keys to my apartment. What am I going to do? I can't go back there. I can't!"

"He has your keys?" Anne asked.

"Yes," Sarah replied. "We … we were friends, I thought. I thought I could trust him."

Elizabeth stiffened in outrage. "Campus Security will get your keys at once. I will see to it myself." She turned to Anne. "I can't believe you were so incompetent that no one thought to ask the rapist how he got in or that no one thought to ask about a key."

"But I understood he went in with her. The question of keys never came up."

"Well, it should have."

"I'll call Director Blatt at once. Don't worry, Sarah. I guarantee you that we'll get those keys back now."

"I can't go back to my apartment until you do."

"I understand," Anne responded. "Believe me, we'll get on it at once."

Just then, a receptionist emerged from the nearby office. "Dr. Snell is ready for you now, Sarah. I'll show you in."

"You go ahead," Elizabeth said. "I have to get back to a class. But I guarantee that you will have your classmates' support fully and totally. Here," she withdrew a card from her purse, "this has my office and my cell numbers. Call me when you're done all this, or if you want someone with you when you give your statement to Campus Security. That Director Blatt is a misogynist, so don't let him bully you. Call me."

THURSDAY, OCTOBER 20, 11:30 A.M.

Alice pulled her C-class Mercedes up to unit 15A of the Dogwood Blooms Motel. It was an old-fashioned, cinder block, one-storey building, but the exterior had been softened by flower beds running the length of the two wings and several copper beeches planted in the lawn. She knew that the rooms opened up onto a pleasant, covered pool area. While the motel was dated, it was well-kept, and the university often favoured it in emergency housing situations because it was clean, and the owners gave the administration a special rate. She got out of the car and knocked on the unit door.

The door was opened by a tall man, about forty years old, wearing a black suit and a clerical collar. "I'm sorry," Alice said. "I was looking for someone else. I must have the wrong room."

"Maybe not," the man replied. "You wouldn't be Professor Gordon, would you?"

"Yes, I am. And you are …?"

"I'm Fr. Mark, Mark Gibbons. I'm the Catholic chaplain. I'm here with Paul. He asked me to come by and talk. He's pretty distraught. I want to take him for something to eat, as he's had no breakfast or even a coffee, but he won't go until he's spoken to you. Please come in."

Paul Anstel, dressed in the jeans he had pulled on so hurriedly that morning, now topped by a plain black T-shirt, sat in the room's one armchair. The only other chair in the room, a small desk chair, had been pulled back from a brown wooden desk and turned to face the armchair. Paul stood up when Alice came in.

"Professor Gordon. Thank you so much for coming. I can't imagine what you must think. Did Mr. Blatt speak to you?"

Fr. Mark motioned Alice toward the desk chair. "Please, take this seat. I'll perch on the bed."

Alice sat down, as did Paul. "Yes, I spoke to Martin this morning. I hope he told you that I couldn't come earlier because I had a class. I'm terribly concerned about all this. Can you tell me what I can do for you?"

"Well, I need to know about this policy they're using, and I guess I need some support. But before you say anything—I know how the university feels about this kind of thing—you need to know that I did not do anything at all to Sarah Yung. I have no idea what she says happened, but I do remember the events of the evening very well, and nothing at all happened between us, not even a kiss."

"What did happen?"

"Sarah was having some troubles with her folks. They weren't happy with her grades, and her father, who's a lawyer, was really unhappy that she was loading up on theory courses, especially courses from Dr. Maryfield. She's also Dr. Maryfield's research assistant this term, and Sarah just adores her. Anyway, Sarah and I have been friends for a long time. My dad practised with Mr. Yung's firm for a while before he went into litigation work—Mr. Yung's firm only does commercial law and no litigation.

"So she asked if I would take her out—dinner and then some drinks after—just to talk. I wasn't that happy about it. To be honest, I have some sympathy with Mr. Yung's opinions about what a lawyer should study. I mean, I'm a graduate student, and if I stay with law, I'm likely to look for an academic position, so the theory is really important to me. But when I was taking my first law degree, I thought I wanted to practise, so I made sure to take all the basic courses that might get me a job. Sarah doesn't want to do that. In fact, I don't think she likes the law at all.

"Anyway, I went to her apartment ..."

"Does she live on campus?" Alice asked.

"No. She's got a bachelor apartment in that tower just outside the campus entrance. It's only a short walk to the law school."

"So you went to her apartment ..."

"Right. She had some beer, so we sat down and had a drink first. Well, I had a drink. Sarah downed two of them, and then she poured herself a shot of vodka before we left."

"But you didn't join her?"

"No, I didn't. I knew we'd have some drinks after dinner, and I didn't want to start so early. Anyway, after that, we walked down to the pub—Angelo's—and shared some wings and a pizza. I had another beer, and Sarah had two Caesars. We argued quite a bit about her program, so we weren't on the best of terms, but still we followed our plan, and after dinner, we got the bus downtown and went to the Zip Bar. She picked up this guy, Arty, who she said was in her Commercial Law class, and she kind of left me sitting while they danced. He bought her some drinks, and I could see she was getting really drunk. She was still mad at me and wanted me to leave her with the guy she had met up with, but I told her I would see her home. By that time, I was worried she was going to pass out, so instead of taking the bus back, I got a cab and took her back to her place.

"When we got there ..."

"Just a second, Paul. Do you know what time that was?"

"Right. We got in the cab about 12:30. It was about fifteen minutes back to her place, so I guess we got to her door sometime well before 1:00 in the morning."

"Okay. And when you got to her place, was she able to find her key or ...?"

"No, she couldn't do it. She was kind of sagging against me. But I have keys to her place and ..."

"You have keys?"

"Yes, I do. I told you; we were old friends. She wanted someone she trusted to have keys, just in case of some emergency or to water her plants if she was away."

"Where do you keep those keys?"

"On my key ring with my own residence keys, the key to my folks' house, and the keys to the library and the law school front door. You know, like faculty, graduate students have those keys ..."

Alice nodded. "Do you still have Sarah's keys, and are they with you?" she asked.

"Yeah. Campus Security took the keys to my residence unit and to the residence building's front door. They didn't ask me what any of the other keys were, including the law school keys, and I didn't tell them. I suppose they might have taken them too, since they told me not to come back to campus until at least the investigation is over."

Alice nodded again. "The Law Faculty is unusual in giving graduate students keys. But we have only ten or twelve graduate students at any one time, so they and the research assistants all get keys. But Campus Security wouldn't likely think about that. So you used your keys to open the main building door and then her door?"

"Right. And to lock her door again after I left, which was a good thing because she has one of those locks that you have to lock with a key when you leave. I wouldn't have wanted to leave her there with her door unlocked."

"Okay, but just back up to the time when you went into her apartment with her, sometime before 1:00 a.m."

"Well, I used my key to open her door. I helped her inside. She has one of those hide-a-bed things because it's a bachelor—just one big room, a bathroom, and a small kitchen—and the bed was still folded up as it had been when we left. I didn't try to open it up or anything; I just pulled the pillows to the one side and helped her to lie down with her head up. I'd helped her off with her coat and scarf and left them on a chair. Then I pulled down the afghan from the back of the couch and tucked her up in it. I got her a glass of water and put it on the table beside her, in case she needed it. I thought about sitting with her for a while, but she didn't seem like she was going to be sick, so I left, locking the door behind me, like I said."

"Did she say anything to you when you left—good night, for example? Did she seem conscious then?"

"She didn't say good night. I thought she was conscious, but she was pretty out of it. I wasn't really sure if she was awake or not."

"And you didn't touch her? Sexually, I mean?"

"No, I swear I didn't."

"How did you find out about … about what you are accused of?"

"My roommate, Richard Prius. You likely know him because he's doing his masters with Dean Haverman. Anyway, after I took Sarah home, I went back to residence and went to bed right away. I was really tired, and, to be candid, I was also pretty fed up with Sarah and her problems, so I just went to sleep. Richard's door was closed, and I figured he was asleep. Next thing I remember, Richard was standing over me, screaming about a rape. Then the Residence Coordinator and Campus Security showed up, and … here I am. I called Fr. Mark because I needed some support."

Alice turned to Fr. Mark, who had been quietly sitting on the bed. "And you know Paul how?"

"Like I said, I'm the Catholic chaplain, and Paul is a member of the Catholic Students' Association. In fact, he's our incoming President this year."

Alice turned back to Paul. "How did Richard become involved with Sarah?"

"I don't know. I mean, he knows her from school. I think he was in the class ahead of her doing his first law degree, and then he stayed on as a graduate student. I don't know how he knew about the assault. I assume she called him.

"I don't know what to do now. I've been talking it over with Fr. Mark, and there just doesn't seem to be a solution. I can be off campus for a while. I can work on my dissertation, and much of what I need, you know, is online. But I am supposed to be in Dr. Maryfield's

Advanced Research Methods seminar; it's a required course for my program. Well, you know that. I should have done it last year, but you wanted me to take some additional courses in human rights and jurisprudence as background to my topic."

"I believe the policy does provide for some campus attendance under controlled conditions, Paul," Alice responded. "I know that unless and until there is some decision in your case by the university, you are entitled to a range of academic concessions. I can speak to the Dean about that and to Dr. Maryfield about class attendance. I would think that we could organize your class times and your coming and going from campus so that you don't overlap with Sarah."

"Please, do what you can." Paul paused before going on. "Professor Gordon, I don't like to ask, but now that you've heard my side of it, do you believe I'm telling the truth?"

Alice hesitated. "From what I know of you, Paul, I find it hard to believe you would do something like this. I understand that Sarah claims she was unconscious when the attack began, and she was too ill and bleary to put up much resistance. Then she passed out again. I honestly don't know more about her story than that."

Fr. Mark intervened. "I've known Paul for the past two years that he has been in Victoria. I can't imagine him doing such a thing. In my ten years as university chaplain, I've heard a lot of stories about sexual assaults. One thing is always common: the man always claims that the woman consented. How often that's true, I can't say, and, given the amount of alcohol or pot they've usually consumed, maybe neither of them is too sure about it either. But this is the first time I've ever heard the accused totally deny any sexual relationship. I don't think that's what someone would make up if they were just trying to excuse themselves."

Paul broke in. "I would never have thought this of Sarah, but could she have made the whole thing up? Or dreamed it, even?"

"I doubt it. My understanding is that it was clear that intercourse happened," Alice responded. "But I don't know enough of the details yet."

"Oh God, you mean someone did have sex with her—and maybe

no condom?" Paul asked. "But wait a minute. If that's the case, there'll be DNA. I can take a test, and they'll know for sure that it wasn't me."

"Maybe. I don't know what Health Services found. But I can find out. As for DNA, that might be possible, but only if the police are brought into it. That might not be the best thing for you; you could be arrested, charged; you might need bail. It would make the whole thing very public."

"I don't care about any of that. It would prove conclusively that I did not touch Sarah."

Fr. Mark spoke again. "Let's not get ahead of ourselves here. Maybe when Sarah's story is told, we'll find out that this is a mistake or that she isn't sure of anything. Paul, I know you want to clear your name, but the less publicity there is about this the better. Even in light of DNA evidence, there're always people who subscribe to the 'if there's smoke, there's fire' theory. If the police become involved then, of course, you will have the evidence. If not … well, maybe it will be for the best."

Paul looked at Alice. "But if she doesn't report this to the police, or the police don't act, or even if they act and the Crown thinks there's not enough evidence to charge, what will the university do? I don't know much about this policy, but what I've heard around campus suggests that if you're accused under it, you're pretty much expelled."

"I think that's a bit of an overstatement."

"Well, I've also heard that there are at least two lawsuits against the university claiming that the expulsions were unjustified. Rumour also says that you were on the policy committee, and you wrote a minority report claiming that the policy did not meet procedural fairness standards … so do you know how it really works?"

Alice smiled. "Trust a lawyer to ask how it really works. I haven't been much involved with the policy's operation. I was on the committee, as you say, but I did not concur in the majority's report, and after that I wasn't involved. I know there have been about thirty cases brought under the policy in the first two years after it was adopted."

"And how many convictions?"

"They don't call them 'convictions;' it's not a criminal trial. The

Sexualized Violence Tribunal receives an investigation report from the investigation department. Then they ask for comments on the report by the parties involved; after that, they make a recommendation to the President about what should happen."

"Right. That's in the policy. Fr. Mark and I just read it online. But my question is: how many of those brought up under the policy have been referred for discipline, and how many have been expelled?"

"I'm not sure. I know that several of the cases were not actual assaults but what I would call sexual misconduct: sexist jokes, the men's basketball team's annual treasure hunt that listed women's underwear as one of the prizes to find, that kind of thing. In most of those cases, there was a short suspension. Where there has been an actual allegation of sexual assault, I think all the men were expelled."

"I rest my case," Paul smiled ironically. "I'd rather take my chances with the police. But whatever the police do, I'll have to deal with the university as well. Will you help me? With the academic issues, of course, but also with advising me as I go through the process?"

"I might not be your best choice."

"No, you are my best choice. You're a lawyer; you know the policy; you know the university; and you're my supervisor. If I possibly can, I need to come out of this without a stain on my record. I almost chucked my PhD program last year, but Fr. Mark persuaded me to come back this year to finish. If there's any hint that I did this, even if I can finish the degree—and that's unlikely—no university would ever hire me, and some other plans I might have would be ruined too."

"Plans?"

"I'm not sure yet. That's why I'm finishing my PhD. But I think I may be called to be a priest."

"A priest?" Alice was startled.

"That's why I try to keep my life away from the hookup stuff on campus. That's why Sarah thought she could give me her keys and talk to me. She's not Catholic, but she knows I take this seriously, and I would never do anything that would stop me from entering the seminary. But now ..."

"If he's expelled for sexual assault," Fr. Mark continued, "he will be ineligible for admission. No priest could serve in a parish or anywhere else with this in his past."

Alice paused and then went on. "All right, I see the problems. Let me deal with the academic concession issue now, and then I'll call the Campus Security Director—we're old friends—and try to find out some details. I'll also call the Director of the Sexualized Violence Unit and see what's happening and what the trajectory is. But in the meantime, I think you had better give me Sarah's keys. She's bound to remember that you have them. It won't do you any good if Director Blatt has to come here and get them back. I'll call him as soon as I get back and tell him I have the keys."

Paul pulled out his key ring and unhooked the two keys. As Alice stood up, they heard a knock at the door. Fr. Mark opened it, and Martin Blatt stepped across the threshold.

"I'm here for Sarah's keys. Why the hell didn't you give them to me this morning, Paul?"

Paul moved to put the armchair between himself and the Director and gripped the back of the chair. "I really wasn't thinking too clearly, Director. I've just given the keys to Professor Gordon."

Martin, who had been advancing quickly toward Paul, stopped. "Well, you didn't do yourself any good by forgetting it. And having keys to the survivor's apartment sure doesn't help your story."

Alice spoke. "I don't think it has anything to do with his story, Martin, other than to show you that Paul and Sarah were friends and that she trusted him. But you're not accusing him of breaking into the apartment, are you? I thought you told me that he went in with her when he brought her home from the club."

"That's all for the investigators to decide. But Paul still didn't do himself any good by holding on to those keys. Alice, will you give them over to me now?"

"Certainly." Alice passed the keys to Martin.

THURSDAY, OCTOBER 20, 2:30 P.M.

"Just a moment, Alice," Hart said, picking up his phone. "Let me call Elizabeth. Since she's the one being asked to make the primary academic concessions, I think we should hear her thoughts."

"I certainly have no objection to talking to her about it, Hart," Alice responded, "but the policy does state clearly that the university will make every effort to preserve the academic standing of any party to any proceeding under the policy until a final determination is made by the President. I read that as meaning that Elizabeth does have to grant Paul a concession here—in some reasonable form—to enable him to complete his course, unless he's expelled before the course ends. I agree that she needs to participate in negotiating a reasonable way to handle this, but I think you need to make it clear that, at this stage, one way or another, Paul's academic progress has to be protected."

"I'm sure Elizabeth is familiar with the policy, Alice, probably more than you, since this touches her area of academic expertise. Let's hear what she has to say before you ask me to make anything clear to anyone."

Alice looked out the window of the Dean's office while he made the call. Hart had one of the best views on campus. When Beacon Hill University had been founded in 1985, it had taken over a series of apartment and office buildings overlooking the park for which it was named. Once prime residential area, the neighbourhood had suffered setbacks in the early '80s, and the university's founder, the legendary multibillionaire, Matheson McBourne, had donated several buildings that he had been able to buy cheap, even for the day. The university, as originally intended, had remained specialized in Law, the Social Sciences, and the Arts. The Marjorie Ataskin School of Law (named after McBourne's wife, who had been legally trained) occupied the tenth to sixteenth floors of the biggest building. Faculty offices were mainly on the tenth floor, but Hart's took up the full corner of the sixteenth and overlooked the beautiful Beacon Hill Park.

The rest of the sixteenth floor housed the Angelo Branca Law Library. When the school had been founded, library materials were only beginning to enter the digital age. Gradually, the footprint of the library, which originally spanned two floors, had shrunk to less than one, shared with the Dean's spacious office. Now, few print books were necessary, as almost all legal materials were online. Efficient arrangements with the other law schools in the province allowed Beacon Hill students access to more esoteric materials not yet digitized. Much of what had been library space was now devoted to computers and individual study rooms, which could be reserved by small groups or individuals for quiet work.

Shortly, Elizabeth knocked at Hart's open door and walked in without further invitation.

"Hi, Hart, Alice. Oh, is this meeting about my promotion package?"

"Nothing so positive, I'm afraid." Hart looked appropriately solemn. "One of the students in your Advanced Research Methods course needs an academic concession. Alice has been asked by the student—it's Paul Anstel who, you know, is one of Alice's graduate students, doing work in the labour and employment law area—to discuss this with me. And, of course, with you."

"Paul Anstel?" Elizabeth exclaimed. "You are not seriously asking me—me!—to provide academic concessions to a rapist?"

Alice's gaze immediately shifted to Hart and then back to Elizabeth.

"How did you know what the issue was?" Alice asked.

"My research student, Sarah Yung, was his victim. That's how. I spoke to her at Counselling Services this morning after Health Services called me to organize an academic concession for her. She was supposed to be presenting a paper in my Feminist Legal Studies seminar tomorrow, and since she's my research assistant, we had a meeting scheduled this morning. Hart, you really can't ask this of me. Besides, what could I do? He can't come to class …"

"I'm not sure we should rule that out, Elizabeth," Alice intervened. "The policy does provide for special arrangements, if possible. Your graduate course runs from six to nine every Monday evening. The basic law degree program that Sarah is in has no classes scheduled during that time. If she wants to work in the library, she just needs to take the elevator past the classroom floors. She and Paul never need to cross paths."

"So she—she!—must limit her movements while her rapist does whatever he wants?"

"Hardly. We will tell Paul that he must go directly to the classroom and leave the building and the campus directly after. He will be restricted from the library. She will only need to avoid the elevators for a short period and stay off the one classroom floor for three hours a week. It seems reasonable to me."

"And what about the safety of my students in the graduate seminar?"

"We don't have any evidence that Paul is a risk to anyone. You know, Elizabeth, if he were arrested for this—and I don't know if he will be or not—he would be out on bail or on his own recognizance very quickly, and the only likely restriction on him would be a no-contact order for Sarah."

"The psychological safety of students in that seminar is at risk. Most women have experienced incidents of sexualized violence. Having him in the class will be devastating to them. I won't put them at risk."

"But they don't need to know at this point. You'll be there to make sure all is well; we can tell him to avoid contact with other students and not to talk about it. Until the investigation is complete, confidentiality will be respected other than for those who have to know."

"So Sarah is to be silenced? That's what that means: shame and blame, shame and blame. Don't speak; don't tell. But by all means—by all means," Elizabeth's voice took on a sarcastic tone, "protect the guilty."

"I'm not shaming or blaming anyone," Alice responded, raising her voice. "I'm trying to work out what we should do in a very difficult situation. Paul completely denies any sexual relationship with Sarah.

He further says that he would never have done such a thing because they did not have that kind of friendship. Also, he may want to become a priest, so he keeps Catholic moral teachings with respect to sex."

"And that really convinces you?" Elizabeth became even more strident in her tone. "A priest? Someone who thinks women are nothing? Only existing for bearing children? God, this just makes it clearer. Rape's about power, not sex. Here's this man who's fed on Catholic bigotry against women; he has his chance, and he takes it—his chance to enforce his dominance and white privilege on a woman who won't accept the patriarchy."

"Colleagues!" Hart intervened. "This really will not get us anywhere. Elizabeth, I think Alice is correct that we need to arrange, at least for now, academic concessions for this young man. Whether he's guilty is not up to us at the moment. But, Alice, Elizabeth is right as well. This won't be kept confidential if Sarah intends to talk about it, and she's almost certain to tell someone who will tell someone. Anyway, I don't think we can have him in class."

Hart turned back to Elizabeth. "Can you send him notes from your classes by email? Can he complete assignments without going to class?"

"I suppose so. It would make me ill to have to mark any assignments or to have any emails from him at all. Right now, I feel like I've been stepped on and trampled in the gut just thinking about what Sarah's suffering. I should be on sick leave if it wasn't so important for me to be here for Sarah. But I suppose I can have my admin assistant send Paul notes from the lectures. And I can also give him the take-home assignments I used last year. I changed the structure this year to be more in-class work. He could do those for his course credit. But I will not mark any of his assignments for now. When he's expelled, as he should be, this will all be irrelevant."

Hart smiled. "Absolutely. Thank you so much, Elizabeth. Don't think we can't understand how horrible this is for all of us, but," he hastily went on as Elizabeth looked likely to speak again, "especially for women in our community. Don't think I can't understand that. Absolutely.

"Now, that seems to dispose of the matter; I have a meeting to attend. I'll leave it to you both to work collegially to see that our agreement is put in place.

"May I see you, Elizabeth, for just another moment? There's a technical issue we should discuss about the scheduling of your book launch. Alice, thanks for your cooperation and your help. Paul should be grateful to you."

Alice left the office and made her way to the elevators.

Hart turned to face Elizabeth. "Sweetie, that wasn't the smartest thing you've done. I know you don't like Alice, but we agreed last night that she is the ideal person to chair your Promotion and Tenure Committee, and I still think that's right. But please, try not to push her too far."

Elizabeth pulled a Kleenex out of her sleeve and blew her nose. "I'm very deeply distressed, Hart. You should know that. And then to have to listen to that misogynist bitch. You should have backed me up. For two cents I'd go on sick leave right now and leave you to figure out what to do with my classes."

"Now Elizabeth, you can't do that. Now's the time to go for your tenure and promotion. Sick leave only delays things. We've got a great setup, and next year, who knows? My term as Dean will be almost over, and the next Dean …"

"Are you saying you don't think I have a strong case for promotion?"

"No, no, absolutely not. But, sweetie, you know the prejudices of the university. Your work is largely in the area of community activism, and it's still controversial counting that as scholarly work, and …"

"I know. I know. I'm just so distressed."

Hart moved toward her but stopped. "We need to be careful. It won't help either of us to have rumours start. I've got a meeting now, but in half an hour, I can meet you at your place. We can talk. Darling, don't be so upset. I would never have made you take that man back into your class. But I can't ignore university policy."

Elizabeth glared at him and turned to walk out. At the door, she paused. "All right, come over later. But not until eight. I've got some things to do first. You really are such a coward."

THURSDAY, OCTOBER 20, 3:00 P.M.

Alice reached her office and unlocked the door. "Idiot," she thought. "There's no way Elizabeth should be able to bait me like that. But that fool, Hart, believing every word she says about how sick this has made her. And poor Paul. If he really does want to be a priest, it's not likely to happen now. It's pretty clear that Elizabeth will make sure this is all over campus. But maybe he's guilty. After all, what do I know?"

She was thinking so deeply, she failed to notice George standing behind her until he spoke her name.

"George, you surprised me. Come in. I've just had a ghastly day!"

"What happened?"

"One of my graduate students, Paul Anstel, has been accused of a serious sexual assault."

"That's terrible. Have you spoken to him?"

"Yes, and he says he's totally innocent." George raised an eyebrow. "I know," Alice continued, "but something both Martin Blatt and the Catholic chaplain, who's a friend of Paul's, said makes me wonder. They both said that in any sexual assault case they've seen, the man always admits the sex but says the woman consented. That's not what Paul is saying. He says he didn't do it at all, and he's also saying he would submit to a DNA analysis to prove it.

"But then I've had to come from Hart's office and a meeting with him and Elizabeth. Turns out the alleged victim is one of Elizabeth's own students, Sarah Yung. And you can imagine how she reacted to the idea that she should make some arrangements so Paul doesn't lose his grade if he should be allowed to continue here."

"I can imagine."

"And I think she's going to make sure that Sarah broadcasts this all over campus. She seems to think that the alternative is a form of blaming the victim instead of just reasonable discretion. It's pretty clear she will take this up as a rallying point. I hope whoever is handling this from the Sexualized Violence Unit has lots of political smarts, or the university is going to hear about it. But if they do have lots of smarts and Paul is innocent, it won't work too well for him."

"Are we sure a sexual assault actually took place?"

"I understand that we are. But I need to find out the details."

"Do you have to get involved with this?"

"I think I do. I'm going to call Paul now to tell him what we worked out for his seminar with Elizabeth. She agreed to let him finish the course remotely—assuming, of course, that he's not expelled before then. And then I want to phone the Sexualized Violence Unit Director and find out when the investigation will take place. And who will do it. Then I want to phone Martin and see if he has a full statement from the survivor."

"Will he give you the details?"

"I think he will. Paul has asked me to assist him, and the policy does provide for the accused to have support—no lawyers, but support."

"May I point out that you are a lawyer? As well as a professor, of course."

"True, but I am a faculty member, and I don't think they can disqualify me on the basis that I also hold a professional qualification. I think the Faculty Association would have something to say about that."

"Well, make your calls. But when you're done, why don't you let me cook dinner for you tonight at my place? We can talk about it then. You know, obviously if an assault occurred and Paul did not do it, someone else did."

"I know," Alice replied. "I also know that Paul had keys to Sarah's apartment. I wonder if there are other keys around, or what Paul did with his when he went home that night. But before that, I wonder how convinced Sarah is that her attacker was Paul. And how she could have been assaulted and not know who did it."

"Those all sound like good questions. But what about dinner?"

"Thank you, George. I'd like to come."

So it began. Nothing really so unusual in our modern day about these cases. There must have been at least one sexual assault a month in residence—likely worse off campus, but no one cared much about that, since what had to be avoided was the headline, "Another rape on campus." Sexualized violence policies were the flavour of the month—well, the year, really—having been mandated by the government. And countless hours were spent debating, consulting about, and writing those policies. Universities hired sexual violence prevention officers, embarked on elaborate campaigns for educating students about the need for consent in sexual relationships, deplored the need for the criminal justice system to hold trials in which survivors were questioned, and gave more than lip service to the credo that women had to be believed. And the sexual assaults just continued on, as before, but now with the added piquancy of lawsuits from men expelled under procedures that committees of university administrators had designed to shield themselves from unpleasant protests by the activists.

Nothing worked. But we could say we were trying. Yes, we were. We continued promoting, as vigorously as possible, the same strategies that had failed in the past. But since they were the only strategies we were prepared to consider, they must, of course, be right. Graham Greene wrote something to the effect that God doesn't learn from experience, or He would have given up on us long ago. I suppose if it's good enough for God, it's good enough for the modern university.

CHAPTER 2

Sarah let herself into her apartment. Anne, the Personal Safety Coordinator, had dropped her off after her session with Campus Security and offered to come up with her, but Sarah had refused. She had the keys now returned to her from Paul as well as her own. The only other keys she knew about were the building manager's master key and the one she had given to her best friend, Melissa, whose apartment was two floors above. There was no need to be afraid, Sarah told herself, and no need to feel this terrible cramping in her stomach. Dr. Maryfield had said that survivors sometimes felt shame, but there was no reason for that. This was not her fault. Sarah hesitated slightly as she closed the door and slid the safety chain into place.

She looked around the apartment. Even with the chain on the door, she did not feel safe here now. This was her own place, and she had decorated it with much love and care. But she looked across the living room at the brightly upholstered sofa bed and shivered. Slowly, she walked over to it. There, on one of the cushions, was a telltale stain, barely noticeable on the dark blue background: the cushion he had shoved under her hips when …

She recoiled, and as she turned, she saw on the end table by the starkly modern brass lamp the orange and white scarf she had worn the night before: the scarf she had seen wrapped around her attacker's face, Paul's face, when she had opened her eyes.

She turned again and walked to the kitchen nook carved out of the large, square room by a granite-topped island that formed a breakfast bar as well as a divider for the room. Crossing from the carpet to the tile floor of the tiny kitchen, she opened a drawer and pulled out a set of tongs. From under the sink, she retrieved two garbage bags. Returning to her living area, she used the tongs to lift the scarf into the one garbage bag, which she tied tightly. Shaking and partly crying, she wrestled the stained cushion into the other bag. She then hid it behind the sofa in the space between the back of the sofa and the wall. She would face that when she was better, take it to be cleaned, and then, perhaps, replace the sofa, although she cried a little more when she remembered how happy its purchase had made her.

Disregarding her tears, she took the bag with the scarf and the tongs to the kitchen and, opening the garbage pail under the sink, dropped in the bag. After a moment, she dropped in the tongs as well. She closed the lid. Standing up, she began to wash her hands thoroughly—once, twice, three times—before drying them on a paper towel, which she also discarded.

The phone in her purse rang. She pulled it out and answered.

"Hi there, Sarah. It's me, Arty, you know, from the club last night."

"Hi, Arty. What's up?"

"Just wanted to make sure you got home all right last night. I called you a few times earlier today, but you didn't pick up. You were having some trouble standing up when I last saw you!" He laughed a little. "Hey, it happens to us all. But that guy you were with was sure some jerk. He wouldn't let me take you home. We were having a lot of fun, I thought. What a spoilsport!"

"Arty, I'm really not feeling up to talking right now."

"Well, okay, but the weekend's coming up, and I thought we might get together. Pick up where we left off. Have some drinks or maybe some pot."

"Things didn't work out very well for me last night. I … I don't think I want to go out again just now."

"Hey, what happened? Was the jerk no good in bed? You know, I think we could hook up, and you'd have a much, much better time."

Sarah shuddered. "The last thing I want is to hook up."

"So that must have been pretty bad. I'm really, really sorry. Sorry I let you go off with that guy. Paul, wasn't it? But, Sarah, really, I'm not that guy. We were having fun. Maybe what you need is a little fun to erase those bad memories. Get back in the game, you know, as fast as you can. What's life for, anyway?"

While Sarah was holding the phone in one hand, she withdrew a bottle of vodka from under her kitchen cabinet with the other. She opened the upper cupboard door and brought down a glass. Still with one hand, she unscrewed the top of the vodka and poured a stiff shot into the glass. While Arty was talking, she knocked it back in two gulps.

"Maybe you're right, Arty. But not tonight."

"Fine, I have to study for a midterm tonight anyway. What about Saturday?"

"Yeah, Saturday."

"I can pick you up at your apartment, say eight o'clock?"

"You know where I live?"

"Sure. My cousin, Melissa, lives up two floors from you. She told me that you're best friends. I noticed you in the Commercial Law class in early September, and then I saw you go into her building one time when she and I were hanging out. She told me where you lived."

"I don't think I want anyone to come here. The place is a mess; I'm a rotten housekeeper. Let's just meet somewhere."

"Sure. Let's meet at 8:00 in the campus pub. We'll see who's there, and then we can migrate downtown."

"Okay, see you then." Sarah pressed Call End. She wondered how many people Melissa had told where she lived. She examined the safety chain carefully. It was sturdy and securely attached to the wall. Anne had assured her that Paul would not come near her. She said he would stay far away. But Sarah took one of the high chairs from the breakfast bar over to the door and wedged it under the knob. She had read somewhere that this made opening a door almost impossible. After she finished, she poured herself another large vodka and sat down in the blue easy chair facing the door. She cried a few more tears and mopped them up with Kleenex from a box on the table beside her. She was fine, she told herself, just as the psychologist from Counselling Services had said she would be; her tears were for the beautiful home she had lost.

Her phone rang again. She picked it up from the table and looked at the call display, thinking she might decline the call. It was Richard. She answered.

"Hi, Richard."

"Hi, Sarah. Look, I just called to see how you are. It was a terrible thing to happen, and I'm so sorry about it. And I wanted to let you know that Paul …"

"I know. He's off campus, and he won't be back anytime soon. But I live off campus, Richard, and, well, and I'm still a bit scared."

"Anyone would feel like that, Sarah. I just want you to know that I'm here for you anytime."

"Thank you. You were wonderful this morning. How did you know I needed help?"

"Well, I didn't exactly, but when Paul got home, I thought he was behaving funny. Somehow, I just felt there was something wrong. So as soon as I thought it was late enough in the morning, I decided I should come and see if you were all right. When I got to your building, I rang your buzzer three times before you answered. I was getting pretty worried by then, but I never suspected that he had … well, you know."

"Yeah. I couldn't have ever thought it either. I'm glad you thought to come. It was a big help to me."

"Would you like some company now?"

"No, I really want to be here by myself at home and get some rest if I can."

"Okay, I understand. But call me if you need anything I can pick up for you."

"What … what do you think's going to happen to Paul?"

"He'll be expelled. He should be in jail. But at least he'll never be a lawyer or a professor. And as for that job with the Supreme Court of Canada, he can kiss that goodbye."

"I heard you applied for that as well?"

"I did. But there are lots of applicants across the country, you know. Not much chance for me."

"I hope you get it, Richard. You deserve it."

Sarah ended the call and took another sip of vodka.

THURSDAY, OCTOBER 20, 6:30 P.M.

Alice stood in George's living room, scotch in hand, as George checked on dinner in the kitchen. His apartment occupied the top floor of a graceful, old Victoria mansion that had been converted into condominiums. Unlike many of the conversion jobs, this one had been done well. The high ceilings with their fir beams had been left intact, and the beams had been finished in the red stain that brought out the wood's glowing grain. The living room, which George told her had once been the master bedroom, featured an original fireplace made of poured cement and moulded to look like tree trunks entwined with ivy. George had also informed her that this style of work had been very popular in Victoria in the early 1900s when the house had been built, but few examples were now left. George had lined each side of the fireplace with glass-fronted book shelves, reaching almost to the ceiling. These were crowded with books, the titles of which Alice was now perusing.

The fireplace, converted to gas, was lit, and its flames reflected on the polished oak floor, which was mostly bare except for a blue and gold Chinese rug that occupied the centre of the living room. The room was warm and spacious. Gregorian chants played on the first-class sound system concealed in the oak buffet on the opposite side of the room.

"This room is just beautiful," Alice had commented after she had given George her coat and accepted a scotch on ice in a crystal highball glass.

"Thank you. Now, relax for a few minutes while I stir the lamb ragout and add the last ingredients."

Five minutes later, George returned.

"It must be wonderful to come home to such a restful environment," Alice commented as they sat down on the comfortable leather sofa, facing the fire. "And you have such a large selection of books. I love a room lined with books. But I didn't realize you had an interest in philosophy and human rights. You've got a great collection of recent titles."

"Ah, being a commercial lawyer is just my job. Philosophy and human rights—those are my real interests."

"But you don't teach in those areas—or write in them either."

"Well, my interest is a developing one. I will write in the area, I think. In fact, I'm planning that for my next book. Mind you, I haven't got past the concept stage yet."

"There's a lot about you I obviously don't know, even though we've been colleagues for thirty years."

"Not surprising. Being colleagues, or even allies, doesn't mean the same as being friends, and I think we're just now starting to take that step. But of more urgent concern, I hope you won't mind that I've asked another guest to join us tonight."

"Of course not. Who's coming?"

"Fr. Mark, the Catholic chaplain. You told me you had met him today."

"I had no idea you knew him. And I'm very surprised you would ask him for dinner."

"He's the son of an old friend. I've known him since he was a baby.

And why wouldn't I ask him for dinner?"

"Well, Catholics aren't noted as 'gay-friendly,' are they? In fact, maybe except for their Pope, they despise gays."

"I don't think that's quite true. I mean, if I had been born without an arm or had MS, he wouldn't despise me. Why should he despise me for being gay?"

"You're not seriously telling me that your sexual orientation is like being born without an arm or having a debilitating illness?"

"Why not? Most people have two arms; most people are heterosexual. It's no slight to them. And as for debilitating, well, I can't say I've had the happiest of love lives."

"Come on, George, a lot of heterosexual romances self-destruct too. Sexual orientation is who we are in a very profound way."

"True, but Catholic doctrine doesn't teach that one should despise different sexual orientations."

"Well, maybe that's what they say, but as soon as you fall in love—form a relationship with another man—then you're evil."

"No, not evil, but certainly they think acting on a same-sex attraction is a sin."

"So? That's the same thing, after all. You're not giving me that old wheeze about being able to make a distinction between what you are and what you do, surely?"

"Again, why not?"

"But it's totally discredited."

"Funny that sexuality is then the only area of life where that's true. I mean, suppose I stole something. Would you say that because of that act I was necessarily an evil person? Mightn't I be a good person who did something wrong—something I could be sorry for and not do again?"

"But it's different for sexuality, surely. You can't deny your need for love."

"I don't see that it necessarily is that different, Alice. Of course, needing love is more important than needing something material that you might steal. But my actions, even my sexual actions, are not who I am in total, and what I do can be changed, even if who I am cannot."

"I really can't believe we are having this conversation. Do you have any idea what your colleagues or your students would say if they heard even part of this?"

George smiled. "Of course. I'd be mobbed. Students would claim that they couldn't feel safe in my classes. Hart would have my tenured head posted on a pike outside the school. So much for academic freedom, by the way!"

Alice took another large drink of her scotch. "You believe it, my friend."

"Well, you notice I'm not proclaiming this in the law school news-letter or in my next lecture! And I'm talking only to you, who I hope is indeed becoming my friend. But I am trying to tell you how Fr. Mark sees it and that I can understand it and not despise him."

Alice let out a long breath and took another drink. "You're just playing devil's advocate, then, aren't you? I should have known."

George smiled. "I'm not inviting Fr. Mark here to convert either you or me. He called me late this afternoon to check you out. He wanted to know if you could be trusted to help Paul. He really believes in the young man's innocence. I suggested he join us so we could have a strategy meeting tonight." He looked at Alice's glass. "You're looking empty there. Can I freshen it?"

Alice looked with surprise at the almost-empty glass. "Goodness. Well, perhaps better not … oh sure. Please do."

Fr. Mark arrived and, after a few pleasantries, their host called them to the table. Like the rest of the apartment, the dining room was fur-nished with antiques, wood softly glowing by candlelight. The table was covered with a linen cloth the colour of daffodils. Yellow candles in a multibranched candelabra lighted a dinner setting of white modern china, and a bowl of yellow and bronze carnations formed the centrepiece.

After they were seated, the wine poured, and the salad course before them, George opened the topic that was on all of their minds.

"So, Alice, I understand that you were looking into some details of the incident with Paul Anstel. Fr. Mark is hoping he can help as well. While we eat, perhaps you can bring us up-to-date on what you've found out."

"I called Martin Blatt, the Director of Campus Security, and I also called Rebecca Connaught, who heads up the Sexualized Violence Investigations office. Martin was willing to give me some details once I assured him that Paul had officially asked for my help.

"The police are not involved, at least not yet. Martin urged Sarah to report, as did the Personal Safety Coordinator. But as a law student, Sarah has heard a lot of horror stories about women who report rape, as well as what you read in the papers. Many of them all too true, unfortunately. She said she'd think about it, but she didn't seem very willing. George's and my colleague, Elizabeth Maryfield, is supporting her and, I would guess, encouraging her not to go to the police but to rely on the campus process.

"There are a couple of interesting things about the assault. Sarah is convinced it was Paul who did it, but she agrees that, until then, they had not had a sexual relationship. She says that she was barely conscious when she got home. She wonders if someone had put something in her drink. But she also admits that a fellow student, not Paul, was buying her drinks, and some of them were doubles. She doesn't remember how many she had. She has a vague memory of being tucked in on her sofa, but the next thing she remembers is a man pulling off the afghan she had over her and ripping down her panties beneath her skirt. It was very dark in her apartment. Blinds drawn, lights off. She also says that she was wearing an orange and white scarf that evening, and the man had tied it around the lower half of his face. He was also wearing some kind of tight-fitting cap. She says Paul was wearing a wool toque that evening. It was chilly."

"So she really can't say she saw his face?" Fr. Mark interrupted.

"No. And she says that she could not identify the man by his feel or his touch. But remember, she and Paul had never been intimate with each other. She is convinced it was Paul, mainly, I think, because he was the last person she remembers seeing. And, of course, he did have her keys, and he did bring her home. She found her door locked in the morning, and since you need a key to lock it outside when you leave, whoever did it had a door key."

"Did Health Services get semen for possible DNA?" George asked.

"Yes, they did a rape kit, and likely there will be DNA evidence."

"But that solves our problem!" Fr. Mark exclaimed. "We can prove Paul is innocent."

"Only if the police get involved," Alice replied. "And it's against university policy to compel any sexual assault victim to go to the police. Supporting them means that they have to call the shots on the process. That's in the policy.

"The university does not engage in forensic testing. That brings me to my call to Rebecca. She says that it's beyond the university's mandate to engage in testing DNA. And, unfortunately, she tells me that her office's caseload is so heavy right now it will be Christmas at the earliest before an investigator can be assigned to this case. Which means that Paul is off campus at least until then. If it goes until Christmas break, nothing will happen until January. Then the usual investigation process is two or three months, another month to write the report, another month until the deadline for responses closes, and then it goes to the President. That all means that we are looking at spring or summer before this is settled."

"That's horrible," Fr. Mark interjected. "Surely the university can move more quickly."

"That is quick, compared to the criminal justice system," George responded. "But I agree that it's hardly ideal to have a student's future unresolved for such a lengthy period. Alice, can Paul continue with his program in spite of this?"

"I think so," she replied. "I believe the Advanced Research Methods class is his only course requirement. With his student ID, he can log-in to anything online that is in the university's database, and that should cover most of what he needs for his dissertation. I can meet him off campus and continue to direct his research."

"But what about the DNA?" Fr. Mark continued. "I think there are private labs. Even if the university won't do anything, and the police are not involved, surely we can have a private facility do the testing. I know it might require some careful planning to make sure it is clearly objective and that no one supporting Paul tampers with the evidence, but why can't we just go ahead and clear his name?"

"I think private testing is available," Alice said, "in Vancouver, if not here. It might be possible. The only issue, I believe, would be the complainant's consent."

"How does that come into it?" Fr. Mark asked.

"The sample is in the possession of Health Services, but I believe that under provincial law, it's the personal information of Sarah, just as her medical records are. Without a court order, such as the police could get if they were investigating a crime, or perhaps what could be obtained if Paul were bringing a civil suit, the only way Health Services would release the sample would be with Sarah's written consent."

"Then let's ask her," Fr. Mark said. "Surely she wants to be certain. Paul tells me that he and Sarah have been friends for a long time. I can't imagine she would want him to be punished if he's not the guilty party."

"I don't think she's planning on coming to campus for a few days," Alice replied. "Not surprisingly, she's pretty distressed. But I have her law school email, and I will email her when I get home tonight and ask for her consent. Hopefully, she'll see the sense of doing this. I assume Paul is willing to pay for the private testing?"

"I'm sure Paul would be willing to do anything to get his life back," Fr. Mark spoke again.

"Good," George said, "looks like we have a plan, and hopefully this will clear up the issues for Paul. But there will still be the question: If Paul is not guilty, who is?"

"I know," Fr. Mark answered. "And it might be even worse for the young woman not knowing who her attacker was. But that's a question, really, for the police or other investigating authorities. And letting her think that she knows when she's wrong is not a kindness. Truth matters, and it matters to the innocent especially. In this case, I believe that both she and Paul are in that category."

THURSDAY, OCTOBER 20, 9:30 P.M.

Richard Prius sat with his friend, Norman Mann, in the student pub. Since it was Thursday, there was no live band, but hip hop blared from wall-mounted speakers, and two large TV screens showed the football game. A pitcher of beer, half-empty, and a large plate of nachos, half-eaten, occupied the table, along with their glasses and plates. Arty Donovan made his way across the crowded room, avoiding the spills on the bare wood floor.

"Hey, Richard, Norman. Thanks for calling. I was about to lose my mind with that Advanced Real Property material. I tell you, it'll be a miracle if I can squeak through the midterm tomorrow. And Professor Bush is a tough marker, so bullshitting my way through is not likely to work. Boy, did I need a break!" Arty pulled out a chair and poured beer into the remaining empty glass on the table. "Great, you got some food. I'm starved."

"Wait just a minute," Richard responded, pulling the nacho plate aside. "You order your own food. We don't have enough for your appetite!"

Arty laughed, deftly removing a handful of cheese-laden nachos as the plate passed out of reach. "Okay, okay. I'll pay my share. Let's get some wings and some more beer."

"Richard was just telling me about Sarah Yung," Norman said, helping himself to another wedge of nachos. "She's in some of your classes, isn't she?"

"Yeah, sure. But what about her? I saw her last night at the bar. She was pretty drunk and pretty wild. Wow, really hot! But some other guy got to take her home."

"Well," Norman continued, "Richard says that after that, she was raped. He took her to Health Services this morning."

"Raped? God, I thought that guy she left with was a spoilsport, but he never seemed like that."

"Richard says it was his roommate, Paul Anstel. You know, he's one of the PhD students."

"Really? What happened?"

"She says she passed out," Richard said. "And when she came to, he was on top of her. She was too out of it to fight him off, and then she passed out again. I only found out when I went to check on her early this morning."

"Oh, one of those cases!" Arty responded. "She does everything but haul him into bed, and then when he takes her up on it, for some reason she's mad at him the next morning."

"She was unconscious, Arty," Richard answered sharply. "It's hardly her fault. You know that an unconscious person can't give a valid consent to sex."

"Valid consent!" Arty exclaimed. "Geez, Richard, you sound like the administration's orientation gurus. Every fall, the same old, same old. Consent! Such a difficult, difficult concept! Here, you stupid little dicks, let us explain it to you. Again, for the forty-fifth time!"

Norman laughed. "Arty, you sound just like that Amahdi woman who runs the annual sessions. Did you get that video they showed this year? Comparing consent to sex like consenting to drink a cup of tea! Done by the British police, I think. 'Just because you wanted a cup of tea yesterday, doesn't mean you want a cup of tea today. And unconscious people never, never, never, want a cup of tea!'" Norman laughed again as he mimicked the British accents in the film.

"As if we weren't able to figure out for ourselves when they want it and when they don't!" Arty added. "And nowadays, sex is just like having a cup of tea. About that important! Now as for that little Sarah, I'm sorry she was upset. But have you seen what she wears to classes? Boy, the other day, her skirt was up to her panties, and her blouse was hanging loose with the boobies almost falling out. I don't know how I kept my pants zipped through the class!"

"You and every other guy there," Norman replied.

Richard put his glass down. "I'm not very comfortable with all this, guys. I mean, women can wear whatever they want, can't they? It doesn't mean they're asking for rape."

"No, of course not," Arty replied. "But you have to admit that most of the women in our classes date, and they sleep with guys, and they want sex. And the good old university administration makes a great big deal out of the whole thing when it's just fun. I'm sorry Sarah got hurt. She seems like a fun girl. I was thinking of taking her out. But if she's making a big fuss, I guess I should rethink that. I mean, I think women should dress how they want and have sex when they want it and not when they don't. The guy was a jerk, like I thought. But she can dump him the way most girls do with guys when they don't like the moves. She doesn't need to make a song and dance about it."

"How can you talk like that? She was raped!" Richard persisted.

"Yeah, well, I'm not talking in public about this because I know how people like Doctor Elizabeth Maryfield would take it," Arty replied, stressing every syllable of the professor's title and name. "Or should I say MERRYFIELD, as in m- e- r- r- y-field! As if she doesn't make very merry herself, especially when the Dean's around. But nobody else is allowed to have fun but her."

"Maryfield and the Dean?" Norman asked, incredulously.

"Oh yeah," Arty replied. "My sister has a condo in the same building as dear old Dean Hart's. Says she sees Dr. Maryfield there at very unusual hours."

"I should be going home," Richard said.

"Look, Richard," Arty said, "I don't mean to be a pill, but sex is good, clean fun, right?"

"Right," Richard replied, "but ..."

"So why make a big deal out of it unless you're in it for something else? I mean, Maryfield screwing the Dean makes sense. He's got the power, and she wants it. Power's what it's all about. Power games. What's all this elaborate stuff about consent but the women in the university exercising power? Hell, what's the law about but forcing people to do what you say? Now, I'm not comparing this to some poor woman who's dragged off the street at knifepoint. But in this kind of a case—hey, it's just about who has the power and which poor bugger's going to be expelled as the unlucky one. You know how the Romans handled their troops for discipline? No matter guilt—they just lined 'em up and killed every tenth man. Decimated, they called it. And that's what the university does to us. Just gets every tenth guy who does something a woman doesn't like."

Richard, who had half risen to leave, sat down. He refilled his glass from the dwindling pitcher. "I suppose you're right, Arty. Power is what it's about. And Paul is certainly going to be expelled."

"Tough for your roommate," Norman added.

"Well," Richard answered, "if you think I'm a bit of a prig, you should see him. President of the Catholic Students. Talks about being a priest. But maybe he'll deign to take a job at the Supreme Court of Canada instead. Too good for us. Hypocrite. Whatever the reasons they expel him, I'm not going to cry."

Am I being fair? I ask myself this again. Some of this, of course, is only speculation, based on what I experienced myself, and how I thought others had reacted. Never mind for now; a friend is coming, and we will go for a walk. I look out through my study window at the pale November sunshine. Yes, sunshine, readers. Even in November, there are some sunny days. And my friend and I will take advantage of them. Friendship. We all thought we had friends. Maybe some of us did. But mostly, it seems to me now, we were all just groping for some theory that would reconnect us to a reality we could not understand. We didn't realize that the theories were another part of the unreal. So they didn't have to make sense; they didn't have to be consistent; they certainly didn't have to be true. They just had to make us feel better. They had to be what everyone believed.

THURSDAY, OCTOBER 20, 10:30 P.M.

Paul, still in his jeans and T-shirt, picked up the wrappers from the burger and fries and threw them into the lined garbage basket in the motel's kitchenette. He placed three empty beer bottles in the recycling box. Fr. Mark had dropped the food and the beer off on his way to a dinner appointment. Paul didn't feel he had the courage to open the motel door and walk down the street to the bus. He knew he would have to leave the room sometime, but he could imagine the story of his crime spreading across campus. If he met anyone from school, he would wonder whether they knew and what they knew. Fr. Mark had promised to stand by him and help, and so had Professor Gordon, although she had been unclear whether she believed him or not. No one else had called. That might mean they didn't know. Or that they did.

The TV was on. It had been on all day. Paul found the noise helpful. He had watched talk shows in the morning, soap operas after lunch, reality TV in the late afternoon, game shows in the early evening, and cop shows in prime time. Late night talk shows were just beginning. He knew he should call his parents in Toronto, but it was too late now. Earlier, he had kept hoping that this was a misunderstanding and would be cleared up. And then they would never have to know.

The unit's phone rang. Paul picked up, hoping it was not some accuser or some new disaster.

"Paul? Fr. Mark here. I hope you weren't asleep yet?"

"No, Father, thanks for calling."

"I wanted to let you know that I've had a good meeting with Professor Gordon and another of your professors. We think that there's DNA evidence. Sarah has not gone to the police, so the main issue is how to get it tested. Professor Gordon says that Sarah will have to consent, given that there's no search warrant or court order."

"Yes, I suppose that's right," Paul responded.

"So that's the good news. Professor Gordon promised that she would email Sarah tonight. Maybe by tomorrow, the samples will be on their way to a lab. And then you can put this behind you."

"I hope so. But what if Sarah won't consent?"

Fr. Mark was resolutely cheerful. "I can't imagine why she wouldn't, Paul. She must want to know the truth. Something like this happens, and you can't rebuild your life on lies. If she's going to have any chance to put this dreadful experience behind her, she'll have to know. But if for some very remote and unforeseeable reason she did refuse, well, then we will have to think of something else, for example, how someone could have accessed her apartment after you locked the door. It would have had to be someone with access to a key: one key if they were already in the building, and two keys if they were not."

"I suppose Sarah is the only one who would know who else had keys. I wish I could talk to her, tell her I didn't do it."

Fr. Mark's voice sharpened. "You are not to go near her, Paul, by phone or in person or by email even. If she doesn't know now, she soon will know that you're claiming innocence. If we need information from her, you will have to stay out of it. Understand?"

"Yes, Father, of course you're right. I just feel so—I don't know. Sad. Desperate. Anxious."

"Pray, my son. God is always with those who seek the truth, even in their suffering. Remember that when our Lord hung on the cross, He opened paradise for the thief who spoke the truth."

After he hung up, Paul turned off the TV, opened his suitcase, and removed a leather pouch. From it, he pulled the silver rosary his mother had given him as a Christmas gift, a rosary blessed by St. John Paul II. He dropped to his knees and began, "In the name of the Father, and of the Son, and of the Holy Spirit ..."

FRIDAY, OCTOBER 21, 3:20 A.M.

Hart turned over in his bed. He opened his eyes. She stood in front of the window, silhouetted in the moonlight that radiated through the light blinds and sheer curtains. He could see the flow of her hair down her back and the curve of her shoulders under the silk robe. The sheen of the silk reflected the pale light.

"What are you doing up?" he asked groggily. He looked at the bedside alarm clock. "It's just past three in the morning."

"I'm thinking." He saw her turn toward the bed. He could not see her features in the shadow, but he heard the excitement in her voice.

"Oh Hart, this is such an opportunity. I've been rethinking the assignment for my class in feminist theory. Sarah's exposé of the misogyny and exploitation of women on this campus will form the centrepiece of a whole new book, or, perhaps, even a film. Every student will select a project that will challenge the culture. I can make some suggestions: picketing the Board of Governors' meeting to demand gender parity on the Board, staging performance art to challenge the inclusion on campus of religious bigots, plastering the campus with posters demanding we believe women. I've thought of a dozen ideas without even trying. I'll record and compile it, and it will be the best piece of work I've ever done. I'm so excited about it. It will guarantee my promotion to full professor in a few years. Who knows? I might even replace you as Dean after your next term!"

"Elizabeth." Hart sat up and propped up a pillow behind him for support. "Look, it's time to get some sleep. You haven't even got tenure yet, and you're already making yourself Dean!"

She laughed. "I know, darling, but it's not too early to plan.

Scholarship needs time to grow and flower!"

"And be careful," Hart continued, barely noticing her interruption. "Some of those things—protests at the Board, disruption of religious services—well, they could be illegal. If not illegal, they could draw the wrong kind of attention. You can't afford that when you're seeking tenure."

"Nonsense," she replied. "First, even if they're illegal, no one will complain. The university won't call the police. In fact, Campus Security will likely assist us by making sure no one interferes. It's protest, darling, and for a progressive cause. Second, let them dare deny me tenure when I'm engaged in cutting-edge research. The faculty women on this campus and in all of Canada would be in an uproar. It would be a clear breach of academic freedom. No, even Alice will be afraid to deny me promotion."

"Well, it won't do me any good with the administration. Even if they are afraid to shut you down—and you're likely right about that—they won't like it. And they don't like Deans whose faculties cause them embarrassment. Hell, Elizabeth, I need the support of the Provost for my reappointment next year. Don't make a scene. And at least come back to bed so we can get some sleep. I've got an early meeting at breakfast with the other Deans to talk about the new diversity plan."

"You get some sleep. I'm going to pour myself a glass of wine and sit down at your computer to get these ideas down while they're fresh. And remind me tomorrow to speak again to Sarah. She must capture her experience as fully as possible. It will form the heart of the project."

Hart groaned and slid back under the covers. "Well, just be quiet when you come back to bed. I thought you wanted to slip out early in the morning so no one would notice you. Being up half the night isn't going to make that very easy."

"Really, Hart. Who cares? You're the one who's so worried about anyone finding us out. Anyway, I don't have a class until afternoon tomorrow, so wake me up when you get up. I can throw on my clothes and get back to my place for some more sleep in the morning."

FRIDAY, OCTOBER 21, 11 A.M.

"I need to speak to you immediately." Elizabeth stood in the doorway of Alice's office. She had knocked and then at once stepped inside. She was breathing rapidly, her breath in short gasps that made her speech broken, and she held a piece of letter-sized paper in her hand.

Alice looked up from her desk in some surprise. "All right. I don't have any meetings just now, so come in and tell me what the issue is."

Elizabeth took two steps toward the desk and held out the paper.

"This is the issue," she said loudly. "Sarah sent it to me early this morning." Her voice rose to a higher level. "How dare you behave like this? How dare you persecute this poor young woman? How dare you support a rapist? Well, I know you're no feminist, but I would have thought that even you would have contempt for men who use violence against women. I would have thought, even you ..."

Alice stood up. Elizabeth's voice had begun to break again, and she brushed away tears from her cheeks. Alice had also begun to tremble with shock and anger.

"What are you talking about? If we're going to talk about 'how you dare,' how do you dare to come in here screaming at me? In my own office, in the middle of work?"

"Look at this," Elizabeth's shaking hand again thrust forward the paper she held. "Can you tell me that you did not send Sarah—a recent survivor of sexual violence—this hateful, hateful email?"

"Let me see that." Alice took the paper. She skimmed it and put it on the desk.

"You are correct that this is a copy of my email. I sent it last night. But it's hardly hateful. It simply tells Sarah that Paul has said that he is innocent and that he wants the chance to prove it. Then it expresses sincere sorrow for the dreadful experience she has had but also makes the point that it is important for her to know the truth of what happened. And then I ask her to give consent for a private lab to test the sample taken from her yesterday at Health Services so it can be compared to Paul's DNA. What on earth is hateful about that?"

"You don't believe her. That's what's hateful. She's told everyone that Paul Anstel sexually assaulted her, and you don't believe her."

"I don't know. And from what I understand of her statement to Campus Security, she doesn't really know either. Yes, Paul took her home, but she cannot identify the man who raped her. It was dark; his head was covered …"

"By a hat such as Paul wore earlier …" Elizabeth interjected.

"Yes," Alice continued, her voice steadying, "and a hat such as is worn by hundreds of male students on cold fall evenings. And the lower part of his face was covered by a scarf that belonged to her. And since she and Paul had never been intimate, nothing in the man's touch or feel could identify him to her. I don't believe she can be sure."

"Well, she is sure. And I am not going to have her upbraided, insulted, and persecuted. I have spoken with her this morning, and her resolve is strong. I can tell you now that she is not answering your email, and she will not consent to the release of her private property to you so that her rapist can pull some legal trick."

Alice's exasperation took over. "Don't be silly. What legal trick could there possibly be?"

"All kinds. Read the papers. See what happens to women who try to find justice. Well, I won't be a part of that system, and I won't allow Sarah to be victimized by it. Take your filthy email and be damned."

Elizabeth turned and rushed from the office, her hand shielding her face from anyone passing. On her way down the hall, she narrowly avoided a collision with George. Barely stopping to murmur an apology, she pushed by, turned into her own office, and slammed her door.

George continued on to find Alice's door still open and Alice sitting, staring into space.

"What happened?" he asked from the doorway. "Elizabeth nearly ran me down. Was she in here with you?"

Alice laughed slightly, and her voice quavered. "You could say that. She was certainly here. Accusing me of persecuting Sarah. Oh, and she was here to deliver Sarah's answer as well. It's 'no.' Apparently, we are supposed to believe her whether she has any evidence or is even that sure herself. I know Elizabeth feels strongly about sexualized violence—well, I can't blame her for that—but it's not as though I suggested or have thought that Sarah was lying. And maybe there are facts I don't know. But they aren't facts she told Campus Security, and on the basis of those, I can't see how she can be convinced that it was Paul. But oh George, it was an ugly scene."

"Let's get out of here and go across to the park."

"To the park?"

"Sure. Don't you ever go for a walk in that gorgeous piece of nature across the road?"

"No, I don't. I mean, I love to look out the window at the trees, but when I'm here, I'm in my office or in the classroom. I'd never think of going elsewhere."

"Think of it now. I find it's very soothing to take a stroll among the flowers, watch the kids play, go down to the duck pond and feed the ducks and the swans. It's beautiful. It's good for your soul, especially when you've had to face a tough scene."

"I suppose so. All right, I don't have a class until after lunch. Did you say feed the ducks? I don't have anything to feed them."

"Waterfowl food in my drawer right next to the scotch," George replied. "A lot of people feed them breadcrumbs, but they're not good for them."

Walking in the late October sunshine, Alice and George crossed the road and entered the park. Following a path lined with red-leafed maple trees and walking through crisp fallen aspen leaves, they came to the duck pond, where several small children stood with their care-givers watching the ducks. As George predicted, some of them had breadcrumbs that they dropped or threw, depending on their age and dexterity, to the waiting ducks. The water was placid, rippled only by the wakes of the ducks as they traversed the pond from one feeding source to the next.

"Let's sit for a while on this bench," George suggested. "It seems to have dried in the sunshine, and it's quite pleasant here out of the wind."

"I don't know what to do next," Alice said as they sat down. "I was so sure Sarah would give consent. I still can't understand why she wouldn't. Perhaps I should email her again. After all, Elizabeth has no right to speak for Sarah. Sarah must be at least twenty-three or four and is entitled to speak for herself."

"I agree it's worth trying again. But perhaps you should see her in person. She'll be back in a day or two. I understand that Angus Maillot gave her a deferral on her Philosophy of John Rawls seminar midterm exam that was on for today, and she told him by email that she would write it on Tuesday. She must be planning on coming to campus at least by then. If you speak directly to her, you may have more success. At least Elizabeth won't be speaking for her and putting words into her mouth."

"I can't see what Elizabeth is getting out of this," Alice remarked. "It seems unbelievably stupid to antagonize me by calling me names when I'm chairing her Tenure and Promotion Committee."

"I think she believes she's on solid ground there. The other committee members will be impressed by her actions, I think, and will see them as evidence of her progressive commitments. But alternatively, she may be just so involved with this issue that she's lost all sense of proportion."

"She was so rude. It was horrible. I've never been attacked like that, even by colleagues who disagreed with me."

"It's the new reality," George replied. "You don't want to hear something, so you shout it down."

"But reason would say …"

"Reason doesn't enter into it, Alice. People like Elizabeth are driven by blind faith. Raising any question about Sarah's report of the situation is heresy and can't even be listened to or considered."

"If Sarah won't consent, we have to think about the keys. Assuming Paul is telling the truth, he locked Sarah's door, but, of course, he couldn't put up a chain or safety bolt, if she has one, and he took his keys with him. Could anyone else have taken those keys later? Where did he put them when he got home? Anyone with a key to his place might have been able to take them. And did anyone else have keys to Sarah's apartment? What about other people in the building? What about the resident manager, if there is one? We need answers to those questions."

"Well, Paul can supply the answers to some of them. But Sarah will have to tell you the answers to the rest. In the meantime, I suppose we should get back and have our lunch. Are you going to the Faculty Club?"

"I brought a sandwich, but maybe it would be better to get something hot. I feel chilled in some way."

"I've kept you sitting here too long. The sun's gone behind that oak tree, and the breeze has picked up."

"No, I think it's just shock from the scene."

"Well, come and have a bowl of soup with me at the Club," George suggested, "if you've got time before your class starts. Then I'll call Fr. Mark and tell him that we're temporarily at a standstill. He'll have to tell Paul, I suppose. It won't be a happy discussion. When do you see Paul again?"

"I'll see him late this afternoon. I don't expect he's made much progress on his work, but we should discuss his next chapter and what he plans to do with it. I'll ask him about the keys. But I hope Fr. Mark will have broken the news to him by then. Tell Fr. Mark that I haven't given up hope. If I can talk to Sarah, maybe she isn't as blind as Elizabeth to the uncertainties in the situation."

FRIDAY, OCTOBER 21, 1:00 P.M.

Elizabeth Maryfield sat at the head of the oblong table in the law school's largest seminar room. Seventeen of the eighteen other chairs were filled with thirteen women students and four men.

"I have some news, some devastating news. One of your classmates, Sarah Yung, was raped in the early hours of Thursday morning. She's home now, recovering, but should be rejoining us at Tuesday's class. At that time, I hope she will read to us a draft of what will become her term paper in this course, detailing her experience of violence on this campus."

Elizabeth looked at each student briefly, surveying the shocked faces, as she paused. Two of the women had begun to cry, and one stood up abruptly. "I think I'm going to be sick," she announced as she turned to run for the door.

"This is a truly horrific thing," Elizabeth continued, "but the good news is that Sarah is prepared to participate fully in our efforts to eradicate sexualized violence, trans- and homophobia, and all forms of oppression and hate from our campus. And I am hoping that you will all seriously consider a research project that I am now adding to the syllabus. I intend to produce a book based upon not just Sarah's experience, although that will form a central portion of the book, but the efforts of members of this class to bring to light the rape culture on this campus and its pervasive effects on our lives. We will speak truth to power, as I promised in my course description.

"I have a list of suggested projects here." Elizabeth passed around a xeroxed sheet. "You are free, of course, to come up with your own ideas. You should let me know before next Tuesday's class if you wish to participate in this ground-breaking research. I will have to approve your project unless it's already on this list of suggestions. But if you participate, I think I can safely say that you are likely to receive an A grade in the course, whether an A-, or A, or A+, of course, will depend on quality. But this is the chance you have all wanted to work on the forefront of current research."

One of the women raised her hand. "Dr. Maryfield," she said, "I think some of us have already begun our research papers. If we change now, we'll have to throw away that work. And I think the calendar requires the course evaluation options to be laid out before the course starts. This seems unfair to those of us who are already doing a project."

Elizabeth frowned. "I don't think we can allow technicalities to stand in the way of this opportunity, Janice," she replied. "Of course, you are free to continue with what you are doing—a paper if that's what you want. But that does not mean you have the right to deprive others of this opportunity."

Several students began speaking at once. "No, Janice's got a point."

"What do you mean? Just because she's already started, why should we suffer?"

"I want to change this campus—this is a great chance …"

Elizabeth clapped her hands loudly. "Students! That's enough. Please show respect for me and for the learning environment by coming to order. Janice is perfectly within her rights to raise this issue, and I certainly do not want to disadvantage anyone. If you feel that you have gone too far to change your project now, by all means continue. I will be grading your work on its merits, of course, including your contributions to the supportive climate in this class. Now, let's please look at the essay that is our discussion topic for today. You have the questions that I suggested. Who is prepared to open the discussion?"

As the class ended and the students gathered up their books, laptops, and papers, one of the men walked across the room and stood close to Janice, the woman who had challenged Elizabeth's change of process. Elizabeth glanced over with some concern. The young man leaned over Janice's books.

Elizabeth knew him well—Tyler Jenkins. He had been in two of her other classes and always made a point of dropping by her office to discuss his readings. They shared an admiration for the philosophers whose ideas shaped the progressive thinking to which they were both committed. Elizabeth expected he would be able to persuade Janice to accept the situation. She knew he was popular with the women.

"Don't get involved in this," he said to Janice. "Let those who want to change, change. It's no big deal."

Janice raised her head as she zipped up her laptop bag and picked up the books. "I'm not going to be intimidated by her," Janice responded. "It's not fair, and I'm going to speak to the Dean."

Elizabeth smiled and continued to pack up her notes as Tyler walked up to her. "I'm sorry, Dr. Maryfield," he said respectfully. "I thought I could talk her into seeing the importance of this project, but I'm afraid she says she's going to speak to the Dean."

"Don't worry, Tyler," Elizabeth replied. "This school is dedicated to the pursuit of social justice. That's why you and I belong here. Dean Haverman won't allow this kind of complaint to interfere. We can rely on him."

"That's good to know, Professor," Tyler added. "And I wondered if I could come by your office now to discuss something I was just reading in Derrida's work? I'm not sure I understand the full import of it."

"Of course," Elizabeth answered. "I'm always interested in helping students form their ideas."

FRIDAY, OCTOBER 21, 4:00 P.M.

Alice knocked on the door to 15A of the motel. Once again, the door was opened by Fr. Mark.

"Professor Gordon, please come in. I've just been talking to Paul about the situation. Unfortunately, I've had a packed day with a funeral in the early afternoon, and I wasn't able to leave the family until just a few minutes ago. A drug overdose … heartbreaking for the parents, of course."

"I understand. I assume George was able to reach you about Sarah's response to my email?"

"Yes, he called just before the mass began. But I didn't want to deliver the news by phone, and I wanted some time to talk to him."

Paul called from the room. "Come in, Professor Gordon. I'm afraid I haven't made any progress with my work today, but I appreciate your coming."

"How are you, Paul?" Alice asked, stepping into the room.

"I'm not too good, Professor. I keep thinking this can't be happening. Sarah couldn't believe I would rape her or anyone."

"I haven't yet given up hope of speaking to Sarah directly, or of the possibility that she won't see things the way Elizabeth Maryfield does when she feels a little better and can speak for herself. But in the meantime, has Fr. Mark asked you about who else might have had access to Sarah's keys?"

"Yes, but I don't know who she might have given keys to. I know she has a best friend, Melissa, who lives in the same building, and I expect Melissa would have a key. The building also has a resident manager who likely has a master key. As for my keys, we always left our keys in a wicker basket on the table by our unit's front door. That way, we can pick them up on the way out. Richard could have gotten my keys or anyone who has a key to our unit. That includes at least Melanie Amahdi and her staff, and I think Richard gave a key to his friend, Arty Donovan. They hang out together a lot, and although Richard is a graduate student, they've been in some of the same classes. Arty's on a bit of a tight budget, so Richard has given him free range of our place if he needs to borrow something."

"And, I suppose," Alice added, "any of those people could have loaned a key to your unit door to anyone else?"

"Possible. We're pretty casual in the residences about coming and going. Lots of parties, and lots of people share their keys with friends."

FRIDAY, OCTOBER 21, 4:15 P.M.

"I need to see the Dean as soon as possible," Janice insisted to Hart's assistant.

The middle-aged woman looked up. Her lips were drawn together tightly, and her eyes showed no sympathetic spark. Dean's admin assistants, as she well knew, were the real powers in any law school.

"Dean Haverman is extremely busy just now. And he's booked solid on Monday. I can't possibly fit you in until late Tuesday afternoon."

Just then, Hart opened the door dividing his inner office from his assistant's cubbyhole. "Sandra, I need … oh, hello. It's Janice, isn't it?"

"Hi, Dean. Yes, I'm Janice Fuller. I was hoping to speak with you. I just finished my last class of the day and came straight here."

"Well, I can always spare a moment for a student's concerns," Hart said jovially, smiling while his assistant, Sandra, continued to frown.

"Hart," she said sharply, "you do have a meeting with the representative of the law school sessionals in fifteen minutes."

"Oh, yes. But plenty of time to speak to Janice. You won't be long, will you?" he asked, turning toward Janice.

"No. I won't take much time, I hope," Janice responded. "I just need to speak to you about something that happened in class today."

"Well, come in," he said, standing aside so she could enter his office. "Sandra, please hold my calls. I won't be long. But please bring me the Murchison donation file when Janice leaves."

Inside the large, airy office, Hart seated himself in a comfortable chair by a coffee table and motioned Janice toward the sofa.

"And what's happening that has brought you here?" he asked as she sat down.

"It's Dr. Maryfield's class. Frankly, Dean, it's not what I expected, and if it wasn't too late to drop the course, I would. But we have to do a major paper in her course—there's no exam—and I've selected the topic of feminist influence on mainstream Protestant denominations in Canada. I'm looking at the parallels between the development of women's legal rights and the expansion of women in church leadership roles. Anyway, I've done a lot of work so far."

"Absolutely. Sounds very interesting," Hart agreed.

"Thanks. But today, Dr. Maryfield told us she was changing the course syllabus to add an option of participating in a project that she's interested in pursuing. It's connected to this horrible rape situation she told us about. And while she says that we don't have to participate, and we can continue with our papers if we want, she made it pretty clear that she favours people joining this new project. I think that, first, it's against the calendar rules to change the course syllabus at this late date. And I'm worried my grade will be prejudiced if I don't junk my paper and do something totally different. She gave us this list of suggested topics and a description to be added to the syllabus." Janice handed Hart the paper she had brought from class.

"Well, this is an extremely serious allegation," Hart responded. "Let's take the issues one at a time. Now, first, she hasn't cancelled the paper requirement, has she?"

"No, she's added another option."

"Well," Hart relaxed slightly and smiled, "I think the calendar is about avoiding prejudice to students, not about preventing a faculty member from adding other possible options for them."

Janice reached into her bag and removed her laptop, which she opened. "But it says on page 148 that, and I quote, 'After the add/drop date has passed, no changes shall be made to the evaluation methods of any course.' And that's what she's done."

Hart smiled more broadly. "You should know, Janice, that a literal reading of a legal document is not always the best one. We must look at the purpose of the provision. And, in this case, surely the purpose is not to foreclose a broader range of student learning options but to prevent prejudice. I can't see how Dr. Maryfield's changes violate the calendar. Now your other point, I think, is much more serious. You say that she directly told the class that she would not fairly grade anyone who did not join this new project?"

"No, not in so many words ... but ..."

"What did she say, then?" Hart asked, raising his voice.

"She said she would allow us to continue with our papers if we wanted. That was after I asked about it. But she also said that anyone who joined the project would get an A."

"Would get an A?"

"Well, likely would. At least that's what she meant, and she further said that part of the grade would depend upon the contribution to class climate."

"That sounds very far from saying that you would be prejudiced. In classes such as those Dr. Maryfield teaches, class participation is a legitimate basis for forming part of the grade. I see nothing wrong with that. In fact, Janice, it seems to me that you have brought very serious allegations to me implying that Dr. Maryfield is biased, and you have nothing to support them. That, in itself, is grounds for potential disciplinary action."

Janice's face paled. "I certainly didn't intend … I didn't mean …"

Hart stood up. "No, I don't think you did. You just weren't thinking about all this in the right way. I suggest you continue with your paper, which sounds most interesting, and I am sure, at the end of the day, you will have absolutely no reason to complain if you do a good job. And this little chat will remain just between us."

Janice closed her laptop and put it back into her bag. She stood up.

"All right. I can see that perhaps I overreacted. Thank you for your time."

As the door closed behind her, Hart picked up the phone. Elizabeth answered.

"Hart here, Elizabeth," he began, an edge in his voice. "One of your Feminist Legal Studies students has just been to see me to complain about you."

"Janice," Elizabeth confirmed. "Yes, she told another student after my class that she was going to do that."

"You have put me in a difficult position."

"Hart, I'm quite sure you can handle her."

"Of course I handled her. But I shouldn't have had to. And, Elizabeth, I don't want any more complaints. I've told you that the Provost is not happy when her life is disrupted by Deans. And I am working very hard to build support with her—for you as well as for me. This is the wrong time to cause problems. Not only that, but it would seem that you told your class about the rape."

"I had Sarah's permission."

"Well, you still should have had more discretion. My advice to you is to defer this entire project until next semester. Your promotion and tenure recommendation will be in then, and you will be much better positioned if you include this project in the syllabus of your seminar from the beginning."

"Hart, this is happening now. Sarah needs support now. And now is the time to strike at the campus culture to effect real change. Don't ask me to back off."

"I am asking you to back off. I tell you, I don't need this now." Hart's voice increased in volume.

As did Elizabeth's.

"I won't back off. This is an opportunity I can't pass up. Are you trying to interfere with academic freedom?"

"Of course not," Hart responded, shouting into the phone. "I'm asking you to have some sense. Don't wave that flag at me. Like patriotism, academic freedom ploys are the refuge of the scoundrel."

Elizabeth gasped. "Are you calling me a scoundrel?"

Hart paused and then spoke more calmly. "Of course not. I'm sorry. But I would very much suggest that you drop this matter about Sarah for now."

Elizabeth was not to be mollified. "Well, I won't," she stated emphatically and hung up her office phone with more vigour than usual.

Hart heard the thud as the receiver hit the cradle. His door opened.

"Your next meeting is here, Hart," Sandra announced.

Casuistry has a bad name. It's always thought to mean fallacious or specious arguments. But it's really just what lawyers do: argument based on general rules and careful distinctions. It's what we all do when what we seek is justification, not truth. Elizabeth's class was certainly a turning point. Would it have all been different if only Hart had not resorted to casuistry? Well, he couldn't have known, could he?

FRIDAY, OCTOBER 21, 6:45 P.M.

George and Alice sat across the round wooden table from each other. The pub, a few blocks away from Alice's small house, was cozy with a fire in the fireplace. The pub was divided into seating areas by wooden pillars and short flights of steps separating the floor space into three levels. Several nooks with upholstered benches had been tucked into the panelled corners. Although it was Friday, the room was not full, and the arrangement provided privacy for George and Alice, who were seated in one of the smaller nooks. Alice sat on the bench, and George, in a wingback chair. They had just placed their order with the server.

"I'm not surprised that Paul is disappointed," George commented. "And I'm not surprised that the question of the key appears to be more complicated than it seemed. But even if we get the DNA tested and there's no match with Paul, the question of who raped Sarah Yung will still be unsolved. The list of people who might had been able to gain access to her apartment with keys—and there may be ways to get in without keys, if you have the right equipment—is fairly long, especially when you add in friends of friends. Even if the police were involved, I doubt they could get warrants for DNA testing on every-one who might have been able to get a key."

Alice nodded gloomily as the server put a white wine in front of her and a draft beer in front of George. "The best we can do is hope to clear Paul, assuming of course, that he didn't do it. And the more I see of him, the more I think I believe him. Especially since he is so eager to have the DNA tested."

"I heard an interesting piece of information from a student this afternoon," George said. "He tells me that Elizabeth caused quite a stir in her Feminist Legal Studies class today by telling everyone about the rape. She also is changing the course evaluation provisions so that she can do a project coming out of the event. He's in my Corporate Tax class, and he tells me that one of the students is going to complain to the Dean about the breach of the rules. But you were wondering why Elizabeth was so determined to protect Sarah from finding out the truth. Apparently, she's going to build a major research project around Sarah's experience. She's also going to include what she calls 'performance art' projects from others in the class. My student said it sounded as if anyone who participated would get an A grade, with the implication, he thought, that those who didn't would be considered 'unsupportive' and could count themselves lucky to pass."

"She's out of her mind. That's a clear breach of the rules. Mind you, I've had a look at the proofs for her new book. She's put them in as part of her tenure and promotion package. It's really all student work. Of course, she edits and adds periodic 'reflections' as she calls them, but the photographs are all posters that students produced, and much of the commentary is from recorded interviews of the students explaining their work. I don't see it as her own work, other than perhaps as the editor of a collection. But that's not enough for tenure and certainly not enough for promotion."

"You won't find the other members of your committee agreeing with you," George warned. "Her way of looking at the world is dominant right now."

"But it's not law. It's not even art."

"Have you looked at the university art gallery lately? Gone to any of the visual arts students' exhibitions?"

"I suppose I'm just old, George. But I truly hate how things have turned out. There was a real study of law once. What happened?"

"Well, I'm old too, I suppose. But I don't think my intelligence has taken much of a dive yet. Law was regarded as a trade, and in the early days of university law schools—you remember, even when we were law students, how that was—other disciplines on campus looked down on us as 'mere' technicians. So our academics sold their souls to be part of the elite crowd, and law became more political theory and social science than the theory and practice of objective rules under which people could flourish."

"And social science and political theory have let us down badly," Alice added. "But we've lost our way. Courts have no idea how to decide things anymore. They see precedent as useless, but it's precedent and the bounded exercise of legitimate discretion that made our society what it was: peaceful and prosperous."

"Bounded discretion is the right term," George continued. "Of course, the application of rules always requires discretion. But that doesn't mean it's all discretion, nor is it all about power. At least it didn't used to be. But that was when we had some idea of the common good and not simply the construction of society on identity groups and power relationships."

"Our colleagues would say that it was always about power relationships."

"A wise man once said that a heretic is not someone who doesn't know the truth. It's someone who knows part of the truth and thinks it's the whole truth."

"Who was that?"

"I'm not sure," George laughed. "That's why I said 'a wise man.' But I think it was either C.S. Lewis or G.K. Chesterton."

"They were Christians, weren't they?"

"Yes, Lewis was Anglican, and Chesterton was Roman Catholic."

"Are you religious, George?"

"Was once. Might be again. Have you ever thought, Alice, that if God really does exist, most of what we do on this campus is totally misguided?"

"How so?"

"Well, God's existence would change everything. All our theories of social science, politics, power—what we were just talking about— they've all been constructed on the premise that academic inquiry must carry out its tasks and draw its conclusions as if God did not exist."

"Wouldn't it distort the results if we assessed our work in the light of a particular faith?"

"Yes, if it's not true. Just as it distorts the results to interpret them as if God does not exist, if that's untrue. There is no neutral in this situation. But we pretend that there is. So if God exists, and especially if He is anything like Judaism and Christianity think He is, we're dead wrong. Most of what we've written and produced in the last fifty or a hundred years, especially in the social sciences, is dead wrong. Because the existence of God would mean that there are realities about human nature and human life that we can't change. It would mean that there are expectations of behaviour between people, and there are things that are genuinely wrong because, however much we want them, they do not contribute to our good. And our good cannot be just what we want; it's what would truly lead to human happiness in the long run ... maybe, depending on how you work out the consequences of God's existence in more detail, the long run of eternity."

"Still, that's a matter of faith."

"In a sense, perhaps. And I'm not saying it's not complex; there are different concepts of God, of course, and how His existence affects us. But it's not faith as blind to reason. In fact, there are a lot of arguments suggesting that it is atheism that is irrational, more so than some form of theism. In the university, we wear blinders to those realities. We live in the country of the blind because we will not see; we don't want to see. But here the one-eyed man isn't king—he's despised. Question the idea that law is anything but solely what the state says it is or argue that it can't be just whatever we want to make it for our own vision of justice, and you will be a subject of ridicule and attack pretty fast. Sorry, I'm shooting off my mouth. I must sound like an undergraduate."

Alice paused. "Maybe it's people like Elizabeth who are so certain they are right who sound like undergraduates. It sounds to me as if you've given this a lot of thought. And I've seen your library—you've given it a lot of study too. I'm not sure who's right, but I do see we're in a mess. Look at our students: drug overdoses, suicides, a hookup culture where the importance of sexual relationships is trivialized until, as in the case of poor Sarah, it's not. Then lives get ruined."

The server arrived with their food.

"I'd like to hear more about how you see things, George," Alice said carefully. "I wasn't brought up in a religious home, and I must admit that I've always steered clear of any commitment to real belief. Of course, I wouldn't say I'm an atheist, and I'd like to hope that something continues after death, especially as I get older. But I can't say I know much about religion. Frankly, it always seemed like the kiss of death to anyone's career. I mean, it's a given that no one of intelligence believes in standard religious doctrine any more, at least that's what everyone assumes to be true. I guess I've always been afraid to find out."

"That's kind," George responded. "These things have been so much on my mind lately. It's good to have someone to share them with, and someone who is a bit skeptical is probably just what I need. It's easy to be convinced when you're alone with your thoughts and a book."

Religion. Faith. Belief. Reality? What blinds us and what let's us see? Do we have a choice about believing? Believing in something? No, we don't. Nietzsche thought we could never see or speak truth. And he was right that we all see the world through metaphor and through the structures our minds impose. We cannot escape them, and our sophisticated scientific instruments do nothing but expand the range of what our metaphor and structure can encompass. I know that now. So does it not matter what we believe in? Well, one belief may be as good as another, but one belief will get you tenure while another will likely get you fired. One belief is easy, and another takes effort. One belief will give you escape, while another will put you in jail. We consider all these factors. But are they the ones that count?

I must put on the lights. It's dark now, although it's not time even to begin cooking dinner. The lighted computer screen sometimes tricks me.

CHAPTER 3

The residence common room smelled of toast and coffee. Several students were seated at tables with phones or laptops in front of them. Toasters popped as others buttered their late breakfast. A large urn of coffee was just being replaced with a fresh one by a residence staff member dressed in jeans, as was everyone else in sight. At a table in the corner, three students from Elizabeth Maryfield's Feminist Legal Studies class sat with mugs of coffee and a box of doughnuts, paper towels serving as plates and napkins both.

"So it's against the rules," the young man said, taking a bite of his crueller. "I need an A grade. I'm in competition for a clerkship in the Court of Appeal when I graduate in the spring, and an A at Christmas, before they decide on interviews, would be a big help."

"We all could use an A, Tyler," one of the young women, her hair pulled back into a high ponytail, responded as she dusted sugar off her fingers and then off her blue T-shirt. "Damn, these powdered sugar-coated ones shed all over everything! Anyway, like I said, we could all use an A. I'm off to graduate school next year, and better grades mean a better chance at scholarships and teaching assistant positions. But I'm not happy about making Janice mad at me. And Dr. Maryfield is breaking the rules under the calendar. What if we do something and then the administration nixes the change? Not only have we wasted our time, but we have to start all over with a stupid research paper on something."

Tyler responded, "I'm glad you raised that."

Both the young woman in the ponytail and the third member of the party, a small Asian woman, rolled their eyes and groaned.

"Okay, okay. But I do have an answer. We get the project done now, today. If Janice complains and if, and I mean a big 'if,' the Dean intervenes, we tell him that we've already completed most of the assignment—just have to finish writing it up—and if he cancels it now, we'll tell him that it's unfairly prejudicial. If we don't receive credit for what we've done, we suffer irremediable prejudice to our careers. We're all in third year, so he'll buy it for sure."

The ponytailed woman frowned. "But if she can't get more students to participate? If it gets cut off before they can, how do we know that Dr. Maryfield will keep her word about the A grade?"

"She'll still carry on with her research project; I'm betting on that. This is her bread and butter, her chance for promotion. Maybe she can't finish it this year, but next year, or even in her next seminar in the spring. What is it again?"

"Social Justice in an Oppressive State," the Asian woman supplied.

"Right, Suze," Tyler continued. "So in that seminar, she'll put this project into the course materials. And, if I'm right, she'll want to use our material for her book, and she'll need our consent. Hence, my colleagues, we are safe. But I say we move today."

"I don't really care if I get an A," Suze, the Asian woman, spoke again. "My articles are in place at Humphrey, Standon, and Price already, so as long as I pass, I don't care. But I'd like to get this work done, and if we could do something quick and write it up jointly, then I could get extra time to work on my Corporate Tax course. It's a bitch, and the workload is huge, but my law firm expects me to pass it so I can work in their corporate section as soon as I start."

"Didn't Dr. Maryfield say we had to get her to approve the project?"

"No, Angie," Tyler responded. "Remember, she told us that if we chose from her list, we didn't need approval. I have a great idea based on one of the projects she lists. We need to get some stuff organized, and one of us should bring a cellphone and take photos. Maryfield likes books to be illustrated. But we can do this about 5:30 tonight, write it up over dinner and drinks during the evening, print our photos on my printer, and turn it in on Tuesday morning in class. And it's exactly the kind of theatre Maryfield will love."

"Okay," Angie answered, "I remember that. I'm in. My new cell has a great camera, and it's smaller than a lot of them, so it's easy to carry."

"Good, because we will have quite a few things to carry. Suze, you with us?"

"I don't know," Suze replied, picking up an apple fritter. "But, yeah, I guess. It sounds efficient, and I'm up-to-date with my tax readings just now. I planned on taking today off, but if I can knock off a major course requirement, I guess it's worth it. What's the project?"

SATURDAY, OCTOBER 22, 11:00 A.M.

Paul Anstel closed his Bible. It had been another long night, and he had slept little. After a shower and drinking the two packets of in-room coffee the motel provided, he had worked up his courage to walk to the bus and go downtown for breakfast. He had avoided the popular cafes where university students might go and hoped that few would be out in the early morning after the parties of Friday night. Eventually, he found himself in the food court of the mall, where he ate two bacon and egg sandwiches and drank another cup of coffee. He bought a latte to drink on the way home. Returning to his room, he resolved to leave the TV off. He finished his latte and opened his Bible but found he had little concentration.

He dialled Fr. Mark's number.

"Fr. Mark, it's Paul here. Sorry to bother you."

"Not to worry, Paul. I'm glad to be here for you. Have you had some food?"

"Yeah, I managed to get downtown to the mall and have some breakfast. It was early and not too many people were around at that time on Saturday morning. Lunch is another issue. Do you know if that room you thought your friend had for rent is going to be available in the next couple of days? I really need someplace where I can cook something so I don't have to worry about being out so much."

"He's not sure yet, but I'm asking around for you. There is a small one-bedroom suite in my building that was free the middle of this month, and I don't think it's rented yet. It's likely to require a year's lease, however, and that might be a problem if you move away in the summer. You'd have to find someone to sublet it or pay the rent."

"I might be able to do that. I sure would like a place of my own. But I assume it's not furnished, so I'd have to find some stuff. I'll need to ask my dad for a loan, I'm afraid."

"I'll speak to the building manager today. I can make you an emergency loan if you need it. The Church provides me with some discretionary funds for that kind of emergency. I would think we could find a bed, some chairs, and a little TV for what I can supply. You remember Wendell Ashley, who overdosed last week? I know his parents don't want to take his furniture back to Nova Scotia with them. I'm sure they would sell it reasonably, or maybe even give it to you, since he was part of our Catholic student community."

"Could you see? I hate to bother them in these tragic circumstances, but I assume they won't be here much longer, and it would be wonderful if they could help."

"I'll speak to them too. Even though they're grieving terribly, they realize, as we all do, that some arrangements have to be made. I'm sure they won't mind, and I'm sure you'll feel better if you get your own place. And I assume the residence folks will refund the rest of the money you had paid for the term?"

"I guess so. I haven't thought that far."

"Well, call Melanie Amahdi and ask."

"I don't think she'll be very happy to hear from me. On Thursday morning, she was looking at me as if I was a piece of dog poop that she had to scrape off her shoes."

"Paul, whatever she thinks, I'm sure she'll do her job. And when you're cleared, I'm sure she'll be relieved."

"I wonder," Paul replied.

"Now I know you can't come to mass on campus this afternoon. And even if you could, you might not feel like facing people yet, although I assure you that I've told no one about your situation. And, more importantly, these people are your friends and will believe you when they hear about it. But promise me that you will go to mass tonight or tomorrow. You need to pray, Paul, and keep praying. I truly believe that God will speak to you through this and that He will protect you."

"Thanks, Father. I wish I was so sure. I mean, it's not that I don't think that God can bring good out of this. But sometimes I think His idea of what is good and mine don't really mesh."

"I understand. 'His ways are not our ways,' for sure. But it will be for your good, in the end."

As he hung up the phone, Paul spoke aloud to himself. "Sure, in the end—likely in heaven." He turned on the TV and stretched out on the bed.

SATURDAY, OCTOBER 22, 2:00 P.M.

"Come on, Richard, I need some help here." Arty, beer in hand, stood in the common area of Richard's living unit that he had once shared with Paul.

"I mean, you know Sarah. She must be pretty grateful to you for helping her out. For being on the spot like you were. And she'd likely be really happy to spend some more time with you. I don't want to call and cancel our date tonight. Like, that would look like I held it against her that she was raped. Or that I thought she was a slut or something. You know, I don't mean anything like that."

"But you don't really think she's just making it up?" Richard asked.

"Look, I don't know what I think. How would I know? But I just can't afford to take chances. It's great if a girl knows the game. But does she? If she can do this to one guy, she can do it to another. You come along, and then I'll say I have to be somewhere and duck out. You buy her a drink or two and split. It'll be fine."

"I'm not … I'm not happy with this. But okay, I suppose I can do it tonight."

SATURDAY, OCTOBER 22, 2:30 P.M.

Alice's kitchen looked out onto her small, secluded back yard. Through the window, she could see the sun resting on the deep-red late-blooming dahlias and the shadow of the Gary oak dappling the lawn as its clusters of dry leaves, not yet blown down by fall winds, shifted in the light breeze. The small patio outside her back door was partly shaded, and two cushioned wicker armchairs shared a table between them. In one, George, comfortable in a worn, brown sweater, stretched out his legs and closed his eyes. Alice poured fresh coffee into two mugs and carried them through the screen door into the fresh air.

Stepping down two slightly uneven brick steps, she placed the cups on the table. George opened his eyes.

"Great lunch, Alice. You make a mean Caesar salad, and the buns were terrific. How did you get them made so early?"

"Secret is a quick-rise yeast," Alice replied. "Here's fresh coffee. I hope I didn't wake you."

"No, although this is a pleasant place to drift off."

"Do you have plans for this afternoon?"

"Not really," George replied. "I have a few errands to do, and then I thought I might go to the anticipated mass on campus at five. Fr. Mark gives a short homily and has a gift for connecting with the kids. I enjoy hearing him."

"I didn't know you went to mass. Is this what you meant the other day when you said that you once were religious and could be again?"

George smiled. "I suppose it is. I'm making some tentative steps back toward belief, and the place that seems right to do that stepping right now is the Catholic Church."

"It still seems very strange to me."

"I can understand that. But the Catholic Church is the one that has, I think, preserved best the premodern philosophical tradition: Augustine, Aquinas. And it's that tradition that has started me thinking again."

"But surely modern science has disproved that tradition?"

"Not so. The metaphysical thinking of, for example, Thomas Aquinas, has nothing to do with science. It's a different type of reasoning. It works from taking basic, undeniable propositions and reasoning from them. Science is about taking observations, creating a theory that is tested by experiment, and then making predictions about future events based on the outcomes. They are two distinct ways of arriving at conclusions, and the fact that one exists and works says nothing about the validity of the other."

"You mean that faith and science live in two different worlds, and both can be valid? But, of course, faith is not rational, while science is."

"No, that's not what I mean. Look at it this way. Suppose you want to find out what the angles of a triangle would be if all three sides were equal. You could start with the fact of a triangle with three equal sides, and you could apply a series of logical steps that would ultimately prove that the angles all must be 60 degrees: a geometric proof that, if done correctly, is irrefutable, and in fact, at least used to be taught to every high-school student. Now, alternatively, you could produce lots and lots of triangles with equal sides and then measure the angles of all of them. If you drew them correctly, you would find that the angles were all 60 degrees, and, from that, you could construct a theory that this is always true. But this method could not guarantee that it would always be true. If you were as challenged with a ruler as I am, you might even see variations in your results, although you might recognize that this was because the lines you drew were not exactly equal. The first method, the geometrical proof, is like Aquinas' thinking; the second is what modern science does.

"Neither method is 'irrational.' Both should ideally give you correct results, but the scientific approach would always have to be qualified, unless you can have perfect confidence that what you have observed will always hold true in the future, and science alone cannot guarantee that. In fact, if you throw out Aquinas' metaphysics and take up with modern philosophy, nothing can guarantee that, which means that science, itself, cannot be trusted as reliable."

"But you talk about 'undeniable propositions.' Are there any? And where do they come from?'

"Good point," George replied. "It's true that Aquinas and similar theorists have to start with some assumptions about the world. For example, that we can know reality. Mathematics, like the Euclidian theorem I just talked about, also starts with assumptions—axioms that cannot be proved but must be assumed. And all science rests on certain assumptions, such as the ability of the human mind to understand nature. That doesn't make any of them irrational."

"But that just leaves us all at sea. For instance, the existence of— well, let's say, God—has to be assumed and cannot be proved. At least so I am told."

"Not 'proved' as in we can prove that water has a specific chemical composition, but the metaphysical demonstration, like the geometric proof, is pretty convincing, provided you really understand it and don't misrepresent it."

"What got you thinking about all this?"

"What I'm seeing. Things like this rape. The way we moderns and post-moderns conceive the world, it seems to me, has not led to more happiness but to less. And the more we keep on assuming that we can throw out this moral rule and make up this other one with no regard for the realities of human existence, the worse the situation gets. Never mind worrying that religion is irrational. Our culture is now in denial that there are any realities in human existence.

"Sure, when I was a young man, there were injustices in our lives and rules to follow. And the rule that if you got a girl pregnant, you got married right away didn't always make everyone happy all the time. Throwing out the sexual rules was supposed to mean that we had more respect for people, for their feelings, and for what they wanted for their lives. But the result has been more unhappiness and less respect. While my students would undoubtedly write me off as a nostalgic oldster, I'm not in my dotage. They just haven't seen enough to be able to evaluate the changes. You see, I think there is a rape culture on campus, but I think it's far more pervasive than sexual assault, and I think that rather than addressing the causes and putting out the fire, there's a good chance that we're piling on more kindling by refusing to accept the power and place of human sexuality."

George and Alice sat in silence for a while, finishing their coffees. When they were done, George stood up.

"I could sit here in the sunshine all afternoon, Alice, but unfortunately, I do have to get to the bank. Would you like to meet for brunch tomorrow? I'd be happy to make some eggs Benedict for us at my place."

Alice rose to her feet. "That sounds good, George," she said. "Would eleven work for your schedule?"

"Just fine." He leaned forward and kissed Alice's cheek. Alice smiled.

When George had driven away in his car, Alice went back to her kitchen and began loading the dishwasher. George was certainly a more unusual and interesting person than she had realized. She saw with a sudden clarity how she had pigeon-holed him as a classic gay conservative, of whom she knew a few: men and women whose sexual orientation was accepted in the community but who followed a quiet lifestyle, seeking more permanent relationships and stable familial situations, who held economically conservative views, and who lived with apparently little interest in their activist colleagues. She wondered where their recent friendship was going, since in any other situation it would look a lot like courtship. But that was certainly not on the agenda, and Alice acknowledged to herself that she found it difficult to understand a relationship with a man that was not purely professional but was not romantic either.

His foray into religion was also puzzling. Alice had no difficulty with the few colleagues, mostly Muslims or Jews, who practised their religion, but that was a private matter. George seemed to relate religion quite specifically to what was happening outside his private devotional life, to think that it had something to say to the chaotic world of the university campus, where a misspoken word could mean the end of a career, and an accusation of questioning the prevailing social agreement on morality could mean ostracism.

Alice pressed the wash cycle button. She too had some errands to run. For a moment, she wondered why she bothered. At her age, retirement was only a matter of time, and then what? Working away, perhaps, at papers no one would want to read, doing a little travelling—although, in truth, Alice hated travelling and hated leaving her home—and waiting to die. "I'm thinking like an adolescent," she said to herself. "What I have is the best I could have, and having some stupid existentialist crisis in one's sixties is pathetic."

SATURDAY, OCTOBER 22, 4:00 P.M.

Fr. Mark Gibbons knelt facing the makeshift altar—really a seminar table that was now covered with the altar cloth and with the crucifix set out on it and a lighted candle on either side. He was grateful that the university allowed him this space at noon on three weekdays and from

4:00 p.m. to 6:00 p.m. on Saturdays so he could offer a weekday mass on Monday, Wednesday, and Friday, and an anticipated mass—the mass for Sunday on the Saturday vigil—on Saturday afternoon. It had been debated hotly by the Student Services Unit, who arranged room bookings, and there had been several university officers opposed. Pressure from the Muslim Student Association for prayer space had similarly been viewed with distrust, but ultimately an "open door" policy for religious practice had been approved, provided it was kept to hours and spaces that were not needed for other purposes.

Fr. Mark had been educated at Ontario universities. In Ontario, some colleges within the University of Toronto still maintained more than nominal religious affiliation, student housing for faith-based groups was common, and quiet efforts were made to accommodate religious practice and beliefs. Not so here. Fr. Mark also wondered if the focus of Beacon Hill University on the Humanities, Social Sciences, Fine Arts, and Law contributed to a special dislike of religion because those subjects had serious reasons to be afraid of a religious perspective that challenged their assumptions. The divine foot, to paraphrase a famous philosopher, could not be allowed in the door.

It was his custom to spend the time from 4:00 p.m. until his small congregation began arriving and when he needed to put on his vestments praying for the university, for the students entrusted to his care, and for any particular needs of which he had been made aware in the past few days. The young man who had died of an overdose and his suffering family were high on his list today, as was Paul Anstel, and those who had committed to helping him establish his innocence. He also turned his prayer to George Bush, who had come back into his life after many years and was now in crisis, having been abandoned by his lover, and was questioning much more.

After searching his mind for other names and adding prayers for the souls of his parents and one brother who had died, Fr. Mark fixed his eyes on the suffering Christ and prayed for his own salvation, courage, and perseverance until death. Just as the door to the seminar room opened and his first parishioner arrived, Fr. Mark rose from his knees and made his way to the table at the side of the room to robe for the mass. A young man walked up to the altar, bowed, and joined Fr. Mark.

"Hello, John," Fr. Mark greeted him. "Right, you're my altar server today."

"Yes, sir," John smiled. "And right after this, I'm off to dinner with Linda's parents."

"And how are the wedding plans?"

"Going pretty well, I guess, although Linda and her mom seem to be fighting over everything. But, so far, Linda's winning. I would like to talk to you, though, about what I should say about one issue. Linda wants this dress—she says it looks wonderful on her. But Fr. Li, who's performing the ceremony, has told us that the dress must be 'modest.' Linda says that's crap and body shaming. Sorry for the language, Father, but I'm just quoting. I kind of get that this dress is not modest by anyone's standard. I know this sounds stupid, but I'm getting worried about it and about how Linda sees this whole thing."

"I can understand how that would worry you, John. There's a very strong cultural pressure to believe that insistence on modest clothing is demeaning to women. But many Christians still believe that in church, even though we have dropped the old requirements of women covering their hair, it isn't appropriate to dress so that every man in the congregation is thinking you look hot. And I know Linda would say that this was their problem, not hers!"

"Exactly, Father. And I don't know what to say."

"Let's chat about it later. What about dropping around to my office on Monday or Tuesday? I know you can't stay tonight; in fact, I have an appointment with someone immediately after mass anyway."

"Okay. Thanks, Father. I'll text you a couple of possible times later tonight."

The robing complete, Fr. Mark and John quietly made their way to the altar. A young Chinese woman in jeans and a white shirt had set up a portable keyboard in the corner of the room and announced, "Our entrance hymn is found in your leaflets on page 15: 'Be Thou My Vision.'"

She struck the opening chords, and the small congregation of twenty-two stood and began singing, "Be thou my vision, O Lord of my heart. Not be all else to me save that thou art. Thou my best thought by day or by night. Waking or sleeping, thy presence my light."

The mass progressed through the first reading, a psalm in which the congregation spoke the response, second reading, and finally, the Gospel. Fr. Mark read from the lectern and, after closing the book, began his short homily.

"All of you are here because you believe in God. You know that believing in God has consequences. But so does not believing. I hear from many of you about the problems you face every day, especially in your relationships. I hear young women telling me that their dates expect sex to follow from an evening out, and young men tell me the same. You wonder if your date cares about you at all or only about getting sex.

"And I hear how many of you wonder about the courses you are taking and what is being taught in them—statistics and studies your professors interpret to prove that our society's current ideas about life, death, and sexuality are all true, while the ideas of the orthodox Christian faith are all oppressive and false.

"I hear many of you asking what meaning your lives can have in a culture where ideas don't have to be consistent and identity is substituted for truth. But I ask you to think: all these things—the disrespect of you as a person, the disrespect for life, the rejection of beauty and truth, the rejection of a culture that, despite all its failures, has enabled freedom and prosperity—all these things flow naturally from a simple idea that we are supposed to accept: that believing in God damages our neutrality and objectivity, while assuming that God does not exist is a neutral position. No, my friends, there is no neutral. To behave as if God does not exist is to embrace atheism and its consequences, which philosophers like Nietzsche saw clearly: only the strong and ruthless survive."

Fr. Mark expanded on his theme for the next five minutes. After the recitation of the creed and the prayers, he turned to prepare the elements for the consecration, the congregation responding, "Blessed be God forever."

George, sitting back near the door, admired again how Fr. Mark could speak in a way that these young people could hear. Even those who had retained their faith in some form, George knew, had serious confusions. The assumptions with which they were brought up were so strong, and the peer pressure so great, that independent thought was a rarity. George wondered where he would go with this. He seemed suddenly to be recognizing the incoherence of many ideas he had always accepted without much question. He wondered if this was some grand illusion perpetrated by decay of his brain.

At the altar, Fr. Mark raised the wine and bread as the great Amen was sung by the congregation. At that moment, as always, Fr. Mark knew that he had done that which he was born to do. As a priest, he had stood in the place of Jesus and had been the instrument through which the elements of bread and wine became the Lord's body and blood. A peace came to him and the sense that in this moment, all time converged in the cross.

George realized he had paid little attention to the actual act of consecration of the bread and wine. Since he would not be receiving communion but asking for a blessing as a non-Catholic and, he acknowledged, a very dubious believer, he was not disturbed. Still, as the congregation knelt and Fr. Mark raised the chalice containing the wine and held above it a consecrated host, George repeated with the congregation, "Lord, I am not worthy that you should enter under my roof, but only say the word and my soul will be healed."

Behind him, as Fr. Mark lowered the vessel, George heard a thud. The seminar room door was thrown open, and it banged across the back wall. He turned instinctively toward the noise, as did everyone else in the room. Feeling as if he was watching a fast-motion film, George saw three people in black shirts, jeans, and black ski masks run through the open door. One held high a cellphone, presumably videoing the process. The other two held bags from which they pulled balloons filled with something that appeared red and various smaller objects that George could not immediately identify.

"No to homophobia. No to oppression. No to rapists." Three voices chanted. The balloons were thrown randomly, as were the smaller items, one of which, George realized as it hit the floor in front of him, was a red-soaked woman's sanitary pad.

Fr. Mark, seeing the entrance, immediately pulled the vessels from the altar and covered them with his body as he turned to face the wall, shielding the bread and wine that he had just consecrated from splashes of the red substance and the barrage of red-coated sanitary pads.

Chaos erupted in the room as John attempted to block progress to the altar, and two other young men joined him. Several other students crouched to the floor, half expecting knives or gunshots. The men who had tried to block the assault were hit by balloons in their faces and were covered in a sticky red substance. John grabbed the jacket of the smallest intruder, and a paper fell from a ripped pocket. Before others could react, the three had turned and run from the room, leaving students screaming, huddling together, and a few of the more self-possessed searching their cellphones for a Campus Security phone number.

Fr. Mark turned back to the group and regained his feet. He put the consecrated bread and wine back on the altar table, which now was splashed with red. He moved quickly forward to help those on their knees or desperately wiping the red substance off their faces and clothes.

George, who had been so surprised that the event seemed to have ended before he had realized it was occurring, joined in the effort to soothe the students, some of whom were now crying uncontrollably.

"It's all right," Fr. Mark kept repeating. "It's all right. They didn't hurt anyone, and the body and blood of our Lord was not harmed."

"But is this blood, Father?" one of the young men asked. "What if it's contaminated? Are we at risk?"

"Just wait for Security," Fr. Mark replied. "We'll find out what this is. I don't think it's blood. But you'll get all the medical help you need."

George put in his own call to Security. Like Alice, he was acquainted with Martin Blatt and knew that a call from a faculty member was likely to be given a higher priority than one from a student.

Martin himself arrived in the room ten minutes later. By this time, students were sitting, some comforting those who were still crying.

George and Fr. Mark immediately joined him.

"What happened?" Martin asked.

"We were just about to distribute communion," Fr. Mark related, "when three people with black ski masks broke in and threw balloons filled with some red substance as well as sanitary napkins soaked in what looks like the same stuff. Three of our young men tried to stop them from coming to the altar and were splashed for their troubles. I'm afraid that my priority was protecting the consecrated bread and wine."

George confirmed the general outline of the events. "No one could be recognized," he added.

Fr. Mark went on. "This doesn't seem like blood, but I don't know what it is. My students are concerned because they don't know if it's toxic or not. Three of them were badly covered, including my altar server, who tried to stop them from getting to the altar. I think they should be taken for medical attention, and we need to know what the substance is."

"Right away, Father," Martin replied. Martin turned to the three young men. "My officers will take you to Health Services. I'm sure they will do everything possible to protect you, and we will find out what this stuff is, although I agree with the Father that it's not blood. Wrong colour; wrong smell."

"Thanks, sir," John spoke up. "There is one thing. When I tried to grab one of them, I ripped a pocket on their jacket. This fell out." John passed over a folded sheet of paper. It was the revision to the syllabus for Elizabeth Maryfield's Feminist Legal Studies class.

A few minutes later, ski masks stuffed into pockets and bags dumped in a convenient garbage bin, Tyler, Angie, and Suze were laughing as they made their way into the residence common room, now deserted and dark.

"Okay!" exclaimed Tyler. "Done. Did you get some good video, Angie?"

"Perfect, including a shot of Professor Bush just standing there like a dimwit. The look on his face was hilarious."

"I'm not very happy that the bozo in the white robes ripped my jacket," Suze complained. "I just bought it, and now I'll have to junk it."

"Oh, quit complaining," Tyler responded. "Now, let's all go over to my apartment and look at the video. We'll download it onto my computer for editing and pick out the still shots we want. Then I'll take my laptop to the pub, and we can do the written commentary over a beer and some food. I'm starving."

My lamps are shedding a gentle glow over my desk; my electric fireplace does not crackle and spark, but I find its warmth comforting, and I think it is pretty, although my friend laughs at me and says that I have no taste! I tell my friend that the ban on wood fireplaces has left us with few choices. Would he think it preferable to play a DVD of a burning log on my TV?

I have written into the night, chasing the dark. If I can hold it down, describe it as I saw it then and as I see it now ... will the night end? But how I see and understand it now, of course, is not how I saw and understood it then, so perhaps the fight is futile after all. Even so, I will write on.

SATURDAY, OCTOBER 22, 7:00 P.M.

Hart was tossing the salad when his intercom buzzed. It was Elizabeth, of course, and after some wine, they would eat and then adjourn to the living room for brandy and sex. It had become their normal Saturday routine.

He did not want to break it off with Elizabeth, but she was beginning to worry him. "She's becoming overconfident and reckless," he thought as he mixed in the dressing.

Hart had very clear plans for his future. Becoming Dean had been for one purpose only: to get to know the members of the local bar association and to demonstrate how he fit their conceptions of a progressive, enlightened leader. Likely he would accept another term as Dean, but then, by his fiftieth birthday, he would make his move for an appointment to the bench. Being known and supported by the bar association was crucial for that step. There, as a judge, he would influence the law and be a power in the country for years to come. Since the retirement age for judges was seventy-five, Hart certainly expected an eventual promotion to the Court of Appeal. With a little luck, he might even make it to the Supreme Court of Canada, although the fact that only one judge on that august body was by convention from the Western provinces made that a chancy matter. Still, if he was lucky with his timing, it was by no means impossible.

All this required, however, that there be no black marks against his record. And while progressivism was crucial to his appointment, any misstep that caused damage to his reputation, or suggested that he was unreliable, had to be avoided. He had known that an affair with Elizabeth would be a risk, although at the time, her lovely body and uninhibited passion had seemed worth it. Later, he had also come to value her impeccable credentials as an upcoming power in the legal feminist movement. She liked to push the boundaries of legal scholarship, and Hart found that both stimulating and challenging. Her ideas helped him to stand in the forefront of progressive Deans at the university and on the national front. But her recent behaviour had begun to worry him.

She clearly expected him to facilitate her promotion and tenure, and he had implicitly committed to do so. But when her application came to him for a recommendation, he knew he would step aside and turn the file over to the Associate Dean, citing a close friendship with Elizabeth that would place him in a conflict of interest. Elizabeth, he thought, would be furious. But it was the only way to proceed safely. Should their affair come to light and should he have participated in her promotion and tenure application, it would mean the end of his aspirations. And if the affair then ended, once he could no longer be of use to her, so be it. But until that day, he intended to enjoy the relationship to its fullest. Now he was becoming less certain of the wisdom of that decision.

He opened the door, and Elizabeth, dressed in a long white skirt and a denim jacket, gave him a quick kiss as she stepped inside.

"What a day!" she exclaimed. "I've found at least twenty mistakes in the page proofs, and my eyes are crossed from peering at them. Please," she continued as she sat down on the love seat, kicked off her half-boots, and put her bare feet up on the glass coffee table, "have pity on me and pour me a large glass of wine!"

As Hart returned with a substantial glass of white wine, the telephone rang.

"It's the Provost," he said with surprise as he looked at call display. "It's strange that she would be phoning now, just at dinner on a Saturday."

"Ignore it," Elizabeth instructed. "Get some wine and come over here and sit by me."

"No. I can't do that." Hart picked up.

"Hello, Hart speaking."

The Provost, Amelie Zirdari, spoke brusquely. "Hart, we have a major problem. I've just had a call from our Campus Security Director—you know Martin, of course—who was reporting on an assault."

"I'm sorry to hear that. I suppose on Saturday, assaults aren't uncommon on campus. Was anyone hurt?"

"No, but this wasn't the common case of a couple of students getting drunk and mixing it up in the residence. These people—three of them—broke into the weekly Saturday Catholic mass during the celebration and threw balloons filled with a red substance—not blood, thank God—and disgusting feminine hygiene products, also reddened, at the altar and over three of the congregation, including the altar server."

Hart felt the floor drop out of his stomach. What had Elizabeth talked about the other night: disruption of misogynist religious ceremonies? Surely …

Before his pause had become noticeable, Hart responded, "That's dreadful. But how can I be of help?"

Amelie continued, "The young man who was serving at the altar grabbed one of the assailants and tore his or her jacket. A paper dropped out, which was identified by one of your professors, George Bush, as at least purporting to be from a class taught by one of your other faculty members. The paper was a list of preapproved projects for credit, one of which was 'performance art protesting the use of campus space by misogynist organizations.' It seems a logical conclusion that these protesters were attempting to fulfill a course requirement. One of the things they were shouting was 'no to rapists.' I think you've had an incident of rape in your student body this week."

"Amelie," Hart replied, "I can't believe that any faculty member of ours would approve such a thing."

"Well, the name on the syllabus paper was Elizabeth Maryfield. And while the description does not precisely mandate what happened, it certainly suggests a category of actions that would fit. Look, I won't keep you further now. But I want to see you at 8:30 tomorrow morning in my office. I've called an emergency meeting with Martin, yourself, and Melanie Amahdi from Student Services. I'm sorry, of course, to disrupt your Sunday, but the students must be identified and appropriate discipline applied, and I want you there to talk about what happens to Dr. Maryfield. She may not have intended what happened, but it appears she set up the situation so that it could happen.

"God knows what we'll do if the paper gets hold of this. We have enough student scandals already, and while there may not be a lot of Catholics at the university, there are certainly a few in government. Whatever their feelings about the regressive nature of the Church, you can count on them to be shocked and scandalized by something like this, especially when it suits their policies of trying to cut back on our grants. I'm sure I also don't have to tell you that we have a major project appeal in for upgrades of several of our buildings and additional wings on two. And that reminds me—our communications people do not want anyone talking to the press. If a reporter calls you, refer them to communications. We'll work on a statement tonight, just to be ready in case. I know I can count on your support, Hart."

"Fine. Fine. Of course, I'll be there tomorrow." Hart hung up the phone. He turned to Elizabeth.

"It appears," he said coldly, "that some of your students disrupted the Catholic mass on campus tonight by throwing bags of unidentified liquid and some kind of feminine products at the congregation."

Elizabeth smiled. "Really? How great! I can't wait to see what they bring me on Tuesday."

"Well, hold your enthusiasm. The Provost is furious. What the hell were you thinking of, encouraging students to behave in this disrespectful way?"

"Disrespectful? Oh, come on, Hart. An organization that promotes homophobia, transphobia, and misogyny can hardly be subjected to 'disrespect!' Besides, how do you know it was my students?"

"One of them dropped the syllabus amendment you circulated in class. I understand from Amelie that the similarity between one of the suggested projects and what happened is striking."

"Nonsense. Doesn't prove anything other than that some progressive students are sick of the university pandering to repressive groups. Good for them."

"Well, if they expect to receive credit for this assignment," Hart stretched the word assignment in a sarcastic tone, "they will have to turn it in. And then you'll know."

"Are you expecting me to betray my students? To subject their work to censorship?"

"Elizabeth, I can't seem to make you understand that there's theory and then there's the real world. I have to live in the real world, and so do you. The Provost knows that this was a part of your course, and she wants to discuss with me what consequences there will be for you."

Elizabeth picked up her wine and waved it airily. "Garbage and horse feathers. I was extremely careful in how I set out that option. I did not target religion, never mind any specific religion, and I certainly did not talk about interrupting services. But if some of my students have decided to call the Catholic Church on its discriminatory doctrines, then that's their right. They were simply exercising academic freedom."

"Assaulting a priest and his congregation at worship?"

"Really, Hart. You may sound progressive sometimes, but you don't get it. Now, you say it was an assault. Was anyone hurt?"

"No, apparently not, although depending on what the substance was that they threw, there could be consequences. But even if the substance was harmless, you know that legally this was an assault—a criminal act."

"Minor. As theorists such as Naomi Klein have shown, destruction of property is an acceptable act in an oppressive society based on capitalist greed."

"Elizabeth!" Hart sat down beside her and grabbed her shoulders as if to shake her. "Listen to me. If this embarrasses the university, if this causes an outcry in the ministry for advanced education, if the public are outraged and donors are discouraged, I don't care how progressive or justified these things are. The Provost will not support your tenure application, never mind promotion. And if I can't satisfy her that this will be dealt with properly, it will mean the end of my chances for reappointment as Dean."

Elizabeth put down her glass and removed his hands from her shoulders.

"Don't touch me like that, Hart, unless you mean to follow your reactionary comments with violence against women. Let me tell you a few truths about reality. In this university, I will be a hero for what my students have done; they said something in a dramatic way that needed to be said. Simply carried the consequences of theory into the real world. And the Provost will not dare to do anything to me. If I'm not promoted now, there will be a stink across the academic world that will make a loss of a few paltry donors seem trivial. Screw up your courage and tell the Provost to go to hell."

Hart slumped forward on the love seat and put his hands over his face. "You really don't understand how this works, do you? You just don't get it. No one is going to make a martyr out of you or out of me. But if this causes trouble, the Provost will make sure that we're ruined. Oh, maybe you will get tenure. She might feel that that's a sop to be thrown to the women's caucus on campus. But promotion? No, believe me, there will be a reason why it's 'premature.' And it'll be 'premature' for the next ten years. And as for me, who'll give a damn if a white straight male doesn't get renewed as Dean? No one's going to the barricade to defend me."

Elizabeth looked at him with contempt. "It's all about you, isn't it, Hart? You don't give a damn about a just society. You just want what you want."

Hart, now blazingly angry, stood up and shouted, "If you can't see that there's nothing else in the world that counts for anything—all that crap about a just society and equality. Where does that get you, and why should I or anyone else care? In a hundred years, we'll all be dead, and who cares about what happens next? Sure, we need to play the game. Sure, we need to talk the talk so that no one realizes how our entire system depends solely on the integrity of the players, and that the players know damn well that there is no such thing as integrity!

It's like the monetary system. The only thing standing between us and ruin is a fiction that we must support. But we know it's fiction. And we know that when the chips are down, we'll do whatever it takes to get what we want now. And nothing, nothing else matters."

Elizabeth stood up. "That's totally untrue. The future does matter; it's all that matters."

"Crap again. Why? Tell me one good reason why it matters."

Elizabeth paused. "Because evolution has selected us to care: it's in our genes. The human race has to believe in the future, and we've been programmed to do that. I care."

"Well, you care for bloody nothing then, because then there's no reason at all why anyone should care. It's all just mechanical, and I guess that particular facet of evolution skipped me. In fact, I think it skipped most people, including you. It's simply that commitment to a just society is your road to success. Well, my darling Lizzie, here is where our roads to success diverge."

"I think I should leave."

"I think you're right," Hart replied, crossing the room to his buffet and pouring himself a glass of wine from the open bottle. "Don't let the door hit you on your way out."

As soon as the door closed, Hart set down the wine glass and, after a slight hesitation, picked up a highball glass, poured himself three fingers of rye, dropped in one ice cube, and sat back down on the sofa.

The situation was out of control. Elizabeth was a menace. She had shown herself determined to pursue this insane project, and she had to be stopped before she ruined him. But he could not think of how.

Elizabeth, shaking with rage, stepped out of the elevator in Hart's building and onto the street. Although earlier the day had been sunny, the clouds had gathered in the late afternoon, and some rain had fallen. The October evening was cool with the wind again picking up. She paused for a moment, leaning against the building door to collect herself. The entire relationship had been a mistake. Now Hart was planning on throwing her under any passing bus, especially one driven by the Provost. There would be a fight. There had to be a fight. All she had ever wanted was to make society better. And somehow, Hart's angry assertion that there was no possible reason for that to be important had to be proved wrong.

Pulling out her phone, she found a nearby hotspot and logged in. Quickly, she googled the number of the local paper, the *Victoria Times*. She called and received an after-hours message for voice mail.

"Hi. This is Dr. Elizabeth Maryfield from Beacon Hill University. I'd like to speak to your reporter, Sam Angelo. I have a story about a rape at the university that I think he'd be interested in. Please have him call me at this number as soon as he can."

SATURDAY, OCTOBER 22, 8:00 P.M.

"Hi, Sarah." Arty met Sarah as she approached the door of the student pub. "How're you doing? Hey, I heard about what happened! Look, I'm really sorry. I know I said that before, but, of course, I didn't realize how bad things had got with that creep."

"Thanks, Arty," Sarah replied. "I'm feeling a little better now, but I don't think I'm up for a long evening or …"

"No, no, I understand. In fact, I thought that Richard might join us for a drink and then we'd go our own ways for the evening. I can really understand how you don't want to be out late or … anything. Richard's feeling pretty upset too, so that's why I thought it would be a good idea for him to come. Get you both out. And I know you and Richard are friends."

"Yeah, he was a big help. I'll never forget that. I'm sorry Richard's upset. He was great to take me to Health Services and all that."

"Good. Well, he's got us a table inside, so let's go and meet him and get a drink and some food."

"Sure. I haven't had much appetite. But I'd love some wings and some fries. And maybe one of the martini specials."

"Sounds fine," Arty responded as he and Sarah walked through the door into the wall-to-wall noise of a crowded room where, after the third (or fourth) beer, voices naturally were raised, causing others to shout louder, until even the music coming at full blast from a live band with their electronic gear was hard to distinguish over the noise.

They found Richard at a corner table tucked behind the band and at the far side of the open space that formed the student pub. As usual, the bare wood floor had several spills, and the smell of beer prevailed over the smell of the deep fryer. The odd paper napkin joined the general clutter and was kicked by passing feet into the aisles. They sat down with Richard, and a waiter appeared quickly to take their first drink order.

"Good to see you out, Sarah," Richard said. "How's it going?"

"Not too bad," Sarah replied. "I can't thank you enough for …"

"Hey, you already did that. Let's just try to forget about all that and have a drink and some food. I'm starved."

"Sure, that's what we should do. But Richard, just one thing. My mind's a bit foggy on what happened after … well … you know. I know we talked on the phone. I think you said that you came to check on me because Paul was behaving weirdly when he got back to your place."

Richard shifted uncomfortably and kept silent while the waiter put a pitcher of beer on their table and two glasses, as well as a martini glass with a blue liquid in it next to Sarah.

"Look, let's not talk about it right now," he said. "Better to forget it happened."

"Richard," Sarah replied, "I can't just forget it. I'm certainly willing to drop the subject, and believe me, I don't want to dwell on this. But just tell me what happened when Paul got back to your unit, and I'll leave it for the rest of the evening."

"Uh, okay, I guess. Well, I'm not sure what time it was because I'd been asleep. But I heard the door, and I looked out and saw him. It was dark, so I called out something—can't remember exactly what, but 'hi' or something, and he called back. He sounded, well, upset. I can't remember what he said, but something like, 'mind your own business.'"

"And that's it?"

"More or less."

"More or less?"

"Yeah. Sarah, really, I can't remember exactly."

"But it was something that made you worried about me? You knew he'd been with me?"

"Sure. He'd talked about meeting you and the trouble you were having with your parents, and he told me how you two were going out to talk about your course selection for next semester, and how your dad was upset about what you wanted to take."

"And what he said when he came back made you think something was wrong?"

"Sarah," Richard laughed a bit, "whatever courses you're taking, don't bother with Advocacy. You're already really good at cross-examination. But come on, drink up. Let's not talk about this stuff anymore."

"Sorry," Sarah responded. "I know I have to put this out of my mind. It wasn't my fault, and I just have to get on with my life."

The din in the pub became even louder as three people at the next table, crouched over a laptop, broke into a roar of laughter.

"It's sure noisy in here," Sarah remarked, "and those people at the next table are screaming. I wonder what's so funny."

"Probably cat videos," Arty laughed.

"Wait a second, that's Tyler from my Feminist Legal Studies class, and I think the two with him are Suze and Angie, who are also in the class. I don't know any of them very well."

At that moment, Angie noticed Sarah at the next table. She got up and walked over to stand beside Sarah.

"Hey, Sarah. Good to see you out. Dr. Maryfield told us about what happened. It's gross. She's revised the whole syllabus so that we can support you. And wait 'til you hear what we did tonight. Hey, performance art!" Angie, her words slightly slurred, pumped her fist into the air. Tyler rose from his chair and joined them.

"Angie, don't spoil the surprise. Sarah, are you going to be in class on Tuesday?"

"I expect to be."

"Well, you'll find out then. But we're all behind you a hundred per cent. We're going to make this campus aware of what's going on here."

"Thanks," Sarah said, "for your support. But I'm not really sure I want a big thing made of this."

"But," Angie continued, sounding puzzled, "Dr. Maryfield says you're going to write it all up and make it your major paper in the course."

"I don't know," Sarah said. "I know she told me I should do that. But I'm beginning to wonder if it would be better just to forget it."

"Forget it?" Angie shouted. "Forget this? No way, no way ..."

Tyler took Angie's arm. "Come on, Angie, this isn't a good place for a debate. Let's get back to Suze and our work." He led Angie back to their table.

Sarah turned back to Richard and Arty. "Does this whole campus know about me?" she asked.

"Well," Arty replied, "I hear Maryfield's been talking about it."

Sarah stood up and put a twenty-dollar bill on the table. "Sorry, I'm not feeling too well. I think I want to go home."

Arty also stood up, awkwardly. "Well, okay. Uh, do you want me to walk you there? Or what about Richard—he could take you."

"No," Sarah replied, noting Arty's hesitation and Richard's look of surprise. "I'm not far from campus, and it's not late. I'll be fine. Take my drink out of that, and I'll get the change later. I'll see you in school Monday or Tuesday."

Sarah turned and walked quickly away from the pub. The air outside was cool and damp, but a stiff breeze had temporarily blown back the clouds from the earlier rain. She pulled her jacket closer around her shoulders and zipped it up. Stepping briskly, she crossed the avenue and turned toward her home.

It wasn't right, she thought to herself. She knew something that she couldn't recall specifically, but she knew something was off. Then her mind turned back to Tyler and Angie. And to Dr. Maryfield. Dr. Maryfield was supposed to be supporting her, but she had spread the story of Sarah's experience to her classmates and to whom else? Sarah mentally rebuked herself. Shame was not warranted; it was a stereo-type from which she had to free herself. She should not mind people knowing. She should not be afraid to speak out against a world in which women could not freely dress as they wanted, drink what they wanted, and have sex when they wanted without men believing that they were there for the taking. Objectification—that's what it was. As she walked, Sarah gave herself the feminist lecture.

She turned into her building and put the key in the lock, looking quickly behind her. When she reached her apartment door, she looked carefully back down the stairs before she unlocked it. Then she opened it only as far as necessary to allow her to slip inside and closed it after her at once, throwing the bolt, fastening the chain, and moving the chair, which she had set to one side, back under the doorknob. She gave a relieved breath. Crossing to her kitchen, she pulled out the vodka bottle and poured a shot into a glass. She would have to stop this if she was going back to school Monday, but she still had another day, and there was no point suffering when a couple more drinks would let her sleep.

As she put the bottle back on the counter, she again tried to recall what was bothering her about how Richard had responded to her questions. Was it ... ? Sipping her drink, she took out her cell from her purse and called Campus Security.

"Hello, I'm trying to reach Director Blatt. Is he on duty?"

The assistant at the other end of the phone replied that he had been called out on an emergency and might or might not be returning to the office before he went home.

"It's Sarah Yung calling. He told me I could call him whenever I needed to. I wonder if you could give me his cellphone number."

"Oh, Ms. Yung. Yes, Mr. Blatt said that if you called, I should give you the number. It's 250-213-4356."

Sarah put the number into her phone and pressed Call. On the third ring, Martin Blatt answered.

"Yes, Sarah. Is there something I can do for you?"

"Mr. Blatt, I realize this might be confidential, but there is one thing I wanted to ask you. It's about what Paul told you in his statement."

"Well, Sarah, I'm not sure at this time that I should break any confidences. I understand you haven't yet decided whether to report this to the police. They would want to hear from you without any—well, influence—and that would include knowing what Paul has said to me."

"I understand. But this isn't really about what happened. It's about what happened after."

"Why don't you ask me, and I'll see what I can do."

"Thank you. What I want to know is what Paul told you about getting back to his unit and what happened then."

The night is fading now, and there is some light in the sky. It's clear outside still, and the stars I could see earlier have faded. I am watching the full moon setting over the hills just as the light begins to brighten.

Have you guessed yet, dear readers, who in this story wears my face? I hope you have not. If you have guessed, I have failed … failed to change and failed to exercise my craft. My craft is that of storyteller. Yes, I am a published novelist, although the name you see on the spine of this book will not be the name you would recognize. Nor, of course, is my name in the story. But I have written through the night more than once and told many stories, all of which were this story. And one day, I thought, "Maybe if I tell that story, the real story, the story behind my stories. Maybe if I tell it once, I can stop writing it." Perhaps I will then write other stories. Or perhaps not. They say that inspiration only comes from pain, and as I try to stop the pain by writing this real story, will the pain go and then the inspiration, the drive to write?

SATURDAY, OCTOBER 22, 8:35 P.M.

Alice sat in front of her television, feet on a well-worn leather ottoman, wrapped in a blue chenille dressing gown. A glass of red wine sat on the table by her chair. She was watching a favourite crime drama and enjoying the quiet evening. From time to time, her thoughts strayed to George, wondering again why he was suddenly so interested in her company and where his surprising interest in things philosophical and religious would lead. The telephone, right by her glass of wine, rang. She pressed Pause on the remote and picked up the phone.

"Alice? It's George."

"Hi, George. What's up?"

"I'm at Paul's motel room with Fr. Mark. There's just been a very disturbing incident. It looks like Elizabeth Maryfield has encouraged her class to commit acts of vandalism, and I think it's likely connected to Paul's situation and the rape. I'm calling to suggest that we bring our brunch forward to 10:00 a.m. and that Fr. Mark join us. I think we need to consider how best to persuade Sarah to release her medical samples. This is starting to get out of hand."

"What happened, George?"

"I don't want to get into detail tonight, but Fr. Mark is pretty shaken up, as am I. Three black-masked students threw balloons of red liquid and red sanitary napkins at the altar during this evening's mass."

"That's horrible. It … it wasn't blood, was it?"

"No. Campus Security folks think it was red-dyed hand soap. But it made quite a mess, and students were very distressed. Fr. Mark and I have just come from giving Campus Security our statements, and I'm driving Fr. Mark home, so we stopped to let Paul know what had happened. The attackers were shouting various things, and one of them was 'no to rapists.' One of the people had a syllabus page from Elizabeth's class that suggested a project of performance art against misogynist organizations; the page made reference to a 'recent rape involving students.'"

"Okay, sure. I'm fine with 10:00 a.m., although I'm not sure other than what we discussed that there's much to do. But I would appreciate some advice about how to handle things if I'm going to see Sarah on Monday or Tuesday."

Alice hung up the phone and turned off the TV. She sat for a while, sipping her wine. Soon it would be time for her to go to bed. Another night, another step toward death. She hated the nights most. She shook her head and turned the TV back on.

In Paul's motel room, Fr. Mark and George spoke quietly to the young man who sat with his head in his hands.

"It's no good. The easiest thing to do is for me to drop out. They can't carry out any investigation without me, and they won't bother. I can find a job. I mean, I do have three degrees already, and …"

"I wouldn't advise that," George spoke. "Once, your leaving would have just shelved the whole thing, but not now. Failure to cooperate is a disciplinary offence under the policy and can result in a notation on your transcript. Anyone who sees your transcript is bound to ask questions. Once you tell them, they'll wonder why you didn't stay and see it out. And while we may have no faith in the university's processes, other people don't know how things work here. Your degrees will be useless to you, and you'll wind up doing something tedious and boring and wasting your talent."

"True," Fr. Mark agreed. "And except for the misery you are undergoing, there's nothing to be gained by quitting now. We are going to talk to Sarah, this time, face-to-face. I still don't believe she wants to go on without knowing the truth. Now, we've had a long, difficult day, so let's pray, and then we'll leave you to get some rest."

They knelt on the spartan motel carpeting as Fr. Mark prayed for safety through the night and God's guidance in the days ahead. He prayed for comfort for Paul and for Sarah, and for wisdom. As they rose, Fr. Mark clasped Paul's hand.

"If it gets bad—if you can't sleep, and you even feel you can't pray— just keep saying, 'Jesus, I trust in you.' It's a prayer He'll always hear."

SATURDAY, OCTOBER 22, 9:30 P.M.

Arty and Richard sat in the pub as the waiter brought another pitcher of beer.

"Well, that didn't go so well," Arty observed.

"I can't blame her," Richard responded. "It was probably just too soon for her to be out. And that little idiot from the next table—why the hell can't they just leave it alone now?"

"I get the feeling that Maryfield has something planned. You know how she is about rape culture. Looks to me like little Sarah's going to be her poster girl."

"That's disgusting. Really, they just need to drop it. It happened; we know who did it. Now the university just needs to expel him and get on with things."

"Not gonna happen, buddy," Arty replied. "That little crew over there, Tyler, Angie, and Suze, are three of Queen Maryfield's most loyal subjects. Besides, what do you care? You did your good Samaritan act; now just forget about it and let's get some more food."

"I just want to see the mess dealt with quickly and that creep Paul to get what he deserves."

"Man, so what's this hate over Paul?"

"Nothing. But if he got that job with the Supreme Court of Canada, it would be a travesty. Once this gets out, he'll have no chance."

"What's the job? I didn't see it on the postings?"

"You wouldn't because you're still in the undergraduate law program. The court is looking to fill a new position with either a new masters or PhD graduate in law to supervise their clerkship program. It's just an appointment for two years, but boy, after that, every law firm and every law school in the country will want you. Plus, you'll know all the judges on pretty much all the courts, and the odds of getting a judicial appointment in ten or fifteen years go way, way up. It's a quick pass to success."

"Did you apply?"

"Of course, along with every other graduate student who's near finishing their program. Paul did too. But as a PhD, he might have the edge, although the competition's open to both degrees."

"Sounds like pretty poor odds of coming up with the prize."

"Maybe, but last week the odds got better. The selection committee narrowed the list to eight. Both of us, Paul and me, are on it."

"What a chance. And now your odds could be one in seven. Much better."

"Yeah, well, I wouldn't care, of course, if I didn't know Paul was such a hypocrite. And a Catholic! Come on, personal beliefs have got no place in the law or in the policy of the country. We have to use law to create a just society, to include the poor and the oppressed and all those that Paul's precious religion would persecute. He's a hater, all right, but he pretends he isn't. Says he thinks there's some moral law—crap. We know that's just an excuse for bigots. But under human rights law, the selection committee can't even ask about your beliefs, so if Paul is out now, it's not just for my benefit. It'll be important for the law and for us all."

SUNDAY, OCTOBER 23, 1:00 A.M.

Tyler and Angie leaned against the door of his apartment as he fumbled for his key.

He laughed and kissed her again as he managed to pull it out of his jacket pocket. His other hand slipped down her T-shirt to fondle a breast. She sighed, returned his kiss, and then pushed him away.

"Come on and open the door. I'm cold out here."

Tyler snuggled closer to her. "I'll keep you warm, here or there."

"Stop it, Tyler," Angie again pushed away his hand. "Let's get in. You got something good to drink in there? Or maybe some pot?"

"No drugs, honey. Told you a million times. No drugs. But I got some real good scotch that Dad gave me. It's expensive stuff."

Angie pouted, tossing her head and flipping her long hair as she sniffed. "You're just stupid about the pot thing. It's going to be legal soon, and even if they catch you, which they won't as long as you don't do something stupid, the Law Society doesn't even care any more. But OK, let's have the scotch."

Tyler managed to get the key into his lock and open the door. As they went in, he put his backpack with his laptop in it on the desk just beside the door, which he then closed, sliding the bolt.

"We did a good piece of work tonight. Maryfield's going to go over the moon when she sees our footage and reads our commentary. We're gonna put this campus in flames!" Tyler threw his arms over his head exuberantly.

"We turn it in Tuesday, right?"

"Right. And we'll get everyone in the class excited about these projects. She'll get lots for her new book, and we'll get A grades."

"You know, I don't think I realized until tonight that you live in the same building as Sarah."

Tyler shrugged. "Sure. Lots of law students live here. Melissa Crawthorne's upstairs another floor; Sarah's one down. And two or three others from either the graduate classes or the classes behind us live here too. Just a very legal place."

"Melissa? Don't you hang out with her?"

"Sometimes. She's a fun girl."

"Fun like me?" Angie accepted the plastic glass with scotch as Tyler sat down on the sofa beside her with his own tumbler.

"Yeah, fun like you. You jealous?"

Angie laughed. "Not if you can show me a good time, Tyler. And not if I get an A in Dr. Maryfield's class. If that goes down right, I don't care who you play with. But," she continued, sitting up straight and pulling away from Tyler's arm, which he had wrapped around her as she lay back on the sofa cushions, "one thing worries me a bit."

"That is?"

"I didn't like how Sarah behaved tonight. It was like she didn't want to help. And, if I understand this thing right, if she doesn't help, the project won't work."

"Oh, come on. She'll do what Maryfield wants. Let's forget it and drink our scotch, and then I'll show you my bedroom."

Later, as Tyler slept, Angie stared into the half-dark of the room. Streetlights showed through the cracks between the old roller blinds and the window frame, giving enough light that she could distinguish Tyler's highboy, the closet door, the bathroom door, partly open, and the pile of clothing on the one chair in the room. She thought about how much she wanted to get away from this town, this university, and this life. And all that was about to happen.

She imagined how she would feel getting on the plane for Toronto, everything she cared to take with her in one carry-on roller bag. And then a small apartment by herself—no more stupid roommates—and respect. She'd be a graduate student in the country's most respected program in Feminist Legal Studies, bound for a PhD and academic success. Then she saw herself graduated, teaching in a university, but more importantly, making a difference in the world, just like Dr. Maryfield. No more sleeping around then. No more feeling like shit the next morning. No, anyone who ended up in her bed would be a lucky and rare guy. She thought about sitting in a faculty office. Maybe she'd get hired at U of T. They had beautiful old buildings, and beautiful old offices with real wood floors, and ivy climbing the stone walls outside the windows. Just like a movie. And this A in Dr. Maryfield's course (she always addressed her as "Doctor" Maryfield in her mind; disrespect was for jerks like Tyler) was what she needed most. Angie drifted away on the comforting thoughts. Soon.

SUNDAY, OCTOBER 23, 8:30 A.M.

Amelie Zirdari, Vice President Academic and Provost of Beacon Hill University, sat at the head of the conference table in her office. As was appropriate for the second most important official of the university, her corner office was the second-largest on campus and well-appointed. Faculty offices might sport metal desks and spartan chairs, but Amelie's office was furnished in antique oak with comfortable wingback chairs by the desk and proper office chairs with adjustable back supports at the conference table. Hart looked around, appreciating the style and the comfort. Had he not set his ambition on a judicial appointment, being Provost would not be a bad life. Well, having a back-up plan was always useful, he thought, provided he could slip through the various crises that were bound to arise between now and the end of a second term as Dean. One of those crises was on hand now.

Amelie smiled, not too broadly and not too cheerfully. Her smile was adjusted to be welcoming, but to recognize the gravity of the occasion. "Thank you for interrupting your peaceful Sundays to join me," she opened the meeting. "Now, I think most of you know each other, although I would like to introduce Ralph Goodline, who has just joined us this week as our Vice President Human Resources. I think, Ralph, that you have met Martin Blatt, our Director of Security, and likely Hart Haverman, our Dean of Law, but you may not yet know Melanie Amahdi from Student Services."

Hart smiled at Ralph, adjusting his smile to be pleasant but not effusive. Ralph had been meeting with all the Deans, since their hiring practices and the regulation of the faculty members in their units technically fell under Ralph's portfolio.

"I asked Ralph to join us," Amelie continued, "because we will likely need advice on a matter of workplace discipline in this issue. I think you all have a basic understanding of the facts, but, Martin, would you please review the security report of the incident and tell us about any recent developments."

Martin opened his file. "Thanks, Amelie. I don't think I need to review the basic incident, as everyone received my email setting out what happened last night. Further analysis of the red goo indicates that it was, as we suspected, simply clear liquid hand soap that had been coloured with red food colouring. Fortunately, no foreign substances appear to be present, and therefore, although some clothes and the altar linens have been spoiled, likely irredeemably, no one has been injured, and there is no threat to the health of those attacked. Other than psychological injury, of course."

Amelie interrupted. "Excuse me, Martin, but just let me elaborate that we have contacted the Catholic chaplain and made it clear that the university will replace the damaged robes and linens and also make available counselling services to the students present on a priority basis."

"Yes," Martin continued. "Thank you. We conducted interviews with all those present last night. No one could identify the trio who broke in, but the altar server, as you know, ripped one of the assailant's jackets, and a syllabus amendment page from Dr. Elizabeth Maryfield's class was found, presumably dropped from the pocket. The page suggested that students could engage in what was called 'performance art' against misogynist organizations as part of a course requirement. It also made reference to a rape alleged to have occurred where the victim—sorry, survivor—was a law student, as was the accused rapist. We followed up first thing this morning with emails to the students in Dr. Maryfield's classes, asking them to contact us. None of them answered our email. Well, it was only 8:00 a.m. on Sunday, and most of them would be sleeping off Saturday night, but we expect to hear from at least some of them during the day today."

Amelie turned to Ralph. "Assuming, as seems very likely, that the incident last night was a result of the syllabus project, can you brief us, Ralph, on what steps we can take with respect to the faculty member involved?"

Ralph cleared his throat. "As you know, Amelie, faculty discipline is a touchy matter. Looking at the syllabus page—thanks for emailing a copy to me, Martin—I think this would be a very marginal case. Nothing here indicates vandalism, and nothing suggests targeting Catholics. The reference to the rape is very unfortunate, but no names are mentioned, and if I understand correctly, the survivor has given Dr. Maryfield permission to talk about her situation."

Amelie turned to Hart. "What do you know about this, Hart?"

Hart shifted in his chair, which seemed less comfortable now. He knew he needed to proceed with caution. "Not a great deal, Amelie," he replied. "I was aware of the syllabus change. A student came to discuss it with me, but as far as I could see, it simply broadened the options open to the class and was absolutely a progressive move. I didn't see any objection, although I am sure that neither I nor Dr. Maryfield would ever have thought it would lead to vandalism. As you know, Dr. Maryfield's work is provocative, but I am sure she would not cross the line to criminal activity. That some students misinterpreted her suggestions is ..."

Amelie interrupted. "Hart, I'm not asking for a defence of Dr. Maryfield. Ralph has given his opinion that we are unlikely to have a clear case for discipline against her, and that settles it. What about the rape issue?"

"Well," Hart went on, "I do know that the survivor is Dr. Maryfield's research assistant this term and is in her class. I understand that the young woman is willing to have her experience used as a case study in the class and, indeed, will likely write her term paper on the experience, so, unfortunately, the fact of the rape and the identity of the survivor are already widely known in the school."

"I see. All right, this is what must happen. Hart, you need to speak to Dr. Maryfield at once and have her clarify with her class that, while 'performance art' may be acceptable, what she means by that is putting on a play, or having a peaceful demonstration (with permit from the university), or even building a sculpture somewhere—I'm sure we could find space—but not, definitely not, any form of vandalism or other criminal or illegal activity."

Hart nodded. "Of course."

"And," Amelie continued, "Hart, you will also tell her that she is to report immediately the students who committed this outrage to you for disciplinary action by the university."

Melanie leaned forward. "Now really, Amelie. Don't you think that's an overreaction? I mean, these students were acting in good faith, maybe foolishly, but they were relying on a faculty member's guidance and acting under the great emotional stress of knowing that one of their colleagues has been raped. I think we have to make allowances for the trauma, and ..."

Amelie waved her hand and interrupted. "Possibly. If this was a response to trauma, it would go to the severity of the punishment. But we cannot turn our backs on illegal activity."

Hart spoke again. "Melanie has a good point here. But, of course," he added quickly, "the fact that the action was criminal in nature does make a major difference. However, I wonder if we have given enough thought to the publicity that will inevitably happen if we try to discipline these students. They're bound to appeal, possibly even to seek some form of judicial remedy against the university. And we also have to remember that they were acting arguably within the boundaries of academic freedom. Absolutely, we must keep that in mind. The Student Union and the Faculty Association could easily take actions to defend them on that basis. There could be a lot of sympathy for their plight, acting in the cause of social justice."

Amelie frowned. While she supported academic freedom fully, of course, she also had lain awake many nights worrying about campus disruptions. Allowing even a small act of unsanctioned rebellion could lead others to assume there would be no penalty, and then the entire campus could be disrupted with much worse publicity. Still, Hart had a point about publicity, and that it would come at once rather than being something to be feared in the future.

"Well," she responded. "I see your point, Hart. And I'm prepared to take advice on this. But there are two things I am going to insist on. I want to know the names of the students involved, and I want to speak to them personally about the gravity of their conduct. Second, I do not want them to receive credit for these actions in Dr. Maryfield's class. They must do some other project or assignment. This will not count toward their grade."

"But, Amelie," Hart protested, "academic freedom. You can't interfere with Dr. Maryfield's rights to decide how her class will be graded."

"Two things, Hart. First, it's up to you to make sure she does what I expect here. If she genuinely never intended vandalism, she should be willing to take the reasonable step and insist that it not be rewarded, even if not punished. Second, from a technical reading of the calendar, this syllabus amendment was illegal. No, don't interrupt with your legal opinion. The calendar is written plainly, and it says that grading methods cannot be changed at this stage. I've got enough legal knowledge to know that, at the least, it's a reasonable interpretation to say that this new assignment is not permissible under the rules."

"But the Faculty Association will grieve ..." Hart attempted to make another intervention, but as he saw the expression on Amelie's face, he allowed his sentence to fade out without completion.

"Fine," Amelie said as she rose from her chair. "Hart, I'll expect to hear from you shortly about the students' names and about the outcome. Dr. Maryfield is to clarify the meaning of this assignment and report the names to you of any students involved in this incident. She will also inform them that they receive no academic credit for this outrageous act. Thank you, all. I hope I haven't too greatly disrupted your weekend peace."

Hart drove from Amelie's office in the direction of his condo. His mind was only half engaged with the traffic, which, fortunately, was still light early on Sunday. He turned off into the parking lot of Amber's, a coffee shop he knew that also served light breakfasts on the weekend. Inside, the place was half full with people enjoying their lattes, pastries, and morning papers. He ordered bacon, scrambled eggs, and a large coffee and sat morosely eating as he tried to decide how to tackle Elizabeth. He had not told the Provost of her reaction when she had heard of the incident. That would have been foolish. But he had doubts as to whether Elizabeth would see the reason for cancelling her project or that she would understand how close they were to a public mess that could damage them both.

Unfortunately, he thought, Amelie was sufficiently old school that she saw a definite distinction between lawful protest and illegal activity, but her own position depended upon the campus remaining peaceful and avoiding too much negative press. That gave him some leverage with her, although he had to be cautious using it, since too much pressure from him could cause her to decide she would be better off with another Dean in his place after next year. But what leverage did he have with Elizabeth? Right now, he could think of nothing.

SUNDAY, OCTOBER 23, 10:15 A.M.

Once again, Alice, George, and Fr. Mark sat around George's dining room table, this time laid with green placemats and blue-and-green checkered napkins. Their eggs Benedict was topped with a small scoop of salmon roe, and George was passing a plate of sliced tomatoes with bocconcini.

"So what's the advice on how I tackle the problem?"

"Surely you can appeal to her sense of justice?" Fr. Mark responded to Alice's question.

"I'm not sure she thinks of justice the same way I do," Alice added. "Being believed is a major issue. I think the problem is for her to be able to acknowledge that she could be wrong. But I have no idea how to approach that without offending her so much that she won't talk to me."

"I don't want to seem cynical," George put in, "but I think you are going to have to start with sympathy. Maybe even an apology for seeming callous in sending your email."

Alice put down her fork. "Well, I'm not unsympathetic. It's a terrible thing. And whatever she did, she didn't deserve to be subjected to violence. But I have a hard time expressing sympathy other than in a perfunctory way to someone I hardly know. If I were in her place, I wouldn't want sympathy from near strangers. And she knows I'm Paul's graduate supervisor, so I expect my sympathy would be far from welcome."

The three sat in silence for a while, enjoying the food.

"I'm becoming more concerned about Paul," Fr. Mark said. "I've told him to stay away from Sarah, but he seems to think he could persuade her that he's innocent. If we can't give him some helpful news fairly soon, I'm worried he'll try to contact her—and add fuel to the fire."

"Elizabeth Maryfield's the key," George said. "If she would back off pushing Sarah, Sarah might listen to some sense. We're not asking anything difficult. All she has to do is sign a simple consent. And then she'd know if her old friend really is a monster or not."

"And who can talk to Elizabeth?" Alice asked. "I certainly struck out on Friday. I've never seen anyone lose it like that at work, and there have certainly been some tense moments in my career."

They went around and around the problem until the eggs were done, the third cups of coffee empty, and no real resolution reached, other than to encourage Fr. Mark to keep close to Paul and for Alice to try to speak with Sarah as soon as she came back to campus. In the final analysis, she would just have to see how the conversation went and do her best to hit the right note. George's tentative suggestion that he try speaking to Elizabeth had not met with optimism.

After Fr. Mark left, Alice stayed behind to help with dishes.

"It must have been very unpleasant last night at the mass."

"Very," George said. "And I wish I thought I had acquitted myself better. There was young John, the altar server, and two other young men who had the presence of mind to try to block the vandals' path to the altar and Fr. Mark. And Fr. Mark was quick to get the consecrated bread and wine off the table and cover them up. But I just stood there like an open-mouthed idiot. I've never felt like such a useless old fool. If the protesters were our students, I'll bet they had a good laugh over me."

Alice dried one of the coffee cups. "I think it's not unusual to freeze when something so shocking and unexpected happens. And look at me when Elizabeth confronted me about the email. I've thought of a thousand intelligent things I should have said, but really all I did was stand there and start to shake."

"We're a pair," George agreed. "But there was one interesting thing for me about the whole experience. When I thought about those vandals doing something to the consecrated bread and wine, something just fell into place for me. That's partly why I was frozen—at least, I'd like to think so. I was just stunned by the certainty that if they had damaged the hosts or the wine, they would have been committing a terrible, terrible act. I realized then that I had come to believe—as Catholics believe—that the bread truly was Christ's body, and the wine, His blood. For real."

Alice was stunned. "I had no idea you were that close to believing, George. I mean, I knew you were intellectually exploring the ideas of the Christian faith, but ..."

George spoke, as she clearly had no idea how to finish the sentence. "I've just told Fr. Mark that I want to convert. I'm going to take instruction and be received into the Catholic Church."

"It's not going to be easy. I mean, we've talked about this. I don't see how you can believe something that will mean you have to give up a major part of your life."

"I know it's not easy. And this won't happen instantly. In my situation, Fr. Mark advises at least two years of study and waiting to see. But I don't see it—at least, not now—as giving up a major part of my life. I'm still who I am. Choosing celibacy doesn't make me less. Look at all the priests, nuns, and saints who chose celibacy and lived wonderful lives."

"And look at the ones who didn't. Sorry, George, but the Church's clergy don't have a sterling record on the celibacy front. For starters, you can't ignore the child abuse."

"No, I can't. And, you're right ..."

Alice shook her head. "I don't want to be offensive, George."

"No, you are right. I won't rush this. But this has been coming gradually, as I've seen more and more of what a culture of secular belief is doing to us and to our students. I don't expect, at my age, to make heroes out of very human people or be disappointed when they fail miserably. But I do know, now, that I believe."

SUNDAY, OCTOBER 23, 11:30 A.M.

Angie slipped out of bed and pulled on the long T-shirt she had worn the night before. It was cool in the bedroom, as Tyler had insisted on opening the window when they decided it was too late for her to go home and they were too tired. She did not like to stay overnight with the men she slept with. It tended to give them ideas that she was needy and would be anxious to be there the next night too. That was not something Angie ever had in mind.

After using the bathroom and seeing that Tyler was still asleep, she tiptoed out of the bedroom, closing the door softly behind her. In his small kitchen, she located the kettle on the counter and a French press in a cupboard above the sink. Opening the refrigerator, she found a package of ground coffee. Putting on the kettle, spooning coffee into the press, she remembered her pleasant imaginings before sleep, but now she felt them tinged with a shadow. Tyler was wild. What they had done was very, very close to a line that Angie had not recognized before, but she was now aware that they would need luck for this to turn out as positively as Tyler asserted it would. But did Tyler even care? More than anything, he wanted—what? What did he want? The only word that could come to her was "wildness;" he wanted disruption and trouble. When that happened, he was happy and alive. Other times, he seemed like he cared for nothing. So he created chaos whenever he could. He reminded Angie of her father, a brilliant litigator who, when not in court, had carried on running battles with his wife, his children, and his law partners until all of them rebelled and threw him out. Then there was a new set of wife, children, and law partners, and more chaos. Even so, he had never broken the law, that Angie knew. And that is what they had done. It felt different than she had expected, and she was more worried than she had imagined she would be. She shivered as she clasped the warm coffee cup.

Perhaps she had been a fool to agree with Tyler's plan, but she was not a star student. Acceptance into graduate school had come only by careful course selection. She had managed her first year with its long list of compulsory courses adequately by very, very long hours of work. She had learned that if you write enough on the exams, you don't do badly. Maybe you're not at the top of the class, but you get solid grades. Then, in her upper years, she had carefully selected only those courses where her ability to intuitively mimic the style and the thinking of her professors got you As. Dr. Maryfield was the best. She had taken three courses from her and had As in all of them. She couldn't afford less in this one.

Sarah was a possible problem, Angie continued thinking. Sarah had not looked grateful for support last night. Her words about forgetting the whole thing made her seem less enthusiastic than Dr. Maryfield had suggested she was, and if she was not willing to be the centre of the project, then ...

Angie decided that she would speak to Dr. Maryfield as soon as possible and make sure this was still on. And maybe she should speak to Sarah as well. She could surely make Sarah see that this was a chance that might never come again—a chance to change the culture of the campus. A chance to make their time in this dinky law school count for something.

Angie took her coffee into the living room and opened the pack she had set on the coffee table the night before. She pulled out her phone and checked recent calls, emails, and texts. One of the missed emails was from Security. God, she thought, they couldn't possibly know. For a moment, the panic hit her stomach, and she felt the coffee push back into her throat in an acrid surge. Then she calmed. No, they had left no clues; all of them had worn gloves, and anyway, none of them would have fingerprints in any system that Campus Security could identify. It must be something else. She pushed Suze's number and texted: Got email. Campus Security. You? A minute later, the reply came: Me too. Call me. Angie dialled Suze's number.

"What's going on?" Angie asked.

"I don't have a clue," Suze answered. "But I texted a couple of other people in Maryfield's class, and they all have the same email. I don't know if anyone has responded yet. I mean, who do Campus Security think they are, leaving us messages at 8:00 a.m. on a Sunday?"

"I don't care about that, Suze," Angie responded. "But could it be about last night? If it is, how does Security know it's connected to us or to Maryfield's class?"

"Well, there is one thing. You know how my jacket pocket was ripped by that bozo in white? I think I had Maryfield's syllabus amendment page in that pocket. I can't find it anywhere today."

Angie gasped, "Oh God, oh God. You mean we're in trouble over this?"

"Calm down. First, even if they connect it to the class, they won't connect it to us. There was nothing at all on that paper other than what Maryfield wrote. But there's another thing. I didn't think anyone would be too upset over this—I mean, social action takes place on campus all the time. We were just a little more original than most. But if I'm wrong, we just deep-six the project and do something else. I admit I'd be a little ticked at wasting the evening, but hey, it's not the end of the world. We had some laughs. And I'm not jeopardizing my future over a stupid project or an A in a stupid course that no one at my future law firm will even look at on my transcript."

"What? Look, if a fuss is made over this, Dr. Maryfield has to protect us."

"Yeah, good luck with that."

Just then, Tyler emerged from the bedroom in his undershorts. He yawned. "Coffee? Great. Lead me to a cup."

"Tyler," Angie spoke, holding the phone away from her ear, "I've got Suze on the phone. We've all got messages to call Campus Security today. Do you think they know something?"

Tyler shrugged. "How would I know. Let's call them and see."

Angie shuddered. "No, wait a minute, let's call Janice."

"Janice?"

"Yeah. She has nothing to do with this issue, but knowing her, little-miss-stick-to-the-rules, I bet she's already called them back."

Angie hung up her call with Suze and was already checking for Janice's number and dialling.

"Janice? It's Angie, from Feminist Legal Studies. Hey, I hear we all got messages to call Campus Security. Any idea what it's about?"

Janice was finishing up her last reading for her 8:30 Monday morning class. She frowned. She did not like to be interrupted, and she did not like to be reminded about her encounter with Dean Haverman, which had left her feeling stupid and guilty.

"Sure. I called back an hour ago. Turns out some idiots broke up the Catholic student mass yesterday evening, throwing some red goo on people. They think it's likely connected to the rape in the law school that Maryfield was talking about on Friday, and they're just canvassing everyone in her class about what they know about these new assignments. Somehow, they know that she suggested performance art and mentioned misogynist organizations, so I guess we're all suspects."

"So what did you say?"

"I don't see that it matters what I said, Angie. But if you have to know, I said I didn't know anything about it, but that I had complained about the syllabus change. Much good that did me. Dear old Dean Hart made me feel like a fool for complaining, and it was clear he'd back Maryfield whatever she did. Of course, that's not surprising, given everybody knows they've been an item for months."

"Really?" Angie asked.

"Sure, at least that's what a friend tells me. Anyway, the only good thing about this is that Campus Security is taking this issue pretty seriously. They're questioning all the students in her class, and my bet is that there's going to be some major pressure on Maryfield to tone things down, at least, and maybe to go back to the old plan."

After Angie hung up, she repeated the conversation to Tyler, who shrugged.

"Well, in that case, let's not bother calling Security. Most people likely won't, and there's nothing that can make us. After all, we have legal rights here, and not being harassed by the campus clowns is one of them. Look, Angie," he added after he saw her expression, "we can feel out Maryfield on Monday and see if she's going to back down or not. If she is, then, so what? We can fight it out, or we can just duck and get on with another project. Either way, we had our fun. So, sure, an A in the course would be great, but—hey, you know we might guarantee that A after all. Maybe if Maryfield won't come through, we tell her that we intend to push it, say that we did the assignment on her say-so, and now we deserve to get credit for it. If we don't, we go public with it. Maybe she'll trade an A for keeping quiet."

"Blackmail?" Angie asked.

"Quid pro quo," Tyler replied, smiling.

Angie gathered her things together after a quick shower and another cup of coffee. She had her own plans gradually solidifying in her mind. No, she would not be a party to blackmailing Dr. Maryfield, but she would talk to her, find out how things were going to go, and she would offer support. Angie could speak to Sarah and persuade her to keep on with the project and bring real change to campus. Dr. Maryfield would be grateful and an A, a well-deserved A, would surely follow, even if she had to turn in some kind of stupid essay on something. Maybe she'd write about her experiences with men on this campus. She had stories to tell that were just as important as Sarah's.

SUNDAY, OCTOBER 23, 1:00 P.M.

Sarah reached again for the vodka bottle. She'd had another night with minimal sleep, half of it spent sitting in the chair, watching the door. Somehow, she had to get over this. Alcohol, no sleep, crying off and on. And last evening … that had been the worst: trying to go out and have fun. Fun? What a stupid, stupid thought.

Richard's response to her questions played over and over in her mind. Then she thought about Mr. Blatt's answers to her question. Someone was lying. Richard said that he was alerted to something wrong when Paul had appeared distraught, but Richard had been suspiciously vague about details; Mr. Blatt had reported Paul's description of coming home, which was very different. Paul said he had not spoken to Richard, who was asleep, as far as he knew. Of course, if Paul had done this awful thing—and, for the first time, Sarah spoke in her thoughts the word "if"—he might lie. But why lie about something as innocent as whether you spoke to your roommate or not? Nothing there would betray Paul. But why would Richard lie?

If—there was that word again—if Paul had not raped her, then who had? Someone still out there. Someone who perhaps still had a key to her apartment. Sarah picked up her phone and dialled her friend, Melissa.

"Hey," she said as Melissa answered.

"Hey yourself. How are you? I've been expecting you to call, but I didn't like to intrude by calling you. I heard from Arty what happened. Gosh, it's just dreadful. Can I help? Do you want to go out for some brunch or something?"

"Thanks, Melissa. I just haven't felt like seeing anyone, and when I did go out last night, it was a big mistake. So thanks for your support, but I really just can't focus today. Yeah, it's pretty horrible. I don't know how you feel about this, but it seems worse because half the law school seems to know all about it. I know it's not my fault, and I shouldn't feel ashamed or anything, but it just seems to keep going around in my head, and people don't need to know everything, do they?"

"Yes," Melissa replied, "I heard that Maryfield was going to make a big, big thing out of this—an example of the rape culture on campus.

You're right that you shouldn't feel the need to hide. But I sure understand not wanting everyone to be talking about it. Arty said you know who did it too."

"Well, I think so. But, Melissa, there are some funny things—things I can't explain. And I never thought that Paul would ... well, anyway, what I called about is my key. I ... I don't mean to be a problem, but I feel really afraid here. I can't sleep; I can't feel safe in my own place, even though I know that's stupid. I've got the security chain on the door and—anyway, could I get my key back from you? For now, I'd just feel safer if I knew where all the keys were."

"Sure. Hold on. It's right here in this drawer ... at least, that's where I thought it was. Oh shit. No, I must have put it somewhere else. Let me think. Look, I'll get back to you when I remember where I put it. Sorry, Sarah, I'm sure it's here."

When Sarah ended the call, she sat again in the chair facing the door. Melissa was a scatterbrain all right. But if she had lost the key, or worse, if someone had taken the key to her place ...

Sarah's terror returned, and she reached again for the vodka.

An hour later, she dressed, picked up her purse, and headed for the mall. She would find something to make herself feel safe again. And on Monday, she would go to Elizabeth Maryfield and tell her to lay off. This focusing on what had happened made everything worse. Surely Elizabeth, who seemed so supportive on Thursday, would understand that.

Then she'd speak to Anne at Campus Security and get her to make sure the law school would let her drop Feminist Legal Studies without penalty. Better yet, she would stop out for the rest of the term and go home. She could come back in January and pick up. It would delay graduation for a few months, but she would be better if she got out of her apartment. Her mind ticked over all she would need to do to go home. Should she try to sublet her place? No, that would take too long. Once she really thought about going home, she wanted to leave today. That wasn't possible, she told herself. There was packing to do and things at the law school to arrange. However awful this was, it was not going to ruin her life. And running off now without arranging a stop out officially could do just that. Her dad would be disappointed in the delay, but he would understand, especially if she could tell him that she could go back in January. She would have to stay a few more days, but for now, she wanted something. Maybe a baseball bat.

In late October, the supply of baseball bats in the hardware store was nonexistent. Sarah wandered up and down the aisles looking for something she didn't know. Something heavy. And maybe something compact that she could take around with her. She had looked at knives in the kitchen and sporting goods sections, but knives were a problem. Police didn't care much for people carrying knives around, and stabbing someone would be awful, Sarah thought. She wasn't sure she could do it, no matter what.

Then she saw it and knew it was just what she wanted. A little hammer for flattening or tenderizing meat. It had a stainless-steel head about four inches in diameter with a handle of about five inches. It would fit into her carryall bag. It would sit, unobtrusively, beside her bed or by the chair that faced the door. And it was heavy. Slugging someone in the arm, on the back, or in a more sensitive area with that would put a quick end to any thoughts of rape, Sarah thought. And she would feel safe … at least until Monday or maybe Tuesday, when she could go home. She carried it to the cash desk and paid $25.98 on her credit card, tucking the receipt into her wallet.

Guesses now? No, I hope not.

Morning has come and gone. I slept for three hours but was wakened by a phone call from my publisher. She was not pleased that I've temporarily abandoned my contracted book to work on something else, especially something that won't be published under my usual name. And, indeed, won't be published during my lifetime, or probably hers. I intend to seal this manuscript when it is finished and leave it with my solicitors. When I die, they can see about publication. The point is just to write it.

But what about my loyal fans who are waiting for my new release? she asked.

Never mind. I will finish my promised book, I hope. And its ending will be very, very different than my other books, once I've written this. In the meantime, I'm hearing the bell from the nearby school calling the children in from lunch break. The rain has started again; so much for the clear morning. Days go on. What a trite thought. I would never write that in one of my best sellers. But they do. Minutes, hours, days. And then life, replaying the stories, rewriting the same stories, again and again.

CHAPTER 4

Elizabeth Maryfield unlocked her office and put down her pack. She unzipped her faux leather jacket and unwrapped the long scarf from her neck, hanging them behind the door. Her office phone was ringing, and she picked it up. It was Hart.

Elizabeth suddenly felt awkward, wondering how they would interact now that it was over between them. She also still felt anger. He had no right to his superior attitude. He was only interested in himself. She really cared about the university. And she felt fear. He would have talked to the Provost by now. The reporter had not called her back. She thought of following up but then hesitated. It was fine to talk about breaking the law, justifiable in the pursuit of social justice of course. And she was certain of being backed up by the women's caucuses in the university circle. But there was no doubt that things could sometimes take a surprising turn. And while she still believed that this project would be a winner, it could turn bad very quickly with the wrong approach. As far as publicity went, she would seek it, since it would make her work more controversial, but she needed Sarah at her side, fully consenting, before she brought in the press. She had acted rashly calling the paper last night. Today she would contact Sarah and secure her full and formal consent.

All these thoughts passed through Elizabeth's mind in an instant as she heard Hart ask her to step down to his office for a few moments, "if you can spare the time," he added, as his usual formally polite manner dictated in dealing with faculty members.

"I'll be there in five minutes," Elizabeth replied.

She reached Hart's office just as his assistant was bringing in a fresh cup of coffee. He motioned for a second cup for her. They both drank it black. It was such a familiar gesture, Elizabeth thought. Perhaps she would miss Hart after all.

When the coffee was delivered and his office door again closed, Hart began, "Elizabeth, I met with the Provost yesterday, and the first thing I want to assure you of is that there will be no disciplinary action against you, absolutely none."

It was the wrong thing to say, and Hart realized it as soon as he saw the scornful smile on Elizabeth's lips. "I should hope not," she replied. "I'm sure the Provost knows I have no guilt in this matter whatsoever."

"True, absolutely true," Hart added, placatingly. "But she does believe that the students need to be told that this kind of action does not fit within university policy."

Elizabeth laughed. "What does she want me to do? I don't even know that it was my students involved."

"True," Hart repeated, "but if they expect credit for it, you will find out because they will have to turn in some kind of documentation of their behaviour. And," he held up his hand to forestall her obvious intent to interrupt, "let me also say that the Provost would not dream of disciplining the students ..."

"I hope not," Elizabeth interjected.

"... of disciplining the students," Hart repeated, "but she does want to speak to them personally to discuss with them the gravity of their actions—the risk those actions pose to themselves and to this university, and," he continued, speaking more rapidly, "she insists that no credit should be given for this project. Assuming, of course, that the students should seek such credit."

"No one, not even the Provost, can tell me how to grade my course," Elizabeth stated. "If she insists, I'll go to the union, and they'll grieve this in a moment."

"Elizabeth, please. I've assured the Provost that you never intended any vandalism to result from your new assignment. But she raises the perfectly reasonable argument that the late change in the course evaluation is against the calendar rules—passed by Senate."

"Don't be silly, Hart," Elizabeth answered. "No one was prejudiced by the change."

"Well," said Hart, "one of your students has complained. The Provost is quite within her legal rights to insist that the calendar rules be followed, especially in light of a serious complaint such as this. Look, you don't have to back down in front of your class; you can blame that little student who brought the matter to me and say I've told you that the change isn't allowed. It's only a couple of days since you distributed the amendment. No one could have put much time into it, so no real prejudice now to say that you were wrong ..."

"Wrong!" Elizabeth exclaimed, rising to her feet.

"No, no, not wrong. Just mistaken about the interpretation of the rules, which I've brought to your attention; and now, in fairness, you have to tell them that you can't go ahead. You can even add it to your syllabus for next term, and then you can qualify the projects to make clear that no illegal acts can be included. It's really very simple if you'll just ..."

"Just back off. Just give up. Just give in," Elizabeth finished.

"Elizabeth, dear, please don't sound so angry. I know we quarrelled last night, but you know I only have your best interests at heart. You can do this project next term, and I know it will be a great success—a major book and contribution to social justice. And if your students have done this and bring it to you, you might even be able to include it in the book, anonymously and with proper qualifications about how you would not condone violence, but how this illustrates the passion your students feel for …"

Elizabeth was thinking quickly. If Hart would be willing to make up their quarrel, it would greatly improve her chances for promotion. Perhaps he was more infatuated with her than she had thought. And he was right—it could be done next term. But then, she thought about standing in front of her class and backing down. She would look like a coward. All her teaching about social justice and fighting against the fascist, racist, and homophobic system would be wasted. No, she thought, I can't. I just can't.

She spoke more moderately, however. "Look, Hart, I agree that I can defer some of this to next term. But I won't take the project off the syllabus, and I won't refuse to grade work that students do for it. The Provost knows she has no right to ask me to do that. I'm going to talk to Sarah today and get her consent to follow up with some publicity on the rape, and then I'll focus mostly on working with her to get the central piece of the book done. You can tell the Provost that you spoke to me and that I'll make sure there's no further trouble coming out of this class. I'll insist that all the projects be approved by me, and—okay—and I'll turn down anything that is illegal, at least for now, until this quiets down."

Hart frowned. It was not what the Provost had wanted, but it was likely the best he could get for now. Perhaps he had more influence with Elizabeth than he had thought. He might gradually be able to convince her that she should give up the names of the students. Nothing much would happen to them, after all, other than a few uncomfortable minutes with Amelie.

"Thank you," he said, changing the frown to a broad smile. "I knew I could count on you to help us out here. And, Elizabeth, I do apologize for seeming to reject your commitment to social justice the other night. I'm very sorry. I was tired, and …"

"I understand, Hart," she replied, smiling. They both stood for a moment looking at each other, and then both spoke almost at once.

"Would you like …"

"Perhaps we could …"

They laughed. Hart continued, "Perhaps we could have dinner tonight, at my place, and make up for the mess I made of Saturday."

"I'd like that," Elizabeth replied.

Returning to her office, she flopped down in her desk chair. Perhaps she had given up too much. But, no, she had Hart back. He would handle the Provost. Her promotion would go through. And she would do this book, including the segment she was likely to receive Tuesday. It would have to be kept quiet for a while, that was all.

She looked at her desk clock. It was now past 10:00 a.m., and she had a class in an hour and a half. She looked up at a knock on her door frame.

"May I come in, Dr. Maryfield?"

"Sarah, how wonderful to see you back! I was just now thinking of calling you to see how you were and to talk about what we might do together arising out of this situation. I have a great many ideas. Things that will make a real difference."

"Thank you, Dr. Maryfield. I'm still not up to much. Not sleeping much."

"Here. Sit down. I'm sure you're still traumatized, and no wonder."

"Yes, I seem to be. And that's what I wanted to talk about. I went out Saturday to the pub with some friends, and they told me that you've been talking about what happened. Almost everyone seemed to know …"

"But only so they could support you, Sarah. Support us in our efforts to challenge the culture on this campus."

"I know. At least, I'm sure that's how it is. But the problem is that I just don't feel that way right now."

"Sarah, you're still shocked. You need to go home and rest. And to write this all down. Writing is very cathartic. I've always found it so. And to think how many women will benefit from your words …"

"But that's my point, Dr. Maryfield, I don't want to write it out. I don't want to think about it. And I really don't want everyone knowing about it, talking about it. God, I just want to forget it!" Sarah pulled a tissue from her pack as she began to cry. "See, I can't even talk to you."

"But, Sarah, you can't let this go by. You must …"

"And you see," Sarah continued, "now that I've thought about it, I can't really even be sure that it was Paul who did this. In fact, I heard something, something that makes me think it was someone else."

"Sarah, they're just getting to you. Causing you to doubt yourself. You mustn't give in to this."

"It's not that. But I've been talking to some people, and … well, there's a contradiction that makes it seem as if … as if someone else I know did this, not Paul. You see, even if I wanted to go on with this project and write about it, what could I say? I may have wrongly accused someone, and even if I think I might know now who it was, I can't be sure. And I'm afraid."

"There is nothing to be afraid of. We are all supporting you. We need you as a catalyst to turn this campus around."

"No, Dr. Maryfield, I've made up my mind. I want to stop out. Anne, the Personal Safety Coordinator at Campus Security, has told me that I can have a stop out for the term or longer and then come back, maybe in January, or maybe even in September. I've talked to my parents, and I can go home. My dad says he'll pay for some therapy …"

"Therapy? And what good is therapy if you won't stay and face the issues?"

"I can't help it. I've thought it all out, and this is what I want to do. I came by this morning to tell you. I'm going to be packing over the next couple of days. And to say I'm sorry that I won't be able to continue as your research assistant this term. I …"

Elizabeth gripped her hands tightly together. Her immediate impulse was to scream, to throw something, to smash something. It was so unfair. Sarah was the key, the key to her major chance to make her name in the academy. She had risked a lot for this chance, and now because of a silly little girl, she could see the chance disappearing and herself left with the fallout.

The sympathetic tone in her voice was dropped as she coldly responded. "Well, then, that's that. But running out on your responsibilities isn't going to look very good on your record, Sarah. Adults, mature adults, take their promises seriously. And you promised me a bibliography on the topic of rape culture in universities. I'm very much afraid that I will have to note on your file that you failed to complete your assignment."

Sarah sat stunned for a moment. "But, Dr. Maryfield …"

"No, if you had decided to pursue this other topic arising from your personal experience—work together with me on it—then I would have forgiven you for abandoning your assignment. But now, well, it's quite different now. I know students rely on research assignments to help pay for their education. I can assure you that when you return, you will find very few faculty members willing to hire you."

"Dr. Maryfield, I …" Sarah twisted the tissue in her hands. "Please, you have to understand how I feel."

"Feel? I understand that you have a precious opportunity here, and you are walking away from it. You're letting your own emotional weakness defeat your progressive commitments. You're running away like a frightened child and to where? To daddy—daddy whose patriarchal influence has obviously damaged you beyond repair. Think again. If you leave now, if you reject this chance, there won't be another. I'll see to it."

Then Sarah's anger surfaced and rose over her distress. She sat up straighter in the chair. "You're simply saying this to me because you want to use my situation for your own benefit," Sarah stated.

"You little slut." Elizabeth could now barely contain her fury. "You have no right to say something like that to me. I am entitled to your respect …"

Sarah stood, picking up her pack. "Fine. I apologize if I am too emotionally weak. And I'm almost two-thirds done your precious bibliography. A few more hours in the library will complete it. You'll have it before I leave for home." Sarah turned to the door and spoke again, "But I think I'll save my respect for someone who deserves it." And she left the room.

MONDAY, OCTOBER 24, 9:50 A.M.

When Elizabeth left, Hart sat at his desk for a few moments to collect his thoughts. He had not achieved the objectives set for him by the Provost, but he could assure her that Elizabeth's class would cause no further trouble and that Elizabeth would be personally vetting all student projects in the future. As for the names of the students involved, Elizabeth had no knowledge of that, and now, with Campus Security asking questions, she was never likely to know, as law students—being a practical bunch—would not attempt to get a grade for something that would get them into trouble. Hart brightened. So, after all, he had done all that could be done, and the matter was very likely settled.

Hart picked up the phone. "I'd like to speak to Amelie, please," he told the receptionist in the Provost's office. "It's Hart here, from the law school."

When Hart was connected and had explained that, while he had not found out the names of the students and he had not received an assurance from Elizabeth that she would not grade work resulting from this incident, he could promise that the matter was taken care of. Amelie was not impressed.

"It sounds to me, Hart, as though you have not managed to do a thing we agreed to."

Hart refrained from mentioning that he had not agreed but had rather been told. "But the same goals are achieved, Amelie. There won't be any more projects of this sort because Elizabeth will be approving them and, as I assured you yesterday, she will not tolerate illegal activity. And since Campus Security is now on the case and all her students know it, none of them are going to stick out their necks. That means they can't reveal their part in this, and that means they can't turn in the work. So they will not be graded on it, just as you requested."

"And what about the privacy issue for the student who was raped?"

Hart thought quickly. He did not recall that Amelie had asked him to do anything about that. "Privacy issue? I'm sorry, but I wasn't aware there was one. As I mentioned yesterday, Elizabeth is the student's professor in her theory class and, I believe, somewhat of a mentor. She is willing to work with Elizabeth to prepare a paper that will be the centrepiece of Elizabeth's new academic book. My understanding is that this is an entirely consensual arrangement ..."

Amelie interrupted. "I'm not comfortable with this, Hart. Not comfortable at all. It looks much too much like exploitation. This girl surely can't want her name out there for all to see. I mean, while no one blames her in the slightest for what happened, does she want everyone to know that she got so drunk that she couldn't resist a rapist and passed out again afterwards? And even if she is willing, what about her parents? Or what about the future? In this kind of case, it would hardly be surprising if, a year or two down the road, she turned around and sued us for failing to protect her privacy."

"But, Amelie, this isn't a little undergraduate. The young woman is over the age of majority. She must be twenty-three or twenty-four."

Amelie gave a little snort. "That's hardly a mature age, Hart. Okay, technically, if she consents to all this publicity, she may be within her rights. But given the trauma, the influence a professor naturally has over a student, and given her youth, I wouldn't put it past a court to say we had failed in our duty to her. And then, I'm also not very happy about one of our faculty publishing a paper that focuses on a rape among our students. What will parents of future students think of that? Especially if it gets in the newspapers. I'm not happy about this at all."

Hart's digestion took a turn. Just when he had convinced himself he was over the crisis—Elizabeth handled deftly and even coming back to his bed and Amelie placated—now the Provost was asking him to tackle an even thornier issue. Hart knew how passionate Elizabeth was about this project. Without the rape as the central story—well, there was no project.

"No, Hart, the more I think about it, the more convinced I am that

Dr. Maryfield cannot be allowed to continue with this subject, at least not right now."

"But, Amelie, I really have no way of stopping her."

"Nonsense. Cite the privacy concern. And tell her that if the girl is of the same mind in a year, I'll give the project my blessing. I can probably even find a few thousand dollars in funding for her. But we must not victimize our young people, especially not when they have already been hurt and are vulnerable. The right thing to do is to wait. Tell her that you have consulted with legal counsel, who have advised caution. That's certainly the truth; our legal counsel always advise caution. Tell her that ethics approval from the university board of human subjects' research will be needed and will not be forthcoming unless she waits for at least a year. Tell her whatever you have to."

Amelie hung up the phone. Hart let out an exasperated groan and ran his fingers through his hair, tugging it by the roots. Yesterday's tasks had been bad enough, but this? This was purely impossible. Elizabeth would never give up Sarah's participation. Never. Hart saw his reappointment slipping away. And, at least for the moment, he could think of nothing to do about it.

MONDAY, OCTOBER 24, 11:00 A.M.

Elizabeth's class was at 11:30, but instead of working on her notes, she still sat at her desk, staring into space. Her anger had been slightly relieved by hurling a book across the room at the door closing after Sarah. How dare she? The hackneyed phrase stuck in her mind. Hackneyed or not, that was the nub of the issue. How dare she? She, Elizabeth, was a faculty member, using her legal training not for earning big dollars in corporate law firms in Toronto but pursuing justice and equality for all, just as she had planned to do in law school. Sarah's father, she knew, was a rich corporate lawyer who had undoubtedly brought up his daughter in the worst possible way. But rather than standing firm for the causes she had been taught were just and rejecting her capitalist background, Sarah was running home to daddy. Running away. Giving in to the stereotypical picture of the rape victim. Slinking away, Elizabeth modified her sentence in her mind.

Elizabeth looked at her clock. In half an hour, she would have to deliver a lecture in her Professional Ethics class. The class was focusing this term on activist lawyering—the idea of a lawyer as an agent pro-vocateur, finding cases that would upset the system and undermine the capitalist economy. In fact, acting just as she was acting in inspiring her students to challenge the misogyny on campus. But this betrayal, as she now characterized Sarah's behaviour, would make her task much more difficult. She thought briefly about cancelling the upcoming class and phoning in sick. She needed time to think. And if she phoned in sick, she could use that as an excuse not to see Hart tonight. The last thing she wanted right now was to have to admit to him that her plans had gone wrong.

As she was about to pick up her desk phone and call the front office, she heard a knock. Perhaps it was Sarah, having thought better of her cowardly behaviour. "Come in," she called.

The door opened as Angie stepped forward.

"Excuse me, Dr. Maryfield, but I really need to speak to you."

Disappointment sharpened Elizabeth's voice. "Angie. I'm sorry, but I have a class coming up, and I'm not feeling well. Can't this wait?"

"I'm really sorry. But I'm quite upset, and I thought you might be able to help. It's about what happened Saturday night."

Elizabeth hesitated. "Well, I must make this phone call to the front office, but just wait outside for two minutes, and you can speak to me before I leave for home."

Angie backed out of the door, closing it after her. Elizabeth dialled the central office and informed a junior clerk that a notice should be posted cancelling her 11:30 class today as she was ill and going home shortly. Then she called Hart's private office line. She was greeted by his voice mail.

"Hart. It's Elizabeth. I'm afraid I need to cancel tonight. I'm ill. Some kind of flu or maybe food poisoning. It just came on suddenly, and I'm going home. Don't call me, as I'm going to bed. But I'll talk with you tomorrow."

When she put down the receiver, Elizabeth went to the door and beckoned Angie to come in and sit down.

"Now, what's this about?"

"Have you heard about what happened Saturday night at the student mass on campus?"

Elizabeth smiled. "Sure. Some unknown people took some well-justified social action against a group of regressive, right-wing haters."

Angie smiled back, relieved and pleased that she had correctly understood Dr. Maryfield's perspective.

"Right. Well, ... well, I was one of them."

"Really?" Elizabeth smiled more broadly. "Now, I wonder who else was involved? I've noticed that you and Tyler Jenkins seem to get on very well in class."

Angie shook her head slightly. "I don't want to say without their permission."

Elizabeth responded, "Good for you. So what's the problem?"

"Campus Security is trying to find out who did it. I mean, we did it for your class, you know. And we have pictures and commentary of the whole thing. We want to turn it in, but if we do, what will happen? I mean, we really want to support your project and your important work on this campus. But if the Campus Security clowns get difficult—I mean, none of us want a black mark on our records. I'm off to graduate school, so maybe it doesn't matter as much for me, but Su ... I mean, one of our group, is going with a big corporate firm who might take a dim view of this, and another wants to clerk at the court. So ..."

"So you want to know if you can turn in your work without being afraid that you'll be found out. And you want to know if you can get an A for it without anyone else knowing."

"Well, yes. But really, Dr. Maryfield, we all want to support you. It's your work that's important, and we all want to be a part of this project. To tackle the campus climate, and to put a stop to the rape culture, colonialism, and to homophobia."

Elizabeth smiled again. "I don't see any reason why your group can't turn in the material anonymously. Of course, I will have to know who you are to give you your grades. But I can waive the requirement of a class seminar in connection with the project; we don't have enough classes anyway for everyone to present. And I am very grateful to you for your creativity and your support, but ..." Elizabeth sighed and shrugged, "but I'm very afraid that the project is off."

"Off?" Angie echoed.

"Yes."

"The administration? Or did Janice's complaint? Or ..."

"No, none of those things. You must know, Angie, that I would never bow to pressure to give up my academic rights. No, this is much, much worse. It's Sarah. She's just been here, and she refuses to help out. She's going home. Running away and abandoning the cause. She even thinks that Paul might not have done it, and she has some fantasy that she may know who did. She's doubting herself and doubting us who support her."

"Oh Jesus, I knew it. I saw her Saturday night in the pub, and she said she just wanted to forget the whole thing. But I just couldn't believe she'd give in like this."

Elizabeth smiled again, this time sadly, shaking her head slightly. "It's very hard to understand this degree of selfishness and irresponsibility, I know. But there it is. Unfortunately, without the project going ahead, I'm not sure I can give your work an A grade. I mean, part of the whole thing was supporting each other, and now there's nothing to support. No context. The work loses a lot of its intrinsic meaning, stifled by hatred and repression."

"That's terrible. But we did do the work. Surely our work could still be useful, and it's still worth an A, isn't it?"

Elizabeth enjoyed hearing the anxious note in Angie's voice; she would not be the only one disappointed by Sarah's desertion. "Sadly not. I realize that the work is the same, whether or not it forms part of a larger project, but, you see, we are not atomistic here. We are part of a larger movement, and the success of the movement is crucial to our success. And if the movement fails—well, you must see that the parts become less valuable."

Angie knew this was the moment to make her proposal. She had been right. Dr. Maryfield definitely needed her help and would be grateful for it. Angie leaned forward in her chair. "I think I can help. I can talk to Sarah. I'll bet I can persuade her to go on with this. She just isn't thinking clearly. I know I can get her to see reason."

"I don't know, Angie. I shouldn't ask you to do this. Probably I shouldn't have told you at all about Sarah's plans. We should respect her privacy."

"Oh Dr. Maryfield, how many times have you said that concerns like people's privacy rights shouldn't be allowed to stand in the way of progressive action? I mean, those are totally trivial things that only those with white privilege can afford. We can't afford such luxuries when we're fighting for justice."

"So true, Angie. And thank you so much for reminding me of my true principles. Sometimes, I do get discouraged, and this was a terrible blow to me. But—yes, if you can change Sarah's mind, I will be very grateful. And, of course, it would put the project back on the map and assure your work its proper place. Yes, by all means, see what you can do. She's finishing up some work for me, so you should be able to find her in the library sometime in the next little while."

Angie stood up and picked up her bags. She was sure now that things would work out for the best.

After Angie's departure, Elizabeth picked up her books and packed them back into a worn briefcase. Probably she shouldn't have cancelled the class. She felt much better now. Angie might indeed have some success. And perhaps extending an olive branch to Sarah would be a promising idea as well. Elizabeth was aware that her reaction to

Sarah's defection had been harsh. Had she not been so pardonably angry, she might have been able to talk Sarah back into the fold. Let Angie try, and Elizabeth would also extend an offer of forgiveness. Still, Elizabeth was glad that she had cancelled dinner with Hart. Until this was settled, she wanted to avoid him completely.

As soon as she was clear of the faculty offices, Angie pulled her phone out of her pack. "Tyler? It's Angie. I've just been talking to Dr. Maryfield. She says that Sarah's backing out of the project, so our work may not rate an A grade. But I told her ..." And Angie continued, repeating almost the entire conversation to Tyler. She finished by adding, "I'm going to the library now. If she's not there, I'll keep checking back. Say, do you know anyone who could maybe phone Sarah and find out her plans? Then I would know when to meet her. I'd do it, but she didn't react to me very well last night, and maybe we need some kind of go-between. I mean our grade depends on this, and, at least, I have to try."

Tyler sighed. "You're making too much out of this, Angie. I'd rather just drop the whole thing. And you say that now Sarah isn't even sure that Paul is the one who raped her. Maybe it's someone else? Well, even if she thinks she knows, she won't be sure, and she won't likely say anything, especially if she was wrong once. Who knows? She doesn't sound worth the trouble to me. If she's going home, it'll all be dropped, I bet, and there won't be any issue." On the other end of the phone, Angie protested that she wanted to see what she could do to persuade Sarah.

Tyler continued, "Well, those guys she was with on Saturday, Arty and Richard, you could try calling them. Obviously, they're friends of Sarah's, so maybe one of them knows when she'll be around."

It's been said that faculty politics is so vicious because there's so little at stake. But it's belief that makes the stake valuable, or not. And in my experience, nowhere is belief more prevalent or more certain of its own truth than in the university. The faculty rival the most devout nuns of the early Church in their dedication, whether to social justice, their research (which they often see as the same thing), or their careers, which they regard as just rewards for their commitment to social justice and research. That it might not be worth it, that they might be wrong, that they might not have all the answers, or that they might not even have the right questions—if any of these occurs to them at all, it is repressed as quickly as the doubts of a medieval novice about the will of her superior.

MONDAY, OCTOBER 24, 11:00 A.M.

After her confrontation with Elizabeth, Sarah had gone home, first busing to the mall for a coffee and Danish, and then to the liquor store for another bottle of vodka and some packing boxes. She would leave most of her furniture and effects in the apartment, but she wanted to send home some books and more of her clothes than would fit in her carry-on, so she had arranged for them to be shipped in two weeks. Once packed, they would wait at Melissa's place to be picked up by a moving company that was taking a mixed load to Toronto that day. Sarah had booked a flight home for Thursday morning. Melissa still had not found her key.

When she got home, she began some packing but soon found herself pouring a drink and sitting in the chair facing the door. Her little hammer sat on the table beside the chair. She had slept better last night, knowing that it was in easy reach, and it had fitted into her carry bag this morning when she had gone to see Elizabeth. The memory of their encounter filtered back into her mind as she sat, sipping her second vodka. She was struck by how when the pressure was on, the revelation of Elizabeth Maryfield's motives had suddenly been clear and how easily she had spoken that revelation aloud: You're saying these things because you want to use my situation for your own benefit.

Now Sarah wondered what else she knew ... knew in some interior place that was usually dark but was now beginning to glow with illumination. Who had done this thing to her? Perhaps ... perhaps she did know now. And, in that case, she also knew that she had to act. Picking up her phone, she texted to Paul Anstel's number: Call me asap.

Paul was seated at the small desk in the motel with his laptop open in front of him. It was good to get back to work, to forget some of his troubles in struggling with the next chapter of his dissertation. He too had slept better Sunday night. He had gone to mass in the morning at a church far removed from campus that had a large congregation among whom one visitor was unlikely to draw much notice. He had then walked the four miles back to the motel, enjoying the fall colours and the fresh air, stopping for a sandwich and a beer at a pub part way between. In the afternoon, he had finally been able to focus on the scripture readings, and he read those for each of the days since Thursday, taking his time and praying after each, hoping God would speak to him. He found comfort in the prayers and the Scriptures. Help would come, he now believed—if not now, then sometime. If not in this world, then in eternity. "Jesus, I trust in you," he whispered as he scrolled through the list of scholarly articles that he needed to include in this chapter.

His phone pinged, signalling the arrival of a text message. Paul turned away from his computer screen to his smartphone sitting next to it. He pressed the messages icon and saw the message from Sarah's number: "Call me asap." For a moment, he stared at the screen. He had thought a thousand times of calling her. Surely if he could speak to her, she would realize that her accusations had to be false. He was her old friend, playmate even. And never had there been between them anything but a comfortable sense in that they shared many memories and childhood fun and could talk freely as a brother and sister. That was why she had turned to him to try to handle her father's pressure over her classes. That was why he had had her key. That was a connection that he believed she would know—if they could just talk—that would never have led him to hurt her.

But Fr. Mark, Professor Gordon, and Professor Bush had all cautioned him against talking to Sarah. She's upset, they had said, naturally. She's convinced it was you. We'll talk to her. She'll consent to have the DNA sample tested in Vancouver. But she had not consented, and as far as he knew, she had not even been willing to speak to Professor Gordon but had sent Dr. Maryfield to accuse Professor Gordon of hate speech. And now, here was the invitation. Paul considered first calling Fr. Mark. But he was convinced what Fr. Mark's advice would be. So, Paul thought to himself, it was best perhaps to follow his instincts. He rang Sarah's number.

"Hi," she answered.

"Hi," Paul replied. "You texted me to call you?"

"Yeah. I wanted you to know that I'm going home on Thursday."

"I see."

"I really can't stay here right now. I'm so upset that I can't sleep much. And I'm drinking a lot of vodka to get through the day ..."

"Sarah, you really shouldn't ..."

"Spare me the moral lecture, Paul. Daddy's going to get me some therapy sessions, and I'm going to be all right. But only once I get away from here. Did you know that bitch Maryfield was just using me?"

"Sarah, I ..."

"Well, she was. And don't tell me not to call her names, either, Mr. Holier-than-thou. She wants to use my story in her academic work. To make her name out of my suffering and pain. Isn't that the worst? When I told her I didn't want that, she told me I was weak, cowardly. She threatened me."

"Sarah, that's terrible. You should go to the Dean."

"No," Sarah replied. "I just want to go home. But there are some things I want to do first. First, I'm going to finish her damn bibliography so she'll have nothing to complain about there. I'm going to start work soon. But there's something else, Paul. I'm sorry."

"For what?"

"For telling them you raped me when I'm not sure. In fact, I'm pretty sure you didn't, and I think I know who did."

"Who?"

"No, I'm not going to say. I've made one false accusation already. I'm not going to say a word to anyone, except maybe to the police and Campus Security."

"I don't know if that's a good idea."

"Well, it's what's going to happen. And I will sign the consent for the DNA test. That way, it will at least clear you. I'll do that on Wednesday after I deal with this other stuff. But please don't say anything until I'm gone, not to anyone. I just don't want any more hassles. And I don't want any more talk or any more sympathy, especially not from people like Maryfield who don't give a damn about me."

"Thank you. This means so much to me …"

"Just say you forgive me, Paul. I don't know what I was thinking to assume it was you. I couldn't really see. And then Maryfield got on her kick, and it was all so confusing. I need to sort out all that stuff. I read so much about women rape victims, and how no one believes them, and how they are revictimized by the system. And all that stuff about gender and power … oh, you know. And now I think it's all crap because I didn't feel like that at all, and all the people who were trying to—they said—support me were really just using me. I heard about the mass on Saturday. Do you know about that?"

"Yes, Fr. Mark told me."

"Just another excuse to hate and to act out. That's what my pain is good for, Paul, to those people. I need to rethink … everything."

"I'm terribly sorry."

"I know you are. But can you forgive me? I really have been a dupe. But I know I have to take responsibility for this too. I was swallowing all that stuff Maryfield shovelled out. I should have known better."

Paul hesitated. He had never felt a sentence to be as important as this one. He was not sure what to say. He knew it had to be the truth.

And suddenly, he realized, simple would be best.

"I forgive you," he said. He could hear her crying on the other end of the phone.

"Thank you. I promise that I will go to Health Services tomorrow or Wednesday latest. I'll speak to Professor Gordon tomorrow for sure. And, if I'm right about who did this, I'll also go to Campus Security and the police, I think. I want to do this the right way now. Please let me be the one to tell them and to do this."

"Yes, of course. I can sit tight here for another couple of days," he laughed slightly. "It'll be a good chance to get some serious work done on my dissertation. But I would like to tell Fr. Mark. He's been my main support. I know he'll keep quiet about it until you have the chance to talk to Professor Gordon and to Health Services."

"Thank you again. I guess it would be okay to tell Fr. Mark. Priests are used to keeping secrets. And by Thursday, I'll be gone home, and you can tell everyone."

"Thank you, Sarah. I'm glad you're going home. And I know you don't believe in God, but I will pray for you, now and always. I'll pray that you find what you are looking for."

"If you must—but then pray that I get this all sorted out."

"I will. God be with you."

"Not likely," Sarah answered. "But I'm so grateful that you are."

MONDAY, OCTOBER 24, 4:00 P.M.

Alice folded her books into her briefcase, getting ready to leave her office. She had a midterm to mark over the next few days from her first-year Property class. She preferred to mark at home, although Hart frowned on faculty members not being in their offices until 5:00 p.m. Still, she was going home. Faculty members come and go, and no one pays the slightest attention. Holidays, sick days, days for travel, conferences—none of it was tracked. It was a major perk of faculty life.

Alice thought about reaching home. Once, the idea of going home held a sense of peace and happiness. After her divorce and then during the terrible time after her ex-husband's death, Alice had loved being home. She had taken six-months' unpaid leave, and she had bought her little house, moved the furniture pieces she cherished, polished each one with furniture wax, redone the kitchen to her specifications, cooked, baked—nested, as she thought of it. Now the question crossed her mind: Why?

Nothing very inspiring waited for her at home, except a jar of cold soup in the fridge, ready to be reheated, and a loaf of bread for toast. Supper, a good supper for a cold fall evening, she had thought. Now, it seemed depressing. Her cat would be there waiting. But, somehow, cats were not a lot of comfort. Possibly she should consider a dog, but dogs had to be walked, and she would have to go home at noon, interrupting her workday. And her cat would likely hate it. As she pushed the overloaded briefcase closed, her mind wandered. She was too old, she reasoned, for a midlife crisis. Late-life crisis? But most people found themselves happier, she had read, as they aged. She was established in her career; there was no need to retire. Why couldn't she be happy?

Finally clipping shut the case, Alice pulled on her coat. It was still daylight, as the time had not yet "fallen back," and she was glad to be driving home in the light. And it wasn't raining. There was much to be thankful for.

She reached home and turned on the hallway light. Her tortoise-shell cat, Patches, immediately paced through the hall and into the kitchen, where he complained bitterly about an empty supper dish. Alice first took her briefcase into the second bedroom, which she had converted into an office and den. In the living room, she turned on the electric fireplace to supplement the heat. The room would soon warm up, she knew, but she kept the heat two degrees below her preferred temperature while she was at work, so now it felt chilly. In the kitchen, she poured a glass of wine after explaining to Patches that she was home early, so, no, it was not yet time for kitty dinner. Patches followed her into the living room.

Alice sat down in the wingback chair by the fire and put her feet on the ottoman. She knew she should start marking now. That's why she had come home early. And she also knew that procrastination with marking was fatal. Sure, it was more boring than watching paint dry, more annoying than fingernails dragged across the old-fashioned blackboards, and more depressing than a funeral, to use some clichéd expressions, but avoiding it only made it worse. Alice picked up her novel from the table beside her chair and sipped her wine. Patches jumped onto her lap, turned twice, and settled down with a purr.

"Know what, Patches?" she asked. "I really don't care just now."

MONDAY, OCTOBER 24, 6:00 P.M.

Sarah stared at her computer screen. She was seated on one of the counter-height chairs at the breakfast bar and linked into the library's system. She took another sip from her drink. It was important not to drink too much this evening, as she needed to finish Dr. Maryfield's bibliography, but a couple more surely wouldn't hurt. Tomorrow and Wednesday would be very full days with packing, making a lot of arrangements, and then taking a very early morning flight on Thursday. There were still twenty articles to look at; each had to be quickly skimmed and a brief note written that summarized whether or not each was important and how it contributed to the subject. Fortunately, the library had an extensive digitized collection of journals. Sarah took still another sip and picked up her cellphone to check the time.

No wonder she was hungry. It was 6:00 p.m., and she had skipped lunch. The conversation with Paul had helped. She was still worried, a little, about what had happened to the key she had left with Melissa. Melissa had lots of friends, and they dropped in and out of her place all the time; she also had her cousin, Arty, who apparently hung out there. And Sarah suspected that, as well, Melissa had been pretty close to Tyler, although she had told Sarah that they weren't exclusive. But if she was right about who had raped her, Sarah knew that Melissa's key didn't matter.

Suddenly, Sarah experienced a surge of anger. He had done this to her, and then he had pretended to be her friend. And he had betrayed Paul too. It was not right that he should get away with it. Tomorrow, she would go and sign the consent to have the DNA test and prove that Paul was innocent. But that would not point out the guilty. There would have to be something for police to go on to allow them to get a warrant for her rapist's DNA sample. As it stood, she had nothing. And then Maryfield and her crew, using her like that. They shouldn't get away with that either. Someone from Maryfield's class had desecrated the time Paul held holy. They should pay for that too, and they would; she would never consent to be Maryfield's poster child.

She picked up her phone and dialled Martin Blatt's cell number.

"Mr. Blatt?" she asked when she heard a hello. "It's Sarah Yung calling."

"Sarah. Yes, I'm here. How are you?"

"Getting better. But I've decided to stop out for the rest of the term and go home. I'll hope to come back in January."

"That sounds like a good idea. How can I help you?"

"Well, you know my statement about Paul? I think I was wrong."

"What makes you think that?"

"Well, for one thing, I can't be certain who it was because I was groggy; it was real dark, and whoever it was had concealed his face with my scarf, and even his hair with a wool hat. I'm sure it was no one I had ever touched—like that—before. But it might not have been Paul, and I don't think it was because … because I think it was his roommate, Richard Prius."

"Prius? What gives you that idea?"

"He came over really early on Thursday morning. He said he'd talked to Paul when Paul got home, and it was because Paul was really upset that Richard thought something had gone wrong, and he thought he should come over and see if I was okay. But Paul told you that Richard was asleep when he got home and that he never spoke to Richard. I can't see why Paul would lie. And raping me is so totally out of character for Paul. Then, at the pub on Saturday, I tried to get more details from Richard about what Paul had said, but he was really avoiding giving a straight answer. It was as if he hadn't expected to be asked and, maybe, hadn't made up an answer yet. If Richard, in fact, did it, he would have wanted someone else to be blamed—maybe for Paul to be blamed. I don't know. But coming here to help me would make me think that he, at least, had nothing to do with it."

"But how did he get into your apartment if, as Paul says, Paul had locked your door?"

"Simple. Paul and Richard leave their keys in a wicker basket by their front door so they won't forget them when they go out. When Paul got home, all Richard had to do was to take the keys Paul had left there and come over here. And that would explain the time thing as well. When I first woke up—when it was happening—I thought I saw the digital clock, and it said 2:00 a.m., but Paul says he was home at a bit past 1:00."

"It's possible. But did you know Richard?"

"Not very well. We had met when I visited Paul. He certainly knew me. He knew why Paul was going to take me out that night; he knew where I lived, I think. At least, he certainly could have known that either from Paul or from his friend Arty. Arty's my best friend's cousin, and she lives upstairs."

"It makes sense, Sarah, at least as a possibility."

"I'm calling you because tomorrow I'm going to consent to have the samples from Health Services tested. Paul will voluntarily provide a DNA sample, and that will prove he's not the one. But if Richard isn't on anybody's radar, there would be no reason to get a DNA sample from him."

"Sarah, I'm not sure what you've told me would be anything like enough for police to get a warrant for Richard's DNA."

"Maybe. But maybe if you or the police talk to him, he might say something. I don't know, but maybe some inconsistencies, apart from the stuff about him talking to Paul, would come up."

"It seems a long shot, Sarah."

"But I don't want him to get away with this if he did it. And I want to know if he did. Would it be possible—maybe I could get a DNA sample from him. You know, from a coffee cup or a bit of his hair or…"

"Again, it's possible. But you would have to be with him, and you would have to take precautions not to contaminate any sample. Pulling out a piece of his hair would likely be too obvious," Martin's dry tone made his sarcasm clear.

"What about a paper coffee cup?"

"Yes, it might have enough. But where would you get a coffee cup that you knew he'd used?"

"I'll ask him to have coffee with me."

"Sarah, this could be risky. If he thinks you suspect him of this …"

"He has no reason to think that. I'll ask to meet him tomorrow and get a coffee—just to say goodbye."

"I don't like this much. But tell you what. If you make a date for coffee with him tomorrow, make it at the Campus Café, and let me know the time. I'll have a security officer out of uniform there, and she'll keep an eye on you both."

"Okay, great. Terrific. I'm going to call him later tonight and set it up."

After she ended the call, Sarah walked into the kitchen. She took out a rotisserie chicken from the fridge and ripped off a leg and thigh. Putting it on a plate, she took the last swig of her vodka and, reaching for a wine glass, poured herself a generous white wine. Taking the wine, the chicken, and a paper towel for her fingers, she circled back around the breakfast bar and climbed back onto her chair.

"Okay," she said to herself, "nineteen more articles. Now this one's from the *Journal of Progressive Law*. Let's see. Oh damn."

On her screen she read, "The *Journal of Progressive Law* is not in the university's digital collection. Selected volumes (2005–2016) are available in the Law Library."

"Oh no. And I've got—let's see—five articles from that bloody journal. Well, that means trekking down to the library. Damn it, I really thought I could finish tonight. Well, maybe I still can. I'll eat this chicken and have my wine, and then I'll go off to the library. But I'll call Richard first."

A few minutes later, Sarah had finished her scanty meal and the wine and noted up three articles that were online. All of them were short notes and needed little attention. "Down to sixteen," she told herself. Wiping her fingers on the paper towel, she carried the plate and glass to the kitchen. She rinsed her still-sticky fingers under the running water, dried them on the kitchen towel, and then picked up her phone from the counter.

"Hey, Richard. It's Sarah."

"Sarah! How're you doing?"

"Not bad. Look, I'm calling to let you know that I'm stopping out for the rest of the term. I just can't get it together here, and I think I need to get away, so I'm going home. I'm leaving Thursday."

"That's too bad, Sarah, but look, if there's anything I can do …"

"No, it's all under control. I've just got to finish this research project for Dr. Maryfield. I spoke to her today, and she raised a real stink about me not finishing it, so I told her I'd get it done. But I'll have it done tomorrow, and since I'll be dropping it off at the law school, I wondered if we could have coffee—just to say goodbye and," Sarah hesitated. Her heart was fluttering unusually. She had not expected to be nervous—not with Richard, who always seemed so reasonable— but now, she thought, perhaps not reasonable at all. Perhaps my rapist. She continued quickly, "and to thank you for your help."

"Well, sure. Look, we could meet tonight even—have something to eat?"

"No, I've got to finish this bibliography. And I've just discovered that several of the things I need can't be accessed online, so I'm going to have to go to the library this evening."

"I know you haven't been at school much the last couple of days. Did you know that the library is closing early tonight—at 6:30—for a union meeting?"

"No, no, I didn't. Thanks. But it's still early, and I do have keys as a research assistant. I can get in, and it'll be quiet anyway. I'll get a study room and be done in an hour." But Sarah also thought about how empty the library would be, and she was afraid.

Richard, hearing her voice tremble, continued, "Why don't I come with you? I can do some studying and keep you company, so you won't be worried about anything. It's reasonable you'd be nervous, even though I don't think there's any chance Paul would break his conditions and come on campus. And after, we can get something to eat and say our goodbyes."

Sarah felt panic. Obviously, Richard had no idea that she did not still think Paul was the guilty party. But the last thing she wanted was to be alone with him in a deserted library. The thought of coffee in broad daylight with a security officer watching was scary enough.

"No, no, don't worry. In fact, maybe I won't go tonight. I hadn't realized the library was closed. I can get in tomorrow morning at 8:30, and I'll finish everything else tonight. I'm being optimistic anyway to think I could do all these articles in a couple of hours. And thanks for the invitation for dinner, but I just ate, so I'd better get back to it. But what about coffee? Would tomorrow at 11:00 at the Campus Café work?"

"Sure. I finish my first class at 10:30 a.m., so I'll be ready for a break. But, really, Sarah, I wish you'd let me help."

Sarah laughed, but it sounded forced to her. "Hey, you know us feminists! We can do it all!"

"Okay, stay safe. And I'll see you tomorrow."

Sarah ended the call. She poured herself another shot of vodka, just to stop shaking. She hadn't imagined how hard it would be. But it was okay now. He didn't think she would go to the library, so she could go. Anyway, her fears were silly. Even if he had come, he wouldn't try and rape her now or hurt her; he wouldn't dare even touch her, for fear she would recognize some scent or feel of skin. And he did not know she suspected him.

Sarah pulled on her wool coat and wound the long green, hand-knit scarf around her neck. She slipped her laptop into its carry bag, tucked in her wallet, and then, after hesitating a moment, added the small, heavy meat mallet. She would get this done. She would be finished with this. Maybe she would never come back. Maybe she would meet someone in Toronto and stay there. She could transfer to the law school there. Maybe she would never have to see this place again. She carefully locked her door behind her as she left.

Meanwhile, Richard sat looking out into the dark. He sensed that Sarah was behaving strangely. He wondered why. His phone rang again, and he shook himself out of the mood and answered.

We all have hopes, don't we? Especially when we are so very young. And how we live when those hopes are gone may become what defines us. Do we mourn them? Do we chase them? Do we replace them? Do we learn to live without them? Or do we still, in some secret place, wait for them to be realized, even if under a very different guise?

MONDAY, OCTOBER 24, 9:00 P.M.

Alice was crying. She could not remember breaking down like this since the days after her ex-husband had died. Suicide, the final result had declared. But in those days, not only had there been the loss but the very real possibility that she would be arrested for murder. Why had this come on tonight? She had been feeling alone; she had ditched the soup and skipped dinner in favour of a couple of glasses of red wine and four chocolate truffles. Maybe the brandy had been a mistake. Patches paced up and down the carpet in front of the wingback chair, tail stiff and alert.

It was all too much. She would have to retire, as she knew that she could not put up with five more years of Hart, and he looked all too likely to win another term. She knew he wined and dined the Provost, and the younger faculty—those like Elizabeth—were devoted to him. And he never failed to treat her with courtesy. But she knew. She knew how he thought of her and her work. Old, passed its best before date, out of the mainstream. And why it should bother her, she didn't know. But everything she had loved about the law, about teaching, about the school—everything was being destroyed, hated, discarded. Perhaps this was just the way of one generation with the last. But was there no such thing as truth?

"I'll regret this," Alice thought to herself, but she picked up the handheld receiver of her home phone and dialled. "Martin?"

"Alice! What's up? Are you okay?"

"No, for some reason, I'm not, Martin. I've just been thinking too much. About my ex, about the days after he died, about being alone."

"My dear, you should know that the only reason you are alone is because you chose to be so."

"I know. I know. But right now, I just wish I hadn't."

Martin stood up, holding his cell. He had been answering a few last-minute emails and giving some instructions to his security personnel. He had enough to do, he thought, and he and Alice had been over for a long time.

"It was a long time ago, Alice, and we've both moved on."

Alice's temper flared. "Don't patronize me, Martin. I may feel like a pathetic old idiot right now, but don't rub it in."

Martin sighed. He and Alice had not been a good combination. When one was romantic, the other was cold, and she had never been able to face the fact that the world of the university and scholarship as she had loved it was no more. He had adapted to the new era and the new realities of campus life; she had not.

"Alice, let's not revisit this. We both wanted to be together once. Then we didn't. I'm truly sorry that you are having a bad night, but I'm not the one to call. I can't help you with what's wrong, and I don't even know what's wrong. The world is as it is. And we grow old; we are replaced by a new generation, and it's too bad that the reverence for the old is gone. But, hell, Alice, you never really were committed to anything anyway. You just loved peace. That's all. You loved peace. And for you and those who keep to your ways, there's no more peace."

"Okay, Martin. I'm sorry I called." Alice hung up the phone. Never dial or email, she reminded herself, when you have had too much to drink.

I haven't done that for a very long time, she thought, gathering Patches into her arms.

Her phone rang. She picked up.

"Alice, George here. I just got back from a long session with Fr. Mark, and I haven't had any dinner. I wondered it you might want a snack or a glass of wine and keep me company at our favourite pub. I'd love to have someone to bounce my thoughts off." When there was silence on Alice's end, George hurried on. "Sorry if I'm intruding. I'm just so—I don't know—absorbed in myself, I guess. But I know it's late, and you maybe are already doing something."

Alice thought. She could just push this off, or she could be honest.

"George," she started, "I don't want to lie to you. Fact is that I skipped dinner, and I'm a mess. I've been, well, sort of revisiting my past, and it hasn't been pleasant. And I'm sorry, but driving to the pub is out, as I've had a few glasses of wine and a brandy. So thanks for asking, but I'd better pass."

George was not fazed. "Well, then, you certainly need some dinner, and maybe one glass of wine and some coffee. I can pick you up in ten minutes. Are you dressed?"

"Yes, but, really, I don't know how much use I'll be discussing the finer philosophical points!"

George laughed. "Maybe what I mostly want is a listener. That will be your fee for my service!"

Alice smiled. After the call, she visited the bathroom, repaired her somewhat smeared makeup, and changed into a casual pair of slacks that she knew suited her. Paired with her black sweater and the tunic top, she was ready in eight minutes.

"Be good, Patches," she patted the cat. "Mommy's out tonight."

The doorbell rang.

She opened it and threw her arms around George's neck. "My saviour," she exclaimed.

George laughed. "No, only St. George to the rescue and slay the dragons!"

"And I don't even really know what the problem is," Alice continued after they were seated in their favourite nook. "I have everything anyone could want. And I know generations change. It's stupid to think everything will be the same. I'm sorry. I know you wanted to talk, and I've been babbling—too much to drink, I suppose."

"I don't think you've had too much," George began, "or I would have tried to persuade you not to order a glass of wine. You don't seem drunk; you seem depressed. What's up?"

"I wish I knew. You don't know all the things that happened after my divorce. It was bad. But that's not really it. When it was over, I thought I would have a life. Now? Well, now everything seems hopeless. I'm sixty-three, and how many years have I got? Twenty would be lucky. And, you know, if I felt I was making some kind of contribution, I wouldn't maybe care. Maybe. Oh, I don't know. I'm just maundering."

"You feel our time has passed," George said. "I can understand that, and it makes the idea of death so much harder when you believe you're just thrown on what we used to call 'the dust heap of history.'"

Alice nodded.

"But what I'm exploring is hope. Okay, yes, personal hope that when we die, we might indeed be born to eternal life, as our Evangelical brothers and sisters like to say, but more than that. Hope that there are eternal truths that will win in the end. That all will be made new. That there is an order in the universe that makes law make sense. It's not just the whim of some progressive (or regressive) state; there is a real order that impacts us and creates our happiness or our sorrow. Truth, beauty, goodness, love—they are real. Identity politics, hate, anger— those are shadows, nothings, but as C.S. Lewis once said, 'the nothing is very strong indeed.'"

"Maybe this isn't the time, George. I don't really know much about those beliefs. Never been really interested, I suppose. But I do know that you being here, even though I'm a mess …"

"Not a mess, Alice, just human."

"Well," she smiled as she picked up her Reuben sandwich, "you being here is proof to me that some things are true. But I don't suppose I've given it a lot of thought."

"So think!" George snapped. "You've got a brain—in fact, a very good brain. Use it. Explode the garbage we're fed. Come to see that there is truth, a piece of solid ground to stand on, even if our culture is exploding around us."

Alice smiled. "And now, I should ask, 'What is truth?' And even I know that question was asked by a very famous, or maybe infamous, person long ago."

"And answered by an even more famous one," George added. "But apart from the specifically religious issues, Alice, there is a clear choice here. Either the law is just something constructed by human beings for the convenience or for the profit of those who are in power at the time, or there are bedrock principles that cannot be ignored, except at peril of creating social chaos. Our law schools and our courts have, in the last thirty years, tried out the first theory, and chaos is following. And chaos leads to division, and division to repression. But we've so far just doubled down on the problem. We keep insisting that the solution to the problem is more of the problem. So, in the end, either we will change our direction, or we will fall into some kind of new darkness, but the truth about human beings and our law will still be there."

"I hate it!" Alice replied passionately. "I just hate it! Everything I loved is being despised."

"I can understand that. And it's fair enough to take refuge where we can, with people who believe as we do, and ride out the storm as best we can."

TUESDAY, OCTOBER 25, 8:20 A.M.

Leah Carter, the Assistant Law Librarian, stepped off the elevator on the sixteenth floor. It was her job today to open up and be ready for the students at 8:30. She didn't mind the early fall mornings, and she enjoyed coming in when the law school was still very quiet, certainly up here. On the classroom floors, she knew, there would be some bustle with students lining up for their extra-large coffees at the coffee stand, preparatory for their 8:30 lectures, and faculty arranging their PowerPoint slides and notes in the classrooms. But here, all was quiet. She pulled her large, brass key ring out of her purse as she stepped across the hallway from the elevator to the library front doors. Down the corridor to her left was the Dean's office. It was the only other occupant of the floor.

Through the glass doors of the library, Leah could see the circulation desk and, to its left, the reserve room where materials placed on two-hour loan by faculty members were held. To the right of the desk, the stacks began, with general references and then back to old case reports that had not been digitized. Just out of eyesight was the journal collection, now limited primarily to journals that were not online. Directly behind the circulation desk, a line of closed doors with small, high windows to protect privacy while allowing a little light, indicated the first set of study carrels, suitable only for private study and too small for more than two people. The larger group study rooms were located toward the outside walls of the space.

She fitted the main door key into the lock, turned it, and pressed the handle. It did not move. She turned the key back. The handle opened. That meant, she knew, that the door had not been locked when she had put the key in. Who, she wondered, had been the last person to leave for the meeting just before 6:30 last night? She could not recall. Well, whoever it was had been unpardonably careless. While there were few very valuable items in the library, one could never discount the possibility that students would steal volumes, especially considering the price of some texts or, as had happened in the past, simply out of mischief to prevent others from accessing some piece of knowledge that the thief considered vital for an assignment.

She stepped inside the doors and looked around. Nothing appeared to be disturbed. Of course, only time would tell. There were far too many books, displays, and other materials to be certain. She would interview every staff member as soon as they came in and try to find out who had been so irresponsible. Whoever it was should, at the least, receive a reprimand. She would notify the Dean's office as soon as Sandra arrived.

One or two students arrived at 8:30, and staff all checked in. Leah ensured that the technician whose turn it was to tend the circulation desk was ready for business. "Do you know who left the library last yesterday when we were going to the union meeting?"

The technician thought for a moment. "No, I don't think I do. I left at 6:15 because I was in charge of getting the coffee going for the meeting. Nobody else had gone at that time, at least I don't think they had. Of course, I didn't do a head count."

"Thanks," Leah said. "I have to step over to the Dean's office for a moment. And do you know when the Head Librarian is planning to be here this morning?"

The technician smiled. "I know that Jennifer said she had a meeting with the Provost first thing this morning, and then she has another meeting with the Deans at 10:00. I don't think we expect her until noon."

Leah nodded and, stepping out of the library, headed for the Dean's office.

Sandra was just hanging up her raincoat as Leah knocked on the open door.

"Good morning," Leah spoke. "I don't suppose Hart's in yet?"

"No, he has a meeting with the Deans and the Head Librarians this morning at 10:00. I don't expect him until after that. He usually uses this time on Tuesdays to work on his own research from home."

"That's what I thought. I'm hoping you can give him a message. When I came in this morning, the main library door was not locked. I don't see any disruption, so likely it was just an oversight, but you'll remember that we all left early last night for the union meeting. I'm going to question all the staff about how this happened. Someone was extremely careless, and I know that Jennifer is going to be extremely angry. I would expect we will be asking Hart to put a reprimand on the file of whoever did this."

Sandra sat down behind her desk. "Hart won't like that," she said. "He hates conflict with the union. And I wouldn't bet on your being able to find out who did it anyway. With everyone leaving pretty much at once, everyone will think locking the door was someone else's job. Besides, how do you know it wasn't a faculty member, or a research assistant, or a grad student? They've all got keys, and certainly it wouldn't be surprising if one of them wanted something after closing time yesterday, went in, and then forgot that the library was closed and just left."

Leah shrugged. "Maybe. But I'm going to speak to everyone anyway. You never know what people might remember."

"After a union meeting with lots of calls for solidarity? Good luck."

Sandra's eyes had already moved to her computer screen. With an exasperated sniff, Leah turned on her heel and returned to the library.

As she came through the doors, she saw a male student bang on the circulation desk. The technician appeared flustered and was shaking her head. "I'm sorry," she was saying, "I really can't find the key."

"I booked carrel 101 a week ago for this time. It's locked, and now you tell me there's no key?" His voice raised in volume and pitch. "I must have some quiet space. I can't work at home; I can't …"

Leah stepped forward. "Excuse me, but this is simply not an appropriate way to treat staff. What can I do to help?"

"Find me the key to carrel 101. See," he grabbed the computer monitor and turned it toward Leah, "there's my booking reservation for the carrel at 9:00 a.m. today. I've got a test at 1:30, and I need the carrel."

"You don't have the key?" Leah asked the technician who shook her head. She passed over the keyboard where the keys to the other five private study carrels hung. The key to 101 was missing.

"Very well," Leah said. "Just give me a moment to get the master key from my office."

Returning with the key, Leah and the student walked to the rear of the circulation desk and fitted the key into the door handle of the first private carrel. The technician, still visibly angry, turned to watch as the door opened.

Leah screamed, turning abruptly away and dropping to her knees. She bent over with her hand over her mouth, forcing back vomit. The male student simultaneously exclaimed, "My God!" and also turned away. "Call 911," he ordered the technician. "Someone's here and … and her head's bashed. My God, it's awful."

He staggered slightly and reached a chair set just to the right of the door. Meanwhile, Leah collected herself somewhat, grasped the door handle, and pulled herself to her feet. She closed the door and swallowed convulsively. "Call 911," she repeated to the technician. "Ask for an ambulance and for the police. There's nothing to be done for that poor girl; she's dead. But we must have the police. Call Campus Security as well. They'll have to handle the police," Leah continued, her brain beginning to function again. "And get Sandra to call the Dean on his cell. He'll have to come in right away."

The technician began to shake. "Dead? An accident?"

"I don't know," Leah answered.

"Do you know who it is?" the technician continued, tears beginning to fall down her cheeks.

"I'm afraid so. I'm afraid it's Sarah Yung."

So you know now that I am not Sarah. More's the pity, perhaps, but there it is. A violent death shakes everyone in a community—there's that word again. I'm sure as you've read these pages, you understand that the goody-feeling of saying we are a community means almost nothing. But like those desk toys with stainless steel balls on strings that cost far more than they're worth, it does mean a connectedness where, when one ball hits the next, it hits the next, which hits the next, until the final ball swings back and hits the one behind it, and so on back and forth down the line until inertia stops them all. And that's how it was in the next few days in the law school. Tears, of course. Outrage, of course. Fine phrases that meant nothing, of course. Anything to prevent us understanding the one basic reality that all the niceness, inclusiveness, and social justice cannot protect us from: death. Real equality.

If I sound hard, it's because I have learned to be. Hard with the fictions that we tell ourselves, including the fictions I tell myself … at least, as much as I can. I have learned to value truth. I hope.

Although I hope I am hard about truth-telling and the lies we use to pretend there is no truth so that death can be ignored, I am not and never have been hard or cynical about the tragedy that Sarah's death was. While there was much fake about the reactions, we were all hit by the ball—not a cute little stainless-steel toy, but a wrecking ball that changed many of us forever. Especially, of course, Sarah's killer. Me.

CHAPTER 5

"I can't believe that Sarah's dead. It's a horrible, horrible tragedy. And it's another example of the violence against women that pervades our culture. This university—yes, sorry, of course I understand that I should answer your questions.

"Well, Sarah was in my Feminist Legal Studies class this year. This was her third year, and she had taken Legal Ethics and also Equality Law from me last year. I think she was signed up for Social Justice in an Oppressive State, my course next term. She was also my research assistant, working on a bibliography for me on campus culture for some research I'm doing.

"I found out about her rape just after it happened. It was terrible. They called me from Health Services—who called? I think it was one of the clerks. Sarah was supposed to make a class presentation on an essay I had assigned as reading in class the next day, and we had a meeting scheduled that morning. The clerk was calling to arrange an academic concession for her so that missing the class wouldn't affect her grade. Of course, I soon found out what had happened, and I dropped everything and met Sarah at the Counselling Services office.

"Well, we talked about what happened. She was shattered. And, although that Campus Security officer who was with her objected, I made sure that no one, no one, was going to silence Sarah about what she had gone through. She told me then that Paul Anstel, one of our PhD students, had done it. He had taken her home and come in; she was drunk, and he raped her.

"We don't do anything like enough on this campus to change the culture of sexual violence. Women have experienced this oppression long enough, and I have dedicated my life to—yes, this is relevant, and I'll thank you to let me finish. It's relevant because I had a project planned. Sarah and I were going to do important work together. Not only is her death a tragedy because of its representation of the culture of hate on campus, but also because it puts an end to a life that might have changed so much. The work is so important, officer. You must understand that.

"Yes, I did arrange an academic concession for Paul, although it was against my better judgement. But now that's surely going to be unnecessary. If he's not arrested for the rape, surely he will be for this terrible murder. I mean, he obviously must be guilty …

"Yes, she came to see me that morning to say she was stopping out. We had—oh, I don't know—a ten-minute conversation. I was a little surprised, as I thought we were immediately going to work on her graduating paper—one that I would have included in my next book, subject, of course, to its quality. But with Sarah, I'm certain it would have been a brilliant exposé of this campus, its hypocrisy, its white privilege. I …

"Of course, I had no reason to be angry at Sarah. Well, it was surprising and a little disappointing, but we could have worked over email, and her stopping out wouldn't have lasted long. She would have come back, and really all that was going on was a slight delay in our project. But we would have worked together, and we would have brought justice to this campus. Her death is a tragedy.

"That evening? I went home before lunch. It turned out I wasn't feeling very well—something I ate, I expect. The cafeterias on campus are dreadful. I went to bed and stayed there all night. No, I didn't see a doctor. I was better the next day.

"Yes, I did phone Sarah once that evening. About 7:30, I think. We had a cordial but short conversation, and she told me she was headed for the library, finishing my bibliography before she left. I was just touching base with her.

"The disruption at the Catholic mass on Saturday? Of course, I had heard about it. Yes, I had expanded the methods of evaluation for my class to include some performance art projects, but really, officer, our students are passionate about social justice—equality and inclusion are vital to them—so perhaps a few were carried away. I can hardly be blamed for that. And besides, what they did was hardly very serious. I understand it was red-coloured hand soap—not anything that would hurt anyone. It was a gesture in solidarity with victims of violence and oppression.

"No, I think that's all I can tell you about the situation. I don't have to answer your questions, you know. I'm speaking to you totally voluntarily."

STATEMENT OF DEAN HARTMAN HAVERMAN, GIVEN TO VICTORIA CITY POLICE OFFICER TERRANCE KLEIN, OCTOBER 26

"I can't believe it. You have to understand, officer, that our school is a very cooperative, caring place. We look after each other, especially those subject to historical oppression: our First Nations students, our members of the LGBTQ+ community, our women.

"Well, yes, of course I was shocked by the rape. But the young man accused, Paul Anstel, well, he has consistently said he is innocent, and I am sure that can be proved now that the poor girl's dead. The DNA sample from Health Services can be compared—no, of course I'm not telling you how to do your job. I'm simply noting that it may not be true that the rapist was one of our students. I am absolutely convinced that you should be looking at the wider university community ...

"No, other than what I heard from Professor Gordon and Dr. Maryfield, I had no real involvement with Sarah, poor girl. The Provost, may I say, is very, very distressed by this. I had spoken to Dr. Maryfield about the incident at the mass, but we can't even say for certain it was connected to Sarah's situation.

"Well, yes, I did know that Dr. Maryfield had altered her course evaluation methods because of the rape, and I understand she had Sarah's full cooperation. They were writing a paper together about the experience. It would have been the central piece of a new book. Absolutely cutting-edge work—just what we would expect from Dr. Maryfield, one of our leading scholars.

"No, I realize that the incident at the Catholic mass is assumed to be connected to Dr. Maryfield's class and to her work, but I don't really know that. We don't know who the students were, after all ...

"Where was I Monday night? I was at home. Alone."

STATEMENT OF PAUL ANSTEL, GIVEN TO VICTORIA CITY POLICE OFFICER, TERRANCE KLEIN, OCTOBER 26

"I couldn't believe it when I heard. I'm sorry I was out when you called, but I went to an early mass this morning. Praying for Sarah's soul is all I can do for her now.

"No, I did not rape Sarah Yung. I've said many, many times that I left her fine. She was tucked up on her sofa bed with the afghan. And I locked the door behind me when I left. I knew nothing about her situation until my roommate, Richard Prius, woke me the next morning. He had just taken Sarah to Health Services.

"Yes, I did have her keys. But I am willing to provide a DNA sample anytime. I know it will establish my innocence.

"Yes, I did speak to Sarah the day she died. She texted me. Well, I'm sure you have her phone, so you know she wanted me to call her. And I did.

"I wouldn't call it surprising. Yes, of course, I knew she had accused me of rape. Why do you think I'm off campus and staying in this motel room? But I had wanted to talk to her. We're old, old friends, since childhood. I thought if I could just speak to her, she'd know I would never have done this to her. And when I called—well, the one thing that makes me feel better—if anything could right now—is that I know we had spoken, and I told her that I forgave her. I wasn't sure what to say …

"Yes, she told me that she realized she couldn't be sure about the rape, and in fact, she was pretty sure she had been wrong, and that she now thought she knew who had really done it. She asked my forgiveness, and I gave it.

"No, of course, no one can back me up about what was said. It was a private phone call, and I'm not in the habit of recording phone calls. But she told me that she was going home Thursday, and that Tuesday or Wednesday—sorry, just give me a minute—Tuesday or Wednesday, she'd be going to Health Services to sign a consent to release samples for DNA testing. And she said she thought she knew who had done it, something inconsistent in what someone said to her.

"Oh, and she was also really angry with Dr. Maryfield. Sarah said she knew Dr. Maryfield had just been using her and didn't care about her at all. She said the attack on the Catholic mass on Saturday was just the kind of hate that her suffering was being used to stir up. And she said she was going to have to rethink everything.

"No, she very, very definitely was not going to help Dr. Maryfield by writing something with her. She was furious at Maryfield. Said they'd had an interview that morning where Maryfield wound up threatening her. I told Sarah she should go to the Dean, but she said she just wanted to get away from here.

"No, I didn't go out Monday evening. I ordered in a pizza, and I worked on my dissertation. Then I spent some time praying, and then I went to bed.

"Of course I didn't kill Sarah. I didn't go onto campus. I didn't need to because everything I needed could be accessed from my computer here, and I thought this nightmare would be over soon because Sarah would okay the DNA testing, and then my life would get back to normal. I was happy, not angry. I thought everything was going to work out—poor, poor Sarah. Dear God, I'm so glad we had the chance to talk before ... before it happened."

STATEMENT OF ANGIE (ANGELA) MAITLAND, GIVEN TO VICTORIA CITY POLICE OFFICER TERRANCE KLEIN, OCTOBER 27

"Sure, I'm in Dr. Maryfield's class, and I knew Sarah. But why are you interviewing me?

"Oh, okay. Well, if I can tell you anything that would help.

"But I hadn't spoken to Sarah after her rape. I don't know anything about it, except what I heard in class.

"Well, Dr. Maryfield came into the classroom that day and said that Sarah had been raped. We were shocked. I mean, the whole point of the seminar is thinking about how we can get justice for women—and for this to happen to one of us—well, it was just very, very upsetting and ...

"But some good was going to come of it because Sarah and Dr. Maryfield were going to work together, and we were all going to help change the culture on this campus. The rape culture. The slut-shaming. I mean, guys talk about what we wear, can you believe it? Or how much we drink, or who we're sleeping with. I mean, women are entitled to do what they want. It's men's problem that they can't cope with it. It's just a perpetuation of the patriarchy, along with heterosexualism and transphobia.

"Well, yeah, we were all going to participate. Dr. Maryfield had this great list of projects that would be included in her next book.

"No, of course I don't know anything about that thing with the Catholic priest. But I don't think it was so terrible – sure, I know they threw some stuff, but none of it was harmful. And it was a protest against the misogyny of religion and homophobia too. I mean, if there had never been any of that, we wouldn't have a rape culture on campus. It's the devaluation of women that does it. And that's the history of religion, as I'm sure you know.

"Well, Saturday evening? I spent it with my friends, Tyler and Suze. We were together at Tyler's place first, and then we went to the pub. I saw Sarah there with Richard Prius and Arty, his friend. I don't know Arty very well because he takes mostly the corporate crap—you know, Commercial Law and Real Estate. Richard is an okay guy. He gets it. He's a graduate student, though, with Dean Haverman.

"Oh, yeah, I guess I did speak briefly to Sarah then. Sorry. I was kind of drunk, and I guess it slipped my mind. But we didn't really talk. Later, I went back to Tyler's—that was late, though. I heard later what had happened at the mass, and, sure, I thought, 'good for you, whoever you are.'

"Monday? Well, let me see. I came to the law school, and I had a short meeting with Dr. Maryfield …

"Oh, just about the class and about the work we were going to do. And then I had some classes. And then I went home. I had some reading to do, so that's where I was. No, my roommate was out having a sleepover with her date, and I don't think I talked to anyone. I just had some dinner. I microwaved some mac and cheese. And then I watched some TV and went to bed."

STATEMENT OF RICHARD PRIUS, GIVEN TO VICTORIA CITY POLICE OFFICER TERRANCE KLEIN, OCTOBER 27

"I know. It's horrible. I'm so sorry.

"Right. I went to Sarah's early on Thursday morning last week, just to check on her because I thought Paul seemed upset when he got home after their date Wednesday evening. I wanted to make sure she was okay. And then I found out—well, it was awful. I took her to Health Services, and she was crying. Really, really distressed.

"Yeah, we were together briefly at the pub Saturday night. She had a date with Arty, my friend. But Arty asked me to come along too. Well, we were both a bit worried about Sarah, and Arty … Arty wasn't sure what to think. Anyway, Sarah didn't stay long. Angie from the next table came over and expressed support. I guess that brought it back for Sarah, and she wanted to go home.

"I never saw her again.

"Yes, she did phone me on Monday evening, around dinnertime. She wanted to make a coffee date with me for Tuesday. She was going home Thursday morning, and she wanted to thank me. She talked about going to the library, and I said I'd go too and keep her company. She seemed nervous, and I don't blame her. I suggested we get something to eat after, but she said she'd changed her mind about the library. That she had too much to do at home, and she didn't want to have dinner with me because she'd already had something. We made the coffee date, and that was that.

"No, I didn't go to the library. I stayed in. I believed her when she said she'd changed her mind.

"No, she certainly didn't say anything to me about being mad at Dr. Maryfield. As far as I know, they were working together. And, no, she didn't say anything about Paul. Well, she wouldn't, would she? I think I said that I didn't believe he would come onto campus. I wish I hadn't said that, and I wish I'd insisted on going to the library with her. I was just so wrong …

"Well, of course Paul killed her. He must have. She was ruining his life."

STATEMENT OF TYLER JENKINS,
GIVEN TO VICTORIA CITY POLICE OFFICER
TERRANCE KLEIN, OCTOBER 27

"No, I fucking well won't talk to you.

"You have no rights to insist. I'm a law student, and I know that I don't have to say anything to you.

"OK, I will say this: I don't know anything about Sarah's rape; I don't know anything about the campus mass stuff; and I don't know anything about Sarah's murder. Now go to hell."

I'm glad, now, that I have written my confession: I killed Sarah Yung. I have written that sentence under a hundred (or more) veils, and now I say it outright: I killed Sarah Yung.

My psychiatrist said to me once, summarizing our conversation, "You carry an overpowering guilt about the events of that night, and that guilt—and the pain—have driven you to write, to be able to write in a way that thousands of readers can connect with, and to be a success. Which all drives you, even more, to guilt, because Sarah's death is the root of your success."

I nodded.

"But then, why write?" he asked. "Why not be a failure? Stop writing."

"I can't," I replied. "The pain and the guilt make me tell the story, and tell it again and again."

"And what you want to know, as well," he continued, "is whether, if you lighten the guilt, your talent will wane. Your question is: Can I put this guilt behind me and still write?"

"Yes," I replied. "That's exactly it. If the sun rises, can I still see the moon?"

"Well," he said, "I don't know. Can you?"

That was the last hour I spent with him.

THURSDAY, OCTOBER 27, 3:30 P.M.

Terrance Klein sat in his superior's office while his sergeant, Mark Miller, thumbed through a file.

"I see you've collected quite a few statements already, Terry. Good work. The Provost, Amelie Zirdari, is a good friend of the Chief's, and I can tell you that she's plenty upset over this murder on her campus. With hot competition for students, it doesn't do you much good to have your campus in the news for a rape and then a murder. How's it going?"

Terry looked at his notes. "Well, Sergeant, I still have a few more interviews. I've had some problems with the students in Dr. Maryfield's class. Over half of them won't talk to me at all, and most of the other half were very rude and said they knew nothing."

Sergeant Miller frowned. "Not good. I assume you gave them the usual about helping the police?"

"You bet. But these kids know they don't have to talk to me, and many of them don't trust the police. They think we're the Nazis reborn."

"Do we have any idea of the murder weapon yet?"

"No. The coroner says in her preliminary report that it must have been some heavy metal object. But nothing was found in the carrel. The killer must have taken it with him."

"And maybe brought it with him? That would suggest premeditation."

"True. It seems strange that some heavy metal object would be just sitting around in a study carrel. We certainly can't rule out premeditation at this stage."

"What's your thinking to date?"

"I think it's most likely this guy, Paul Anstel. He was accused of raping the victim. He was thrown off campus, barred from classes. He's a PhD student, so he looked like he'd have a bright future, probably as a prof somewhere. No way that was going to happen if he was turfed out of the university for rape."

"But it seems unlikely he did the rape, doesn't it? I understand he's given a DNA sample, and there's a sample from the rape kit. That could establish his guilt, but more likely, his innocence, since he's said all along, he was willing to be tested. I suppose we haven't got the results yet?"

"No, the lab in Vancouver's backed up. It'll be another day. But, Sergeant, as for motive, I understand that the victim had refused to give her consent for the testing. And she'd refused to go to the police, where we could have had a warrant. There was no way this Paul guy could get the testing done.

"My guess is this. He and the victim spoke the night she was killed. I'm betting that it was far from the cordial conversation Paul Anstel reports in his statement. Likely he begged her to let him clear his name. She refused. Everyone says she was hot to work with this Dr. Maryfield and push the social justice line. She and Maryfield were going to publish a full account of her experience. It wouldn't have done Anstel any good.

"Anyway, suppose she told him she was going to the library. He goes there to try to reason with her. They fight. He hits her, and she's dead."

"The library was closed. How did they both get in?"

"The librarian who found the body tells me that all the faculty, research students, and grad students have library keys. Sarah Yung was Dr. Maryfield's research assistant, so she likely let herself into the library after it was closed. That squares with Richard Prius' description of their phone call and its timing from Sarah's phone. Anstel is a graduate student, so he has keys as well."

"Sounds plausible. I understand from your conversation with the librarian that the carrel was locked?"

"Yeah, but that's simply explained. All anyone had to do was push the lock button inside the doorknob and close it after himself. The locks are all like that on those carrels."

"But the main library door was not locked? If the killer had a key, he didn't use it to relock the main door."

"No, but if Anstel had just killed someone, he might have been too rattled to think about relocking the door. That one requires a key to lock from the outside. He probably wanted to get away fast, before he was seen and didn't want to stand there fiddling with a key."

"Nobody did see him?"

"Not that I've found yet. But, of course, I'm not done with the interviews yet. The whole library staff, however, except for the Head Librarian, seems to have been at a union meeting from 6:30 to about 9:00 p.m. And the Head Librarian had gone home to dinner with her family. The coroner thinks the victim was killed sometime between 7:00 and 9:00."

"Of course, in his statement, Anstel says their conversation was about the victim asking his forgiveness and saying she was not going to work with Maryfield."

"True, but that's what he would say, isn't it? Of course, no one can back up his story about that. No, I think the conversation was very different, and I think he had a motive at least to talk to Sarah, and if she was angry and there was a fight … well …"

"But we were just discussing the murder weapon. If the killer brought some heavy metal object with him—or her, I suppose—then likely the killing was premeditated. But in your scenario, Anstel didn't intend to kill her; it would have happened during an unanticipated struggle. That suggests Anstel isn't your guy, or if he is, that he has a different motivation from the one you've come up with."

"I suppose that's a problem, all right."

"Say, have you talked to Martin Blatt yet?"

"Blatt? Oh, he's the head of their security services, right? No, I haven't, but I will. The victim's phone shows that she called him the night she died, some time before she called Richard Prius."

"Well, talk to him next. And don't write him off. Before Blatt took an early retirement and joined the Security service at the university, he was a damn good cop. A few years ago," the sergeant continued, lowering his voice, "he stopped me from making one hell of a mistake. This guy, Adam Gordon, died under suspicious circumstances. He had an ex-wife, a prof at the university, who had no cause to love him, believe me. Anyway, we were pretty sure she was the one, until Martin stepped in and looked at things a little differently. Actually, turned out it was suicide. We cleared the case, and we didn't lock up an innocent person. But I was younger and not experienced. If not for Martin, we likely would have had egg on our faces when Professor Gordon's defence counsel was through with the evidence. Martin knows the campus. Ask for his help. He'll be glad to assist you."

"Gee, Sergeant, I'm not keen on getting someone who's not one of us involved."

"Martin really is one of us, Terry. He's good, smart, and he knows the people. Ask for his help."

THURSDAY, OCTOBER 27, 5:00 P.M.

"Sure, Terry. I'm glad to chat now. I'm not quite ready to leave yet—usually that's about 5:30, so come in and sit down. How's Sergeant Miller doing these days?"

"Really good," Terry replied. "He and I were just reviewing the facts of the Yung murder investigation. He suggested I ask for your help because, to quote, you're 'good, smart, and know the people.'"

"Glad to help. In fact, as you likely know by now, Sarah called me the evening she died."

"Yes, I was going to ask you about that first, before we get to the other stuff."

"Well, she called because she had decided that she couldn't be sure the rapist was Paul Anstel."

"Wow," Terry exclaimed. "So Anstel may have been telling the truth? Do you know if she had told him that?"

"I don't know. She told me she thought she knew who it was, and she had some pretty decent reasons—although it certainly wasn't an airtight case. But she had the idea that she'd have coffee with the guy the next day and try to get the coffee cup he used for a DNA sample. I offered to have a plainclothes security officer nearby. She was scared all right, but she was going home, and she didn't want him to get away with it."

"No shit?" Terry said. "But you don't know if she had told Anstel about this?"

"No, I don't, but it makes sense she would have. She told me that she was going to sign the consent to have the DNA tested to clear him before she left. It would be surprising if she hadn't told him."

"She texted him, and they had a phone conversation," Terry added, "before she called you."

"Well, that's it then."

"So Anstel certainly had no reason to kill her."

"Nope. I wouldn't think so, unless there's something we don't know."

"Who did she suspect?" Terry asked.

"Richard Prius," Martin replied.

THURSDAY, OCTOBER 27, 7:00 P.M.

Alice and George sat in what they now referred to as "their pub," sipping their drinks. Alice was pale and still holding a tissue in one hand.

"It's the most dreadful thing, George. That poor girl. She was so confused and so alone. Why didn't I try to reach her on Monday?"

"Because we all thought she wasn't coming to school until Tuesday, and had you tried to call her, if she was still as antagonistic as she had been, she would likely have refused to speak to you at all. You did your best, Alice. But there is one positive thing. I was talking to Fr. Mark earlier today, and he says that Paul had a phone call with Sarah in the early evening of the day she died. Sarah told him she didn't believe he was her rapist and that she would go to Health Services in the next day or so to sign the consent for testing the DNA. She asked him not to say anything to anyone, but that she would tell you herself the next day. He agreed. He says he was so relieved; he was sure his life would be back on track in a few days. He says she asked for his forgiveness, which he gave. She was going home—to heal, he hoped."

"That's a relief. I was very much afraid that the police would think Paul was the murderer. But wait a minute. What if the police don't believe him? I mean, he might have said that, but the police are likely to think it's exactly what he would say. And, oh God, he still had his library keys. He could have gone after her. They'll think that's what he did."

"Don't panic, Alice. The police won't jump to conclusions, I'm sure."

"Ha! The police love jumping to conclusions. Let me tell you about …" Alice's cellphone rang. "Sorry, George, but I'd better get it. It won't be long."

Alice answered her cell to hear Martin Blatt at the other end.

"Hey, Alice. How are you? Look, first I wanted to say that I'm sorry I cut you off the other night. You were in distress, and I …"

"Hi, Martin," Alice interrupted. "I appreciate your call, and I know I shouldn't have called on you just then. It wasn't fair. But this isn't a good time to talk about it. I'm just having a drink and dinner with a friend."

"I'm sorry. But just quickly then, there was another reason I wanted to talk to you."

"And?"

"I've just had a meeting with Terry Klein, who's the officer investigating Sarah's death. His sergeant is our old friend, Mark Miller."

"Hmm. Sergeant now, is he?"

"And Sergeant Miller advised Terry to ask for my help. He's brought me the witness statements that they've taken so far and some other things. But, of course, the reason Sergeant Miller asked for my help is because of your case. And, Alice, I'm not so arrogant that I don't recall very clearly that the real reason we were helpful in your ex's mystery was because of you. I know you're Paul Anstel's graduate supervisor, of course. And I don't think Paul is a suspect, not after I told Terry that

Sarah called me on the night she died to say she no longer thought Paul was the rapist. Turns out she called Paul too, and Paul says, quite believably under the circumstances, that she had told him she was consenting to the DNA test. So he had no motive to kill her. The question is, who did?"

"I'm glad to hear that, Martin. Actually, I'm having dinner with George Bush, and he told me the Catholic chaplain said that Sarah told Paul she would give consent for the testing. But I was afraid the police wouldn't believe Paul. I'm not too impressed with their record of believing honest witnesses. But why are you calling me?"

"Because, to get back to what I was saying, I want us to put our heads together over this and see if we can help out in the investigation. I know the people somewhat, but you really know them."

Alice thought for a few seconds before responding.

"I'd like to help if I can, but only if I can bring George with me. He knows the people too, and I'm sure the three of us together will be a better team."

"I don't know, Alice. The stuff I've got is all confidential."

"Martin, I know you. You want to be the one to solve this case. You just love giving the Victoria police a poke in the eye. And you think I'd be a real help. So if you want me, you get George too." Alice smiled across the table at George. He reached over and squeezed her free hand. She released the tissue to return his clasp.

"All right. But let's not tell Officer Klein."

"I wouldn't think of it."

"Can we meet tomorrow morning?"

Alice covered the cell for a second. "What's your schedule tomorrow?" she asked George.

"Not much. Since the Law Student Society persuaded Hart that Fridays should be 'study days' without classes, all I have to do is some research."

Alice went back to the phone. "I have a midterm to mark, Martin. But this takes priority. Can you come to my office at 9:00 a.m.?"

"I'll be there."

Alice ended the call.

"One piece of good news: Sarah had called Martin, and their call confirms that she no longer believed that Paul had raped her."

"That's a relief," George replied.

"I still can't help wishing I'd tried harder with Sarah. George, do you really think that there's some afterlife where we go? I'd like to think that Sarah was somewhere she could be happy. It's so strange. All these kids have everything—most of them live in a comfort that we couldn't afford when we were students. They go out to parties, to clubs, they drink expensive cocktails all evening—you know, even with my salary, I think twice before having more than one cocktail at fifteen dollars a pop—they have all the electronic toys. And they all feel their lives are hopeless."

"It's true that many of them won't have the kind of financial security or the stability of employment we've had, Alice."

"Maybe for low-skilled jobs. But these young people are going to be lawyers." She smiled. "I haven't noticed any decrease in demand for our services lately. In fact, with government's approach that 'if it moves, we have to regulate it,' more lawyers than ever are needed. And, worst of all, I think these kids hate us. They hate me, anyway."

"Why do you say that?"

"A conservative white woman? I'm one of the oppressors. My ancestors stole this country from the first peoples. I'm a 'settler,' as they say. And, even if I'm not religious, George, I can't abide the new moral approach. I mean, I don't like sex-selective abortion, and I think we should have laws about it; I worry when doctors have to help people die, even if it's against their consciences; and I don't think we should be able to shut up people we disagree with. You know, that used to make me a liberal. Now it makes me a bigot."

"Terrible things were done to our first peoples, Alice. And their current plight is still horrendous in many cases. And while I have the same worries you do, I can understand the reaction these kids have to a world that creates so much pain and that they believe has no hope of redemption unless they remake it all by themselves. It's a burden too heavy for any mere human."

"I admire your tolerance. But despite what I feel about our moral lives, just like our students, I have no foundation for my beliefs. I just feel them. Whoever killed Sarah couldn't have had any foundation for their moral beliefs either. Likely they didn't have any at all. And that's eventually, I'm afraid, what it leads to. When you don't have any basis for moral judgements, then why shouldn't you kill if the situation seems to demand it? Why shouldn't you do anything that seems expedient? Maybe that's where I really am heading."

George was thoughtful and paused for a moment.

"I hope you won't think I'm unfair, Alice," he said, "but I think that your feelings result from hundreds—in fact, many more than two thousand—years of moral teachings that came out of the Judaic and Christian faiths. In our generation, there was a wholesale desertion from any real adherence to faith. But the moral teachings hung on for most of us. But the next generation, and the next, they're further and further removed from the root. And the life fades away, just like the life of a flower fades when it's picked."

"You're saying that the only way we can avoid this collapse is through restoring faith in God?"

"Sounds radical, doesn't it? And I'm sure the word 'bigot' would be immediately used by many of our students if they heard me. But if we want to avoid things getting any worse, and if we want to have hope, then I think we have to get back to the idea that human beings bear the image of their creator; that this is what gives us dignity; and this is the basis of our human rights—not some idea of equality imposed by the force of the state. That equality is always going to produce suffering because it motivates the state to act not on a desire to improve people's situations but to manipulate our hatred of those who are richer, more talented, or luckier for votes and popularity. It's the divine image imprinted on the human person that makes us worthy of respect and care. When we recognize that, then balance and real tolerance become possible. And as an antidote for hate, we have to accept that we are loved, deeply loved, by God. Hate never drives out hate."

THURSDAY, OCTOBER 27, 9:00 P.M.

Hart was rebuttoning his shirt in front of the mirror on his closet door; Elizabeth, standing slightly to his right, ran a comb through her hair and adjusted her jacket to sit properly on her shoulders.

Hart smiled at her in the mirror. "Quite a reconciliation, sweetheart," he said.

Elizabeth smiled back. "I'm starving, Hart. We missed dinner, and I didn't have any lunch." She stopped smiling as she remembered the day. "I was just so upset all day. I'm still angry about that snippy police officer who came to talk to me. I certainly didn't have to help him out at all. He could have been grateful that I told him anything."

"I don't expect you could help him much," Hart responded. "It's good that really neither you nor I had anything to do with this. You're not responsible if it was a few students in your class that disrupted that mass, and, anyway, I think the disruption had absolutely nothing to do with that poor girl's murder. Most likely, it had to do with the rape. And, most likely, it was Paul Anstel who killed her. He would have had the motive—either he was her rapist, in which case he would want to shut her up, or he wasn't, in which case he might have killed her to get the DNA tested. She was ruining his life, after all."

"That's pretty much what I told the police," Elizabeth said. "But I got a strange feeling from them. I was surprised they would ask me about the phone call I made to Sarah that evening. And then they asked me where I had been—of course, it's all too ridiculous to think that I would be involved in any way in violence against a woman."

"Of course it is, darling," Hart replied. "Look, I've got a couple of steaks in the fridge along with a package of romaine lettuce. What about steak and Caesar salad?"

"You know I'm not keen on eating red meat, Hart. In fact, I might think about turning vegetarian again. Violence against any living creature is abhorrent to me."

"Well, if you don't want steak, you can have salad alone. But as for me, I want some steak."

"Do you think all this will have any impact on my promotion?" Elizabeth asked anxiously. "How's the Provost taking it?"

Hart shook his head. "I spoke to her on the phone about 6:00 today. She's having fits, and she wants to turn the law school upside down. I have strict instructions to see that we cooperate fully with the police, although how she thinks I can force students and faculty, who certainly have minds of their own, to cooperate I'll never know. It's just another example of how she expects to tell me what to do and then to assume I can do it. Oh, and she says the police have asked Martin Blatt for help, and to top that off, he's going to bring in Alice Gordon, of all things. So she wants us to do 'whatever it takes,' to quote!"

"I've told you a million times, Hart, that you should tell her to go to hell. Why on earth do you want another term as Dean?"

"Sweetie, maybe if I believed in hell, I'd tell her to go there," Hart smiled at his very mild joke. "But as to why I want another term, I would have thought it was obvious. There's so much left to complete in my agenda for the school to secure the legacy of my leadership. We need to carry through our programs and ensure our curriculum is solidly centred on our commitment to social justice. We need to revamp our application processes and focus them more on social justice and less on grades. We want committed students to help us. And I want to make sure your work gets the recognition it deserves."

"Thank you, Hart. That's very thoughtful."

"You're the wave of the future, darling," he said, gathering her into his arms. "But," he continued, "you really aren't involved in any way with this, are you?"

"How could you think that?" she replied.

Later, Hart had removed two rib-eye steaks from the refrigerator and was tossing a salad with a commercial dressing while he sipped a neat scotch.

"Do you ever think," he asked, "that perhaps there is something after we die? I mean, that we survive somehow?"

Elizabeth, nursing a glass of white wine, shrugged. "Of course not. It's just a fairy tale. We die, and we're gone."

"Doesn't … oblivion … worry you at all?" Hart continued, taking a larger swig of scotch. "Damn. Freshen this for me, would you, sweetie?" he asked.

Elizabeth picked up his glass and poured another finger of scotch into it as Hart began to season the steaks and heat the oven.

"Of course it doesn't," she replied. "In fact, thinking about some 'pie in the sky when you die' just distracts us from the struggle for social justice here."

"Religion is the opiate of the people, eh?" Hart said.

"Precisely."

"So that poor girl, who never had the chance to live her life, is just gone and is … nothing?"

"We have to make her life mean something, Hart. That's what immortality really is—having her death serve the greater good."

"But what can mean anything? Why should I care about whether her life means anything? Why do you?"

"Really, Hart. You know perfectly well that we must create our own meaning. Anything else is just wishful thinking. This is how the world is."

"Well, then, I don't see any reason why I shouldn't just do exactly as I please and ignore anyone else."

"Hart, I think we're getting back to our quarrel. I intend to see that Sarah did not die for nothing. Her life and her death will help many of us to turn around this campus and turn around our society. But let's not debate the point."

"Okay," Hart said, searing the steaks. "You and I will never see this the same way. But if I'm going to oblivion in a few short years, then I'm here for me. Social justice is great, but we have to make sure we're on the side of the revolution that gets the good results."

"Hart," Elizabeth continued, "good results will be there for everyone when we have eliminated hate, and the patriarchy, and the family as the site of oppression, and when everyone can be free."

"Free for what?"

"To be themselves."

"And to die."

"And to die, but to mean something." Elizabeth finished her wine. "Let's drop it before we fight again. Honestly, Hart, I know the sex was great—and we both needed something to relieve ourselves from the dreadful days we've just lived through—but please, let's not get back to this issue. I know you're just blowing off steam, but it sometimes really does make me worry that social justice to you is just a way of getting ahead."

"Fine, let's drop it for now," Hart said. "In five minutes, we'll be ready to eat."

FRIDAY, OCTOBER 28, 3:00 A.M.

Elizabeth woke from an upsetting dream, although as she opened her eyes in her dark bedroom, she could not remember the dream or understand what now was causing her heartbeat to accelerate and her breathing to come in gasps. She choked and sat up, breathing more steadily. She looked at her bedside clock and groaned: "3:00 a.m.—hours until morning," she thought. And wasn't there something about 3:00 a.m.? Ghosts walked then, surely, in legends. Didn't Americans have a saying, "Dead as three o'clock"?

She shivered. She was not superstitious, she reminded herself. But the room seemed darker than usual. Heavy cloud cover, likely, she concluded. Pulling her silk robe from a chair beside her bed, she slipped it on and lifted the blind on her bedroom window to peer into the night. The streetlight beneath her condo window was out. That's why it was darker in the room than usual. Her heartbeat began to slow back to normal. So dark, and somewhere out there—in a shipping warehouse, no doubt—Sarah's body lay, waiting for transport in the morning. And somewhere out there—in a hotel room—grieving parents wept and waited.

In a moment, the meaning of the word Hart had used—oblivion—hit her in the stomach. Her heart again pounded in her ears, and pure animal terror pushed its way through her thoughts. Oblivion and the endless dark. She turned to the bedside table and switched on a light. As its beam illuminated her bed and her bedroom walls, she sat for a moment on the edge of her bed. What was it to be nothing? Elizabeth shook her head. She and Hart had drunk too much wine with their steaks and too much cognac afterwards. Now she was wide awake, as the alcohol had dissipated. She pulled her dressing gown closer and tied the sash.

How, how was she going to live with this? No, she thought to herself. Control your thoughts. Control your mind. It's done, and it's over. It's justice that matters. Forget it. Walking from her bedroom into the living room where the shine of the bedroom light dimly outlined her furniture, Elizabeth made her way to her dining area and the sideboard. Turning on another light, she found a snifter and, opening a bottle of brandy, poured another shot. She headed to her second bedroom, outfitted as a home office, and pulled out the page proofs for her book. She would work until the night ended.

FRIDAY, OCTOBER 28, 7:15 A.M.

Alice knelt, somewhat awkwardly, on George's carpet in his living room. Beside her, appearing far more at ease, knelt Paul Anstel and George. Fr. Mark was finishing the prayer of consecration at the portable altar, set on a table that had been moved in front of the fireplace. Getting to her feet by placing a helping hand on the seat of the chair behind her, Alice sat quietly as Paul received the host and the chalice, and George, arms crossed over his chest, received Fr. Mark's blessing. The mass had been celebrated for the repose of the soul of Sarah Yung, at Paul's request. Her family had arrived two days ago, and her body had now been released by the coroner's office. She would be going home today for burial in Toronto. Since Sarah's parents had no religious affiliation, there would be no religious service, and Paul had asked Fr. Mark to celebrate mass privately for him, Alice, and George to pray for her.

After Fr. Mark had spoken the final blessing, George invited them all to the kitchen for toast, fruit, and coffee.

"But, Fr. Mark," Alice asked, "Sarah wasn't Catholic. In fact, I understand she wasn't even Christian. Why are you saying mass for her soul? Doesn't your faith teach that she's doomed to … well, to hell … if anyone still believes in hell?"

"God is infinitely merciful, Alice," Fr. Mark replied. "We can't know what was going on in Sarah's soul. As for not being Christian, it's very difficult today for young people who have no religious teaching, or very simplistic teaching as children, to find their way to the faith. The pressures are all against it. We're ridiculed or worse for our approach to sexuality. The sexual revolution is supposed to be a great step ahead for humanity, even though it seems to me that it's created hell on earth. But watch TV, read the media—no one, or very few—even have the courage to ask serious questions about faith. The reality is dismissed with name-calling and slogans. God understands these problems. Unless Sarah deliberately rejected the gospel, fully understanding what she was doing, there is a good chance that her soul indeed will be with God. We know that she had come to reject the ethos of the people she had been involved with. She told Paul that she was rethinking everything. We know that she was trying to do the right thing by Paul. She was searching for the truth. That counts for a lot. We have every reason to hope that God will give her the chance to find it."

"Thanks for coming, Professor Gordon," Paul said. "The support of all of you has kept me going these past few days. I understand the DNA test results should be back today, so I'm hoping I can be back on campus soon."

"Some people will assume there's something wrong with the testing, Paul," Fr. Mark cautioned, "when it shows you're not a match. It's amazing how scientific evidence today can be rejected when it doesn't show what people already believe."

"I know it's not going to be easy," Paul replied. "But I'm not giving up my studies and running away now."

"Will you move back into residence?" George asked.

"No. One of the people who may not believe me is Richard. He seems to have been implacably convinced that I raped Sarah. I don't understand it, but I don't want to have to try to get along with him any longer.

"Was he always difficult?"

"He sees himself in competition with me. We're both short-listed for the position at the Supreme Court, and he wants it badly, I know. And although he's never said much, I can tell that he has no respect for my faith. He can't believe it's anything other than hypocritical.

"Fr. Mark's building has a vacant suite. I'm going to take that, starting November 1. In the meantime, I'll hang out at the Dogwood Blooms a couple more days. It's pleasant enough, and I'm getting lots of writing done now on my dissertation. I expect to have another chapter, Professor Gordon, for you by the end of the month."

"Excellent, Paul," Alice replied. "At this rate, you'll be done the draft by Christmas. Then, once we've done revisions, we'll send it to the external, and I'm sure you'll be ready to defend by early spring."

"Well, finish your coffees, people," George interrupted. "It's now 8:15, and Alice and I have to be at her office by 9:00."

How? Why? Who? Those are the questions any mystery writer must be concerned with, just as are the police. In criminal law, it's not necessary to prove the why. But for the mystery writer, the why is perhaps the most important question. Who can always be deduced from why.

Has my outright confession in these pages solved anything for me? I am not finished the story yet, so perhaps it is too early to tell. But as a professional writer, I find myself engaged with the characters and their thoughts. You, readers, have perhaps guessed by now the how, but, of course, that was still for Alice, George, and Martin to discover.

FRIDAY, OCTOBER 28, 9:30 A.M.

Papers were spread out over Alice's desk and her low occasional table. Alice sat behind her desk, organizing some of them, while George, at the low table, read through another. Martin Blatt, in a third chair by the desk, waited.

Alice began. "It seems to me that we have three mysteries that likely have connections, but the problem is, we don't know what the connections are."

"Who murdered Sarah is the one I can think of," Martin said drily.

"Yes, of course, but also, who raped Sarah, and who disrupted the mass on Saturday? The murder may be connected to the rape; in fact, it seems a very odd coincidence if it wasn't. And the vandalism is also likely connected to the rape. But is the vandalism connected to the murder, either directly or not?"

"Well, Paul is not the rapist," Martin confirmed. "The DNA results came just before I got here, and the email from Terry Klein confirms that there is no match with Paul's DNA. And, apparently, Paul knew that Sarah no longer suspected him and was going to take steps to exonerate him the next day. So he has no motive to kill her. But the real rapist might."

"But we have no idea who that is," George noted. "Where does this get us?"

"We know what Sarah suspected," Martin replied.

Both George and Alice stared at him. "What? Didn't I tell you the other night? In the phone conversation I had with Sarah, she was convinced it wasn't Paul but that it was Richard Prius."

"Paul's roommate?" Alice exclaimed. "No, you didn't mention that part of the conversation."

"I told Terry," Martin continued. "Sarah thought it odd that Richard told her the reason he came to check on her the next morning was because Paul had seemed upset the night before, but Paul maintained that he had never spoken to Richard that evening. Sarah thought Richard was more likely to be lying than Paul. And Richard could have taken her keys from the basket by the door, where they left all their keys. She also thought that would account for the time disparity. She thought the rape happened about 2:00 a.m., but Paul thinks he was home just a little past 1:00 a.m."

Alice flipped through the papers on her desk. "And," she said, picking up one, "Richard's statement repeats that he had spoken to Paul that night. So if he's lying, he could be both the rapist and the murderer. But why would he kill her? Although, I see from her phone records that she called him …"

Martin interrupted. "The call was because she thought she could get a DNA sample from him by taking a used coffee cup. She had decided to meet him for coffee. She and I discussed this, and I agreed to have an out-of-uniform officer nearby on Tuesday. That's what the coffee date was about."

George broke in. "Might she have given him some reason to believe she suspected him when they talked?"

Martin shrugged. "Possibly. Although I'm sure she wouldn't have done it consciously, but it must have been a difficult conversation for her, thinking what she was thinking."

"Reinterview Richard." Alice made a note on her laptop. "But if he had a motive to kill her, if he thought she suspected him of raping her and no longer believed it was Paul, we still don't know how he found her. He says that although they talked about her going to the library, she told him that she had changed her mind and would stay home."

"He could be lying about that too," George said.

"True," Alice continued, "and he does have keys to the library. Or he might have just taken a chance that she was going and checked it out and found her there. The fact that when he offered to come with her she changed her mind might have made him suspicious. So we have to talk to him again and soon, as he is looking like a prime possibility. But reading through these statements, I don't think he is the only one who was lying to the police."

"What else have you spotted?" Martin asked.

Alice picked up Elizabeth's statement. "Since we now know that Paul was telling the truth about his phone call with Sarah, that she no longer believed he had raped her, and that she did suspect someone else, I think we can assume that he was telling the truth about the entire conversation. She told Paul that Elizabeth Maryfield had fought with her and had even threatened her. But in her statement, Elizabeth says that their meeting was cordial, and that Sarah remained committed to the project. That's very different than what Paul says Sarah told him."

"It's not surprising that someone who quarrelled with a murder victim on the day of the murder would want to cover that up," George commented.

"No, true, and I find it hard to believe that Elizabeth would commit a premeditated murder. If Elizabeth was the killer, I would think it would have arisen out of a sudden argument. But she did know that Sarah was in the library, even called her that evening around the time Sarah was likely heading there. She has library keys as well. But I still can't get over the premeditated angle."

"But we don't know it was premeditated," Martin said.

"We don't?" Alice asked as she again shuffled through the papers. "I thought—here it is. The murder weapon issue. The coroner says that

Sarah was hit on the temple with what was likely a heavy metal object, likely smooth, and possibly made of stainless steel. But no such object was found in the carrel, which was locked, remember. If the killer brought a weapon and then removed it, that indicates premeditation."

"We don't know what it was, though," Martin replied.

"No," Alice continued, "but I can't even imagine any smooth, heavy, metal object that would be found in a study carrel."

George had been looking through a list as Alice and Martin debated the point. "Here's a list of what was in the study carrel," he said. "Of course, there was her laptop, her carry bag with phone and wallet. Now that's interesting. The police listed the contents of her wallet: a credit card, $200 in cash in twenties—well, I suppose she had taken out some money for the trip—a couple of ID documents, including her university student card, and a receipt for something she bought Sunday at a hardware store for $25.98."

Alice looked up from her laptop. "What did she buy? Did the police check?"

"The receipt doesn't say what it is. There's just a stock number. Here," George passed the sheaf of documents over to Alice. "There's a photo of the receipt."

"I doubt the police would bother," Martin said. "I mean, we all push receipts into our pockets or wallets and forget to throw them away. It's likely nothing."

"But she was going home. What would she have bought at a hardware store?"

"Maybe she needed a lightbulb, or toilet paper, or …"

"Let's find out what it is," Alice said, picking up her phone. She dialled the store number.

"Yes, good morning. I'm wondering if you can help me by checking your records to determine what product one of your stock numbers represents? You can? Great. The number is AX4297-C. Yes, I'll hold."

George continued to read the coroner's report.

"Really?" Alice asked. "And can you describe that item to me? I see. Do you have more in stock? Thank you. I expect someone will be down to buy one shortly."

Alice hung up, and George and Martin both looked expectantly at her.

"It's a meat hammer."

"What?" Martin asked.

"A little, metal, heavy hammer, stainless steel, used for pounding or flattening meat. Martin, do we have a complete inventory of Sarah's apartment?"

"We should have." Martin searched through the papers on the table. "Here it is. But it doesn't itemize kitchenware—just says, 'kitchen utensils.'"

"OK," Alice said. "George, let's run down to the hardware store and buy a meat mallet. We should take it to the coroner and ask if it could have been the weapon. And Martin, you get Officer Klein and ask the police to go through Sarah's apartment to see if there's a meat mallet in it. I'm betting there isn't."

Martin looked confused. "But are you saying that the murderer somehow had the same … no, I don't get it. What would a meat mallet be doing in a study carrel?"

Alice pointed to the receipt. "Sarah bought one. Why when she was leaving? It's not the kind of thing you would pack. But a nice, heavy, little mallet that you could carry around? A great defensive weapon against a rapist. I'm going to bet that Sarah bought it for security. And I'm going to bet that she took it with her to the library that night, and …"

"And someone used it to kill her," George added, "which means …"

"The murder was not premeditated but was a crime of opportunity. We need to speak to Richard Prius for sure. He might have just gone to reason with Sarah if he thought she suspected him, and it turned into a fight. But we also need to speak to Elizabeth Maryfield. And there's one more thing that's peculiar."

"Which is?" Martin asked.

Alice picked up the statement from Angie Maitland and gathered up other reports of interviews with students in Elizabeth's class.

"It may be nothing, but there's an inconsistency here. Angie Maitland is the only member of the Feminist Legal Studies class who said anything substantive to the police. Many of them declined to be interviewed; some, like Tyler Jenkins, told the police in short and vulgar terms that they knew nothing. But Angie, she cooperated. It just seems strange. And, to add to that, there were three people who disrupted the campus mass, weren't there?"

Martin and George both nodded.

"I notice that her alibi for Saturday night is with two other friends, Tyler Jenkins and Susan … Lu … I think. They're all in Elizabeth's seminar. They were all together Saturday afternoon and evening. She's the only one who mentions an alibi—maybe nothing, but it seems a significant coincidence—and she's willing to tell that to the police."

"A guilty conscience?" Martin asked.

"A nervous one, at least," Alice replied. "Let's add her to our second interview list."

FRIDAY, OCTOBER 28, 1:30 P.M.

Richard Prius had received the note from Professor Gordon at 11:00 a.m. when he checked his student email. He wondered what she wanted him for and hoped it was to ask for his services as a research assistant. After having taken on sole occupancy of the rooms he had shared with Paul, his finances were strained. Melanie Amahdi had given him a generous break on the rent when he had asked that he be allowed to keep the set of rooms to himself, but it had been to the university's benefit as well, since by this time, students had their housing arrangements, and no one wanted to get into residence. Some rent was better than none. But despite the break, the rent was still more than he had budgeted for at the start of the year.

He knocked at the office door.

"Come in," Alice responded.

As Richard stepped into the room, he immediately saw Professor Bush. "I'm sorry, Professor Gordon," he said. "I thought this was the time you asked me to come, but if another time's better, I can come back."

"No, this is the right time," Alice replied. "I've asked Professor Bush to join us. Please sit down."

Richard sat. "Why did you want to see me?"

Alice put Richard's statement on her desk where he could not help but see it. "Campus Security is working with the police on Sarah's murder investigation, and we're helping," Alice explained. "There are some things about your statement we'd like to review with you."

Richard sat forward in his chair. "I don't see how I can help. I really know nothing about it."

Alice looked into his eyes. "Let me start by saying that the DNA tests have come back and confirmed that Paul is not Sarah's rapist."

Richard's head jerked up. "What? But Sarah …"

"Sarah was mistaken. And she had realized that before she died."

"No, that can't be. I mean …"

"She had another suspect; someone she was quite convinced had lied to her. Lied to her about what happened after Paul got back to his rooms on the night of the rape. Someone who could have got hold of her keys. Paul said he never spoke to you that night, Richard. You said he did and was upset. Sarah had come to believe you were lying and that you were likely the one who raped her."

"No!" Richard exclaimed. His face flushed, and he gripped the arms of the wooden chair in which he was seated. "How could she think that? I … I helped her. She was grateful!"

"But you lied about talking to Paul that night."

"I … yes, I lied. But you have to believe that I did not rape her!" Richard's voice raised in pitch, and his body shook while he tried to control his reactions.

"What did happen that night, then? Tell us."

Richard swallowed. "All right. I knew Paul was out with Sarah. I couldn't sleep. Sarah was ... well, she was beautiful, and smart, and I wanted to be out holding her hand while she told me all about things instead of that goody-goody Paul. I knew she and Paul were likely sleeping together. I mean, he always pretended to be so holy, so good ..." A sneer crossed Richard's face. "Anyway, I heard him come in and his door slam, and I thought to myself, 'There he goes. He's won again.' And then I thought, 'He's home pretty early. Maybe things didn't go so well. Maybe if I show up to Sarah's early and see what happened, maybe she'll ... maybe she'll see me as a good guy.' I still didn't get much sleep, and I got up as early as I thought could work. All the undergraduates had classes Thursday morning, so I knew she wouldn't sleep in. I went to her place; I rang her buzzer until she let me in.

"I swear I was shocked when she told me she'd been raped. She was crying ... it was dreadful. I said, 'Paul did this to you?' And she said, 'Yes, it must have been Paul.' So I took her to Health Services. I was sure that would finish Paul. And he deserved it. I was sure he'd raped her.

"I was so glad when she called to set up coffee with me. I thought that even if she went home for a while, we could email. She'd come to like me, trust me. I never thought ... oh hell, how could she think I'd rape a woman?"

Alice passed a tissue across her desk to Richard as his shoulders shook and a few tears ran down his face. He took the tissue and wiped them.

"You have to believe this. And ... wait a minute. Do you think I killed Sarah as well?"

"Not necessarily," Alice said. "But you have to realize that lying about what happened has made things look very suspicious. Why did you lie?"

Richard swallowed again and wiped his face with the tissue. "I didn't want Sarah to know why I came over. She didn't know how I felt about her. And when she was so sure Paul was the one who raped her—well, saying he was upset when he came in supported her, didn't it? I mean, I believed her, and I wanted to help."

"And you wanted to damage Paul."

Richard sat silently. "Look," he said. "I lied about something that didn't really matter at all. Paul's a hypocrite and a bigot, and I thought he was getting what he deserved. As far as the rape and murder go, I didn't rape her, and a DNA test will prove that, and if I didn't rape her, I didn't have any reason to kill her. I didn't even know she had gone to the library. She told me she wasn't going, and I believed her."

After Richard left, George asked Alice, "Did you believe him?"

"I think I did," Alice replied. "He was genuinely shocked to find out that Paul's DNA wasn't a match, and he was genuinely distressed when we told him that Sarah suspected him. But we'll let the police follow up with another DNA test."

Alice heard another knock at her door. "Come in," she responded.

"Professor Gordon, I haven't been in any of your classes," the young woman stepping through the open door said quickly, "but I know you're Paul Anstel's graduate supervisor, and it's all over the school that the DNA test has proved him innocent."

"That's right," Alice replied. "And you are?"

"I'm Melissa Crawthorne. I was Sarah's best friend. We live … lived … in the same building. I'm just upstairs. And there's something I know that I have to tell. I thought you might know … might be able to tell me who I should speak to."

"Is it about the murder?"

"Maybe. It's at least about the rape. You see, I was sure—well, Sarah was sure, and I believed her, that it was Paul. But if it wasn't …"

"Then you know who it might have been?"

"I think so."

"Come in and sit down," Alice suggested. "Do you know Professor Bush? He's helping me, and I am helping Campus Security with their investigations, so you've come to the right place."

"Thank you," Melissa said, stepping inside the door. She dropped her heavy carry bag on the floor and took the chair that Richard had just vacated. She shook her hair out of her eyes and brushed aside the long bangs.

"You see, a few law students live in this building where I live. One of them is Tyler Jenkins. Do you know him?"

"Not really," Alice replied, "but I know he's one of Dr. Maryfield's students, just as Sarah was."

"Right. Well, in September, Tyler and I met in the laundry room. We hit it off, and he came back to my place for a few drinks. After that, we went out for most of September. Then I told him I was seeing someone else, and I wanted us to stop. That was a lie. Tyler scared me. When we had sex, he was great at first, but then … I don't know exactly, but there was some wild thing. He liked to—be a bit rough. And I thought he was getting rougher. Anyway, I decided I didn't want him around anymore. I never told Sarah, but he was in my apartment a lot then. Sarah had given me one of her keys, just so I could look after her plants if she was away. I gave her one of mine for the same reason. I kept her key, tagged with her name, in my desk drawer. After the rape, Sarah called and asked for it back. She was worried about having keys out there where other people might get them. I looked, and it was gone."

"You think Tyler took it?"

"I don't know for sure. He's the only person who was in my place often. I know he thought Sarah was hot. He made some comments to me about her. She did wear some really cool clothes, and he said she was super sexy and wondered if she would go for a threesome. I thought he was just trying to make me mad, and he did. When we split, he said I'd never been any good in bed anyway, so I was no loss." Melissa choked slightly at the memory. "When Sarah asked for her key back, I told her it was gone. But I didn't talk to Tyler, and I didn't tell her that he could have taken it. Now I wish I had. But I was afraid of him."

After Melissa left, Alice made some notes on her laptop.

"We've apparently lost one suspect and gained another," George remarked.

"At least for the rape," Alice replied. "But I can't see why Tyler would kill her, even if he is the rapist. She had no idea it might have been him. It does solve some of the mystery of how, if it wasn't Richard, someone got into Sarah's apartment. And Tyler could have seen her come home and realized she was too drunk to resist him. I'll send him an email and ask him if he's going to be around the law school on Saturday, and whether he could drop in later in the afternoon. Or maybe make an appointment for Monday."

"Good," George replied. "I feel we have made some progress. I'd suggest talking to Elizabeth now, but I've got a class coming up."

"As do I," Alice added. "Let's grab a glass of wine at the Faculty Club at 5:00 after our classes. We'll consider our next moves. But I'm going to email Tyler and Elizabeth before I go off to class."

FRIDAY, OCTOBER 28, 8:00 P.M.

Alice and George walked in companionable silence from the Faculty Club to his apartment. They had discussed the case and every aspect of it once again over a glass of wine and then over dinner. They had decided that a walk would be a good idea, and since the rain had eased off and the clouds broken, they had covered the thirty minutes to George's building in comfort. Alice had left her car at the university. She would cab home from George's and then to the university in the morning for her car.

"Come in for a nightcap and then I'll call you a cab," George suggested.

"Lovely," Alice replied. "When do you think we might hear from Martin about whether the meat mallet we gave to the coroner this morning could be the same thing that was the murder weapon?"

"Well, Martin said when he called this evening that it looked promising. There was no such item in Sarah's apartment, which suggests your theory is correct, and we're not looking for a murderer who intended to kill, just one who either succumbed to the opportunity or had some quarrel with Sarah that went badly. We should know tomorrow."

"I'd really like to talk to both Elizabeth and Tyler Jenkins sooner rather than later," Alice added.

"Any email replies from them yet?"

Alice pulled out her smartphone as George unlocked his front door. Just then, a man moved out from under the oak tree in the front yard and spoke.

"George?" he asked.

George turned sharply. "Andrew?" he replied. "What on earth are you doing, lurking out here in the dark?"

The younger man stepped forward, smiling. "I was hoping you would come home early, George," he responded. "I've been doing a lot of thinking over the past two weeks, and I would really like to talk to you. But I see you have company."

"Yes," George answered. "I think you've met Alice Gordon, Andrew."

"Indeed." Andrew held out his hand. "Pleasure to see you again. Look, George, if this time doesn't work, that's fine. But maybe we could have brunch tomorrow?"

"Don't worry, George," Alice interrupted. "I wasn't going to stay long anyway. I can just as easily call a taxi from your lobby and wait here for it. I really should get home."

George hesitated, knowing he was being inhospitable.

"Don't worry!" Alice repeated. "I'm sure you two have a lot to discuss, and I'm tired and should be at home. I've got marking tomorrow!"

"If you're really sure, Alice," George responded. "May I call you in the morning about getting together? I know you need to pick up your car."

"Of course."

George let them all into the lobby, and Alice called the taxi company while they all waited.

"There," she said. "It'll only be five minutes. You two go on." And she watched as George and Andrew walked together up the staircase toward George's third-floor suite.

Alice sighed slightly as they turned the corner of the stairs out of her sight. That was likely the last she would be seeing of George for some time, she thought. After all, what everyone wanted was love, and now that Andrew had come back, well, surely he and George would settle their differences.

George unlocked his front door, and they both hung their rain-coats in the hall. George's coat showed signs of wear and one of its cuff buttons was missing. Andrew's was new, stylish, and crisp. George noted the name of Victoria's best men's shop on the label. Andrew smoothed the sleeves of his cashmere jacket.

"Are you going to offer me a drink?" he asked.

"Sure," George answered. "Will you have your usual gin and tonic? I'm afraid I've quit buying fresh limes so …"

"Never mind," Andrew replied as they entered the living room. "I'll manage without the lime. Why don't you make the drinks while I put on the fireplace?"

Making himself at home, Andrew flicked the switch for the gas fireplace, which gave a whoosh as the flames surrounded the artificial logs. He sat on the leather sofa, and George shortly returned. George took the wingback chair to the side.

"Well?" George asked. "You wanted to talk?"

Andrew smiled. "Why don't you sit beside me here?" he asked.

"I'm fine here," George answered.

Andrew smiled again. "I suppose forgiveness can't be quite so easily won," he said. "But I really have come here hoping we can patch things up."

George took a drink of his scotch from the crystal glass. "Your affair with André doesn't seem to have lasted, does it?"

"Hell, darling," Andrew continued, "I never expected it to. Look, this is just exactly what I want to talk to you about. I know we both said some things when we parted, but it was just a quarrel. We don't exactly want the same things, but I think we can compromise. I do love you, George. Don't doubt that. But I'm not monogamous. There's no reason why we can't be together because of that. You can have the comfort and the stability you want. I'll even marry you. I was stupid and cruel about that. But marriage doesn't have to mean stagnation. And if I go off for a day or two, or even a week or two, with someone charming and exciting, it doesn't mean I won't come back. This way we can both have what we want."

George stood up. "It's not what I want, Andrew. It's not what I ever wanted. You should know that I'm talking with a priest. You know that I've been struggling with a lot for a long time. I've finally decided that I should make a commitment to God."

"Oh, damn it, George. This … flirtation … is just insane. Maybe once, in another culture, in another galaxy far, far away … maybe there, God existed, and people dedicated their lives to Him and found happiness. But this is twenty-first-century civilization. We know that sex and our sexual lives are central to who we are. It is who we are. Anything else is a stupid dream, and it's going to fail. One day, you're going to wake up and know this religious stuff was all crap. You'll fall into a terrible mess—fall in love with some young priest and make a fool of yourself. Celibacy is cruel, unnatural, and can't be maintained in our modern world. It's like volunteering to go blind. But when you get your sight back and realize the truth, well, maybe it'll be too late. You'll be alone, and old, and helpless. And, believe me, your God will be damned cold comfort."

"Maybe," George said. "Maybe that's true, and I will come to a time when I believe I've thrown my life away, and maybe there will be no comfort. It's funny you should talk about being blind because I think that's what I've been, what we've all been, for many years. But I see what's happening to me as getting my sight back and rejecting the culture that is blind to anything but its own short-term pleasures, a culture that can't see what is truly good any longer. But whichever of us is right, this is the choice I'm making now."

Andrew took another swig of his drink. He too stood and, putting his drink on the coffee table, reached out his hand and stroked George's cheek.

"Darling, don't ruin both our lives for a fantasy," he said.

George took a step backwards. "Andrew, this may be the most harrowing conversation I have ever had."

"Well, then, stop it, darling, and let's make up. We can go for a nice dinner somewhere quiet and then come back here, and I'll move back in. You know I'm right about this. You've tried celibacy before, and it didn't work for you. It won't work now."

"I tried before when I was very young and unwilling to admit my feelings and acknowledge my sexuality," George said. "It didn't work because it was based on a lie. I know I may not be able to be perfect, but God will …"

"Oh, don't give me the 'God will help me' line. He's got a rotten reputation for helping. Take that precious crucifix of yours that I see you've put up in the living room—He couldn't be bothered to help Jesus avoid being murdered, could He?"

"That's not the point of it, Andrew, as well you know."

Andrew snorted. "It's the truth of it. People who follow your God wind up screaming alone, abandoned, in torture, and knowing there's nothing left. How can you consider believing in a religion that thinks you're scum?"

"I can't argue with you, Andrew. I wish you hadn't come."

Andrew turned toward the door.

"If I can't convince you, then I wish I hadn't come either. I do love you, George. And real, human love is worth having."

"I know," George said. "But you and I have very different ideas of what love is."

Andrew shrugged and left the room. A minute later, George heard the front door of the apartment close. Shaking, he sat down in his chair and sipped his scotch.

FRIDAY, OCTOBER 28, 8:30 P.M.

Alice let herself into her house, and her tortoiseshell immediately came to rub against her legs. Alice scooped up the cat and placed it on a nearby chair while she took off her coat, slipped out of her shoes, and pulled on the slippers she kept by the front door. She tucked her purse into the drawer of the table after removing her cellphone. She threw the lock, picked up the cat again, and walked into her living room.

Why she should feel bereft, she did not know. After all, she reasoned, George would now be happy, at least for a while. And perhaps that was all anyone ever had.

She sat down in her chair with the cat curled in her lap and opened her email on her phone. There were two new messages. The first, from Tyler Jenkins, informed her that he had the flu and would not be at school for a few days. It was short and terse. The second, from Elizabeth Maryfield, was longer. Elizabeth wanted to know what right Alice had to question her about anything, to assert that Sarah's death had been a tragedy in cutting off Sarah's likely contribution to social justice, and to reaffirm that Elizabeth intended to proceed with her project to give meaning to this event. She said nothing about whether the suggested meeting time on Monday would work for her schedule, but Alice interpreted the email as a rejection. Alice sighed. So much for progress. Then she shook her head. No, this was not acceptable. Sarah's death was a tragedy, but justice lay not in exploiting the violence but in exposing it. Her rapist and her killer must be found. Alice began to plan.

Ten minutes later, while she was considering whether planning would be helped or hindered by a nightcap, Alice's landline rang. She reached the phone by the chair and picked up.

"Did you get any replies to your emails?" George asked. But his voice was odd.

"George, you sound ... upset? Are you okay?"

"No, not really," George responded. "Andrew and I ... well, it was a very low-key scene, but it was very distressing to me. He's gone, I should say, and I'm on my second scotch."

"I'm so sorry. I thought you two might …"

"No, Alice. There was no chance of that. But it was very painful. My second scotch is likely to soon become my third and … Alice, is there any chance you could pack an overnight bag and come and stay for the night? I have a very nice guest room," George added quickly, "and it's already made up. I don't expect you to listen to my drunken maunderings, but it would be … helpful … to have someone here to make sure my third scotch doesn't somehow become my fifth!"

"Of course I could come. Just give me a few minutes to pack and get a taxi. And don't worry about maunderings. I maundered a lot the other night when you rescued me from a similar plight."

Forty minutes later, Alice was seated cozily in her blue chenille dressing gown in front of George's fireplace, her ankles curled up on the sofa, and a plaid afghan tucked around her feet. She was nursing a small cognac.

"Do you want to talk about it? We don't have to, you know."

"I know," George said. "And I won't bore you, so I won't say much. Andrew wanted to resume our relationship, even marry me. But he wasn't interested in only me. He made that clear. I used to get so jealous when he was looking at younger men. If it had been irrational, I might have overcome it. But it wasn't irrational because he was interested in them, and he was prepared to go off with them for a day, or a week, or more. He doesn't see that as incompatible with loving me. Once, I was prepared to agree and try to live with the jealousy because, like him, I thought it was just selfishness. Now … well, since last Saturday when I had that … shattering … revelation about what I believed was true … well, I don't want to sound idiotic, Alice, but I've had these experiences: joy and peace, but passion and fire too. They make the kind of love I thought I had for Andrew seem like nothing. I know this sounds presumptuous, but have you ever heard of the mystics?"

"Well, yes, I guess. People who think they have some real

experience of God."

"Yes, and Jewish, Catholic, Protestant, Buddhist, Hindu—all the great religions of the world have reported similar things. I've had—oh, maybe not on the same level as the greats—but I've had that. It's real. And it helps to recognize what's counterfeit."

"Maybe Andrew is just the wrong man for you, George. I'm sure there are other gay men who want what you want."

"Maybe true. But that's not what I want. I know it seems inconsistent with sitting here swilling scotch, but I don't think many loves, if any, would measure up to what I've now known. Andrew was—cruel. He told me that my love is an illusion, that God will leave me comfortless. And I can't say that isn't possible. No one can know their future, and not all futures are happy. And I can't say I will never abandon God. But right now, in this present, is where I am, and where God is. And I can't walk away to the counterfeit. Not now."

Belief shapes us. Everything I write, everything I see is shaped by the beliefs I hold. I asked earlier whether it matters what we believe in, since everything, especially everything we express in words, is always metaphor. Can we choose what we believe? That's a crucial question. "I just believe it" or "I just can't believe it" or "I just stopped believing it." All those phrases assume that belief is something that overpowers us, and sometimes that's true. I think it was true for George in that moment in the makeshift chapel. But after the first emotional flush, what then? Choice, I think. Ultimately, whatever our beliefs, we make them our own choice. Or not. And if that is true, then we take responsibility for the results of our beliefs: for everything we write, and everything we see, and everything we do.

CHAPTER 6

Tyler opened the door to his apartment, and Angie followed him in.

"Let's have another drink, babes," he said. "The scene at the pub was boring tonight. No fun at all."

"Okay," Angie replied. "I'll have some of that good scotch. You're right. It was a bore. No one was talking about anything but Sarah."

"So right," Tyler replied. "I didn't say anything there, but that old witch Gordon emailed me today to say she wanted to talk to me about the murder as soon as possible. She even suggested we meet tomorrow … Saturday, can you believe it?"

"Have you replied?" Angie asked. "And why would she want to meet with you?"

"The only reason I can think of is that she's guessing I was involved in the thing last Saturday. Or maybe she wants me to spill the beans about Maryfield and what's going on in her class. Anyway, it doesn't matter. She said she's helping Campus Security, and they're helping the police. It's a little difficult because I don't want to make her mad. I've got to take one of her classes next term, and a bad mark could be a problem for me. I just said I had the flu and wouldn't be around for a while. Give me a minute while I go to the toilet, and I'll get our drinks."

Angie wandered over to the kitchen area, took off her rain jacket, and dropped it on the nearby chair.

"Do you have any ice?" Angie called to Tyler as she turned to the refrigerator.

"What do you need ice for?" Tyler asked as he emerged from the bathroom.

"If you're going to give me a scotch, I like ice in it," Angie replied as she opened the freezing compartment and reached into it for the ice.

"What the hell are you doing?" Tyler shouted as he suddenly came up behind her.

"God, you startled me," Angie gasped, flinching. "I'm just looking …" As she lifted the ice cube tray, her hand made contact with something cold and small. She put down the ice cubes and pulled out the object. Tyler, reaching from behind, grabbed her wrist and her closed right hand.

"Give me that," he said as he pried open her fingers. There, in her hand, was a small key with a label attached. The label read, "Sarah."

"What … what are you doing with Sarah's key?" Angie asked.

Tyler did not let go of her right hand but solidified his control of her by using his other hand to seize her left arm.

"You're hurting me," Angie said.

Tyler smiled. "I wouldn't want to do that, Angie. Not at all. But I could. I could hurt you a lot. But we've been good friends, haven't we? And you don't want to be hurt. Let's just go into the living room where we're going to sit on the sofa and have a talk."

"I … I think I'd rather leave, Tyler."

"Well, I wouldn't rather you left, babes. After all, you came here for some fun, didn't you? And you haven't had it yet." Tyler let go of her right hand as he moved her around him so he could stand behind her and manoeuvre through the open kitchen into the living room. When they reached the sofa, he pushed her down. "Don't get up," he said. "I'm going to pour us both a drink, and we're going to sit here and discuss the situation."

As he backed away toward the sideboard where the scotch stood,

Angie cautiously stood partway up. In an instant, he was back by her side and had pushed her down again.

"You can't move fast enough, Angie. You'll never make it to the door."

"All right, Tyler, but I don't see why you're doing this. I mean, I don't know ... just because there's a key ... I mean ..."

"You're so right, Angie," Tyler said, pouring two measures of scotch into glasses. "Sorry about the ice, by the way, but I don't think I'll move far enough away to get it. You shouldn't have been snooping. But no, you're right. A key means nothing. And just to make sure you know it means nothing, we're going to spend a night together here. And by the time the night's over—well, I'm betting you'll be totally convinced that a key means nothing."

Angie took the scotch and managed to raise it to her lips with trembling hands. "Tyler, just let me go home."

"All in good time, babes. But before you go, I'm going to make sure you know just what happens when you snoop and get funny ideas from what you find." He sat down beside her with his drink.

"Tyler, don't," she said as he put his free arm firmly around her shoulders. "Let me go home, and I swear ..."

"Sure you do, but babes, swearing is going to mean so much more by morning. Now drink up because I'm waiting for that fun."

"Don't touch me," Angie struggled away from his arm. But he moved quickly to hold her again.

"Now, here's what we're going to do," he said, putting his drink on the coffee table and reaching with his free hand for the waistband of her jeans. He popped open the snap.

"Tyler, don't."

"No, babes, I won't force you. I won't have to." Tyler's arm moved from the waistband to her throat. "I'm just going to push here a bit, and then you're going to take off those jeans, and we'll have our fun. We'll have lots of fun tonight—the whole night—and then, in the morning, you'll have learned a lesson you won't forget about drawing funny conclusions."

Angie felt his hold tightening and her breath cut off. As she tried to struggle, the pressure increased.

"Now, before you lose consciousness, babes," Tyler said, "just nod that you're going to take off those jeans, and be a good girl who consents freely to all the fun we'll have."

Feeling the blackness coming, Angie was barely able to nod.

SATURDAY, OCTOBER 29, 2:30 A.M.

Angie shivered under the heavy quilt. Was he finally asleep? She had tried to crawl out of his bed once before, but he had simply been lying still. Before she could find her clothes in the dark room, he had grabbed her and forced her back to his bed.

"And the door locks with a key, Angie, and I have the key. You can't get out until I let you out. And I'm not letting you out until morning. And don't think about your cellphone, babes. I've got it and put it in a safe place. You can have it back tomorrow. And if you try screaming, well, you can guess how that will go. Now, I don't have to tell you to just open those legs again, do I? I really don't want to hurt you." And, again, she had complied.

She wondered if he would let her go. She wondered if she could get to his kitchen. Was there a knife that would be sharp enough? She shuddered again but very slowly inched her body toward the edge of the bed. As she began to carefully slide her legs toward the floor, Tyler's hand again shot out and pulled her back.

"Naughty girl," he said. "I can see I can't trust you to stay put." He got out of the bed and opened his top dresser drawer. Angie made another effort to rise, but he was too close. As he threw her down against the mattress, he rolled her onto her stomach and tied her hands behind her back with a cord he had removed from the drawer.

"A little bit of bondage always adds spice," he said.

SATURDAY, OCTOBER 29, 6:00 A.M.

Alice was dreaming. George's spare bedroom was airy and comfortable. The bed's feather duvet was soft and warm. She had fallen asleep almost as soon as she had lain down. As her mind was set free by sleep, she found herself in a hallway with many doors. In her hand, she had a large key ring with dozens of keys on it. The keys were all different: some, the old-fashioned keys she remembered from her childhood; some, the modern keys for a deadbolt lock; and some were delicate structures of twined green and brown flower stems. She knew she had to find the right key. She fumbled in her dream, trying to take hold of one, but they kept slipping away from her. One of the doors had a name on it: Tyler Jenkins, she read. That was the door. She must find the key that opened that door.

She sat up, suddenly awake. Alice looked at her watch. It was 6:15 a.m. Too early to get up, she thought, but then the spicy dark smell of coffee floated over top of the clean smell of the sheets. Someone's up, she thought, or else the coffee pot's on automatic. In any event, it would be better to get up than lie back down and try to recapture sleep. Sleep, she suddenly thought. And the memory of the dream returned. Tyler was the key.

She swung her legs out of the bed, pulled on the soft dressing gown and her slippers, and, after visiting the ensuite bathroom, opened her door and made her way down the stairs to the kitchen below. George was dressed and just pouring his first cup of coffee. "Good morning," he said. "Did you sleep?"

"Yes, very well. And you?"

"Pretty well, considering," George replied, passing her the cup of coffee he had just poured and reaching for another mug.

"George," Alice said, "I had this dream, and I'm pretty sure I've made some progress in my sleep toward solving our mysteries."

"Tell me."

"Well, it's Tyler Jenkins. Remember that he's in Elizabeth's

Feminist Legal Studies class. And although he wouldn't speak to the police, Angie Maitland did. She's evidently a friend of his, because in her statement, she said that she was with Tyler and another student, Susan Lu, on the night your mass was vandalized. I thought it odd at the time, and now it just seems a huge coincidence that she was the only one to speak. Plus, there were three of them together, and there were three intruders at the mass. You said one of them was smaller than the others, and Susan Lu is a petite build. I'm betting that Tyler was one of the three students who broke into that mass.

"Now," Alice continued, "we hear from Melissa that Tyler is a very likely suspect for taking Sarah's key. I've been worried about the keys. I dreamed about them. If Richard Prius didn't rape Sarah, accessing her apartment with Paul's keys that he could have taken from the basket after Paul got home, someone else must have had a key. Paul told us that he thought Richard's friend Arty had a key to their unit, and Arty was with Sarah in the pub, so he knew she was drunk. But Paul took her home in a cab. It strains credibility to think that Arty waited and watched Paul's place until Paul got in, opened their unit, took Paul's keys, raped Sarah, and returned the keys. He would have had to be hanging around for quite some time. And why would he? Even if he intended rape, he couldn't have known that Paul wouldn't stay with her and he would have a chance. It would have been stupid.

"But if it wasn't Paul's keys that were used, then we have a problem."

"We do?" George asked.

"Yes, because anyone from outside the building would have had to have a front door key as well as a key to Sarah's apartment. We don't know of any missing keys to the building—although some could be floating around, I suppose—but, again, big coincidence. And whoever raped her would have to know she was home, although I suppose they could take a chance. But again, it just seems another big coincidence that they would choose a time just long enough after she got home drunk so that she would be deeply asleep.

"But Tyler lives in the building. He wouldn't need a front door key. He could have seen Sarah come home and Paul leave. I'm betting Tyler is both the rapist and one of the vandals who attacked the mass. We have to talk to him as soon as we can."

"It makes sense," George replied. "Did he reply to your email?"

"Yes, to say he had the flu and wouldn't be at school for a few days. But his home address is on the police statement. I think that when we walk back to the university to get my car, I'll get his address, and we should go there this morning."

"Wouldn't it be better just to report this to the police? Or to Martin?"

"Possibly. But Tyler might let me talk to him because I'm a faculty member. He's ambitious, I understand. And he's taking one of my courses next term. He's already been to see me about it, and he has the reputation of liking to get to know his professors, especially women. He gets better marks that way, I assume. He's one of Elizabeth's loyal supporters, supposedly. At least, he's taken several of her courses. He's refused to talk to the police, and he's not likely to regard Martin any differently. My suspicions—even the way they fit together logically— aren't hard evidence. I think we should get his address and pay him a visit. If he has the flu, he's likely home; if it was just an excuse, he may still be home for fear of being found out as a liar."

"You think he may be a rapist and a vandal," George said. "Do you think he's also a murderer?"

"I don't know," Alice replied. "But assuming we have the right theory of how the murder was done, he didn't plan it. And that means that he's unlikely to try violence to cover it up—if it was some kind of struggle or accident."

"But how did he get to Sarah? I don't think Tyler is anyone's research assistant, and he's an undergrad. He wouldn't have had library keys."

Alice thought. "The carrels are right across from the main library door, just behind the circulation desk. I would bet if someone tapped on the door of the library, someone in the carrel, especially if they didn't have the door closed, might notice them."

"And why would he kill her? She didn't suspect him. She was convinced it was Richard."

"That I can't guess. Might he have betrayed himself somehow? I can see she might have let him in because she didn't suspect him. Might something have happened later? But you're right. There doesn't seem to be a motive, and that's a point against Tyler as murderer."

SATURDAY, OCTOBER 29, 7:30 A.M.

Angie woke suddenly to the feeling of someone stroking her cheek. She was cramped, and her arms, still tied behind her back, were sore. He had finally slept and, with exhaustion, so had she. Now he was bending over her, stroking her cheek. She wrenched her head away.

"Such gratitude, babes," Tyler said. "But now what I want you to do is to get up and get dressed. We'll have coffee and then we'll talk about the day. I'm going to untie you, but I'm dressed, as you see, and the door is still locked. You can't go home until I'm sure we understand each other. Now, I want you to say, 'Tyler, I had a lot of fun.'"

Angie shook her head. "Well, babes," Tyler said, putting some pressure on her throat, "you can say that, or we can have some more fun."

"All right. Tyler, I had a lot of fun."

"Good," Tyler said. "Now there's another thing you should think about. Just remember that you came here of your own free will. You wanted sex with me, just like we usually have. And you told me, time and time again, that you gave your consent to what we were doing. Just nod if you agree."

Angie nodded. She was now beyond terror. Would he really let her go? Surely not, she thought. She knew she ought to care.

"Good again."

He allowed her to use the bathroom, standing in the open doorway. "Turn around," she pleaded. But Tyler laughed. "So you can hit me with something? Don't be funny, babes. We've got no secrets, and after last night, you don't need privacy."

When she had finished, he locked her in the bedroom to dress while he made coffee. When the coffee was made, he brought her into the living room and passed her cellphone to her.

"Now, just so you really learn your lesson, you're going to call your favourite Dr. Maryfield and tell her I raped you."

Angie shook her head. "No, please," she said, "I swear I won't say a word."

"No, this isn't a test. You see, Angie, you have some lessons to learn. Oh, you learned some last night. But there's one more—a biggie. Angie, babes, you're a believer. You've bought that our culture stinks, that we need justice, and you want to tear down all the oppressive structures. You think this will make the world right. Well, it won't. The world will go on just as it has, and the strong and the tough will win. It's just that they'll be different people. People like me. And you're going to find that out right now when you call Maryfield.

"You see, she won't believe you. I'm one of her faithful students, and I'm going to have a stellar career. Starting with clerking with the Court of Appeal, I'll be on the road to having a position of influence. Who knows? I've talked politics with her, and she sees me as someone who is willing to push the progressive agenda she wants. Do you really think that you, somebody who will never get top grades or a top position anywhere, are going to convince her to throw me away? To bring me down when I'm on my way up? Uh-uh.

"No, babes, you're going to find out that, as far as you're concerned, your Maryfield will abandon her ideals in a second."

Angie looked away. Tyler grabbed her face and turned her back toward him.

"Little true believers have to learn about reality," he said. "And when you've finished your lesson, I think you'll know what you have to do. No," he continued, as he saw Angie flinch back, "I'm not going to kill you, babes. I'm not a murderer."

Angie's eyes widened as she startled.

Tyler smiled. "No, I'm not a murderer," he said again with emphasis. "But when you've learned your lessons well, I think you'll know there's only one thing you can do. So forget that little dream of going off to graduate school; you'll never make it. The only places you can get As are places that don't require any brains. Maryfield likely wouldn't have given you a recommendation anyway. You're too stupid. Now," Tyler pushed the phone into her hands, "do as I tell you. Call Maryfield and tell her I raped you."

Shivering, Angie looked through her recent calls. She selected Elizabeth Maryfield's cell number and pressed the Call button.

SATURDAY, OCTOBER 29, 8:15 A.M.

Elizabeth Maryfield was sipping her second cup of coffee when her cellphone rang. Without looking at the number of the incoming call, she answered. "Hello?"

Elizabeth heard the gasp on the end of the line and a voice, distorted somehow, saying, "Dr. Maryfield, it's Angie. I'm … I'm in trouble, I …"

"Angie!" Elizabeth exclaimed. "You have no right to call this number. It's a private phone. If you want to see me, come to my office and …"

"No, wait. I wouldn't have called but … it's an emergency. I … I've been raped."

"What?" Elizabeth responded, "Angie, if you're trying to replace Sarah in my project …"

"No! I've been raped!" Angie shouted into the phone. "By Tyler. Tyler Jenkins."

"Angie!" Elizabeth exclaimed again. "Tyler? I can't believe that. Now see here, I don't know what you're up to, but if you and Tyler are involved, and you've had a fight …"

"No, he raped me," Angie repeated.

"Don't exaggerate," Elizabeth answered, irritated. "Tyler is committed to the progressive agenda. He's with us. He would never do such a thing. He's going to be a big part of turning this culture around and bringing in real equality. If you two have had a misunderstanding, don't ask me to get in the middle of it. Don't …"

The call was ended as Tyler removed the phone from Angie's hands. She sobbed.

"See, babes?" he asked. "No one is going to believe you. I'll say you consented, and I'll be believed. And your career is now over. Maryfield's not going to give you a reference for graduate school because you're attacking me, and given your very average marks, I can't see any other faculty member helping you anyway. See? It was all a crock. And, like all true believers, you're now abandoned in the cold."

Tyler brought her rain jacket and satchel. "Here," he said. "Now get out and do what you know you have to."

Angie looked at him through her tears. Shaking, she put on her jacket and took her bag. Tyler led her to the door and opened it.

"Goodbye, babes," he said. "It's been fun."

SATURDAY, OCTOBER 29, 8:30 A.M.

Angie stood leaning against the door into Tyler's building. Her mind and her body were cold. From time to time, she shook uncontrollably. She knew what she had to do. She saw in her mind the moment she would have walked onto the plane, her roller bag behind her with everything she cared to save from this life. She saw again the old stone buildings at the Toronto law school and again imagined herself in one of the offices, a respected professor, doing work she loved. She cried again.

What she had to do now was simple. It was only a few blocks to the breakwater, the long extension with the footpath that led out over the deep ocean. It was only a few blocks.

But just for the moment she would stand here, in the cold morning, and remember how she had expected things to be. Again, she saw herself walking onto the plane; again, she saw the ivy-covered walls; again, the comfortable office; again, the respect.

SATURDAY, OCTOBER 29, 8:45 A.M.

"Angie? Angie Maitland?" Angie opened her eyes. She had slumped into a sitting position on the sidewalk, her back leaning against the building wall. Standing over her were Professor Gordon and Professor Bush. She pulled herself up hastily, smoothing her jacket and brushing her jeans.

"Professor Gordon. Professor Bush. What are you doing here?"

"We were coming to see Tyler," Alice answered. "Do you live here too?" As Angie struggled to collect herself, Alice continued, "Something's wrong, isn't it? You look dreadful."

Angie began to cry. "I can't say. I have to do something. I have to. I'm sorry, but please, just let me go." Angie tried to push past Alice, who was standing in front of her. Alice reached out and held her arm.

"No, I think you need help."

"Let me go," Angie screamed as a morning dog walker turned back toward them. "Let me go," she repeated in a lower tone as the dog walker moved on. "I can't tell you."

"Angie," Alice responded, "you're in trouble. I'm not letting you go off on your own. You need to come with us. You look very ill, and you're obviously in a terrible state. I think you should come with us to the emergency room at university Health Services. They can help you. Find out what's wrong."

George had stood slightly back, but now he spoke. "Professor Gordon is right, Angie. You clearly need help. Let us help you."

Angie looked at him. His tone of voice was so kind. She looked back at Professor Gordon, who had taken away her hand but whose face registered great concern.

"I … I have to die," Angie said. "There's no other thing to do. I …

nothing has worked out like it was supposed to. Nothing. I ..." And she fainted. Alice caught her and was almost pulled to the ground too as George stepped forward to support them both. They gently lowered Angie to the sidewalk, and Alice pulled out her cell and dialled 911.

The emergency services siren woke Angie just as the ambulance pulled up to the curb. Angie struggled up.

"Lie still," the medical technician said. Turning to Alice, he asked, "What happened?"

"We were coming to see a tenant in the building. We found her here, outside, only partly conscious, it seemed. We tried to persuade her to come with us to emergency Health Services. She's a student at our faculty in the university—the Marjorie Ataskin law school. She told us she has to die. I think she's a suicide risk."

"We'll take her in for evaluation," the technician said.

"I'd like to be with her," Alice replied. "Can I go in the ambulance? George, could you follow in my car?"

Angie was lifted to a stretcher and strapped in as she lay sobbing. Her bag was put by her side, and the stretcher lifted expertly into the ambulance. Alice climbed in after passing George her car key.

In the building, Tyler had popped a beer and turned on the morning news on his computer. After finishing the beer and reading a report about a conservative speaker shouted down by protesters at a Vancouver university, he smiled, yawned, and decided to return to bed for some sleep. He heard the siren, but it was not an unusual sound in the near-downtown area. He did not draw back the curtains.

SATURDAY, OCTOBER 29, 10:00 A.M.

Alice sat quietly by the hospital bed. Angie was asleep. Her sobs had grown violent, and the emergency-room doctor at the general hospital had sedated her. She was expected to sleep for a couple of hours yet. George had called Fr. Mark, and they had both knelt by her bedside and prayed. Alice had been aware of their peace but also of the uncomfortable strangeness of people behaving as if there was a reality that was unseen and to which they were connected. "Am I the one who's blind? Who can't see what's real?" Alice thought.

After the prayers, Alice stepped out into the hall with George and Fr. Mark.

"I'm so sorry to see Angie here like this," Fr. Mark said. "Her mother and stepfather are Catholics in a parish where a friend of mine is pastor in Kelowna. They've been worried about her and about how she's changed since law school. But she would never agree to talk with me. How can we help?"

"I'm pretty sure I know who killed Sarah and why. We already know the how," Alice said.

"How have you figured that out?" Fr. Mark asked.

"I'm afraid I did something dishonest while she was sleeping," Alice replied. "I looked at her cellphone and her record of recent calls. I have to speak to Elizabeth as soon as I can. My dream was right that Tyler is the key to this. I'm quite sure he, with Angie and Susan Lu, disrupted your mass, Fr. Mark. But I'm also pretty sure that Tyler, whatever his crimes, is not Sarah's killer.

"George," Alice asked as she turned to him, "would you stay here with Angie? I don't want her to wake up alone. But I must see Elizabeth."

"Is it safe?" George asked.

"Yes, definitely, but she has some answers I need to know before I call Martin."

"We'll both stay," Fr. Mark said.

"Thanks," Alice replied, and she stepped back into the room where she retrieved Angie's cellphone from Angie's bag. She pressed Call for the last dialled number.

By this time, Elizabeth was settled in her home office with her page proofs and a stack of student essays. The phone rang, and she noticed with exasperation that it was again Angie. This had to stop.

"Angie," Elizabeth began before hearing the voice on the other end, "do not ever, and I repeat, ever, call me on this number again. I've already …"

"It's not Angie, Elizabeth," Alice said, "but Alice Gordon. I am using Angie's cell. I want you to know that I have it, and I've looked at it. I think we should meet as soon as possible."

"Where's Angie? Did she give you her cell?"

"Angie's in hospital, sedated. We believe she was about to kill herself. I need to speak to you."

Elizabeth's hand shook slightly. "I can't see why. And I can't see what right you have …"

"The Provost has authorized me to help Martin Blatt," Alice replied. "And, Elizabeth, you are enough of a lawyer to know that this could be a major problem for you."

Elizabeth paused. "Very well. I'll meet you in my office in thirty minutes."

"Fine," Alice replied.

SATURDAY, OCTOBER 29, 10:35 A.M.

Alice sat in Elizabeth's office. They had met in the hallway. Exchanging few words, Elizabeth unlocked her door, threw off her raincoat onto one of the chairs in front of her desk, and pointed silently to the other. Alice had sat down.

"Well?" Elizabeth asked, sarcasm in her tone. "What do you need to see me about?"

"I know," Alice shrugged. "I know you lied to the police about your situation with Sarah. I know that she was very angry with you. She believed you were using her, and she refused to cooperate with your projected work any further. I also know that Angie came to your office just after Sarah had left.

"I know that you must have been upset. I don't know what you said to Angie, but I do know that you called Sarah—your own statement acknowledges that fact, and, of course, your call was on her cell—that evening just as she was either at or near the library. And now, I know that six minutes after you say you called Sarah, you called Angie.

"I'm guessing that you told Angie that Sarah was in the library. And I'm guessing that, for whatever reason, Angie went to the library to talk to Sarah and that, somehow, Angie killed her.

"I also know that Angie called you just before we found her collapsed outside Tyler Jenkins' apartment building, the same building Sarah lived in. And I know that Tyler likely had access to Sarah's key and may be the rapist.

"Now, tell me what Angie called you about this morning."

"You have no right to question me," Elizabeth responded angrily.

"Elizabeth, let's look at reality here. If I'm right that Angie killed Sarah, and if I'm right that something that happened between you and Angie precipitated this whole thing, then—well, you are a lawyer. You know you could be guilty of being an accessory if you withhold this information. This isn't a joke, and it isn't one of your classroom exercises. I will be talking to Martin Blatt, who will be talking to the police. Maybe we had better find out the story first."

Elizabeth swallowed. "Angie called me this morning with a preposterous story about Tyler having raped her. I didn't believe her for a moment. Angie was always trying to get my attention. That's why she came to my office on Monday, she ..." Elizabeth paused.

"She told you that she was one of the ones who attacked the Catholic mass," Alice finished.

"How did you know?"

"Another guess, but Angie was one of the only ones who talked to the police about what happened Saturday afternoon. And her alibi was two other students in your class. It seemed a surprising coincidence— her willingness to talk and volunteer an alibi when other students wouldn't, plus the fact that it was three students who attacked the mass. I wondered if that's what she came to talk to you about."

"Well, yes."

"And Sarah and you had just had a quarrel over her participation in your project?"

Elizabeth snorted. "Sarah was a weakling, and she was betraying her principles. She was running home to daddy."

"You were angry, and then Angie came …"

"Angie wanted an A. She always wanted As, and I generally gave them to her. Well, I mean, she did have her theory straight. She wasn't original—I guessed she wasn't the one to get the idea to tackle the Catholics on campus; in fact, I suspected it was Tyler Jenkins, because she and Tyler had seemed tight in class. But I thought she did believe in the cause, and she was willing to sacrifice for it. And then, she was very upset when I told her that she wouldn't get an A for their work because Sarah was backing out. It was perfectly reasonable, and I explained that the value of the work depended upon the whole. I was shocked when she didn't really seem to care about the cooperative project. And then she, SHE, suggested that she could talk Sarah around. I thought it was a good idea. We need to change the culture and expose the hypocrisy and violence to achieve real equality. Sarah's cooperation would have been key."

"And you called Sarah later?"

"I thought if I apologized, she might come around. She had been very disrespectful, but I was prepared to compromise and even admit that perhaps I had been a little hasty. I was willing to take her back into the project. But she was rude and disrespectful again. She was just on her way to the library to check out the last articles for the bibliography she was doing for me. She hung up on me."

"And then you called Angie?"

"Yes. I knew Angie had been trying to catch Sarah all day, so I used Angie's cellphone contact number from her file. Angie, as it turned out, was studying in the common room downstairs. I told her Sarah was on the way to the library and that I would be … grateful … if she could persuade Sarah to see reason."

"And that's why Angie had your private cellphone number on her phone?"

Elizabeth nodded. "I had no idea they would fight ... in fact," Elizabeth's voice, which had dropped and faded, now gained strength again, "in fact, what I did was perfectly reasonable. I could have no idea ..." She trailed off.

Alice was right, of course. And so it ended ... at least this part ended. But I had still to face what I had done and face being alive. And to face whatever came next, without the comfort of my dream ... no airplane, no roller bag with everything I wanted to save from this life, and no respect. I wondered if now that my mystery is solved, I should appear in the first person for the rest of the story ... Angie's ... my story. But I have decided against that because this is also the story of Alice and George, Elizabeth, Hart, and Tyler, Paul and Fr. Mark, Martin Blatt and Dr. Zirdari, believers all. And Sarah's story. I do not forget that.

SATURDAY, OCTOBER 29, 11:30 A.M.

Angie opened her eyes. Alice Gordon got up from the chair in which she had been sitting.

"Angie," she said, "I know. I know what happened, and believe me, you can get through this."

"No," Angie replied, her voice rising. "No."

"Listen to me," Alice spoke firmly. "I know Tyler raped you, and I know he raped Sarah. He will not get away with this. There's DNA evidence from Sarah's rape."

"I won't ... I won't ..."

"You don't have to. But when you have time to think, you may want to."

"You don't know …"

"I know you met Sarah outside the library and went with her to her study carrel. What did you do with the meat hammer?"

Angie looked startled. "I threw it off the breakwater after … Oh God, after …"

"Don't tell me anything more," Alice said. "George Bush is getting you a very fine criminal lawyer. He should be here soon … with the police, I'm afraid. But believe me, Angie, we can get you through this. Your life does not have to be over."

"But all I wanted … I just wanted to go to graduate school. To become a professor … to be like Dr. Maryfield. To make a difference. I didn't mean … Sarah was angry; she pushed me. I saw this little funny hammer on the desk, and she grabbed it and swung around … I didn't …"

"Don't say more," Alice admonished. "I can believe there was a struggle. It may have been self-defence. There are a lot of possible defences. But we will, believe this, we will help you get through this."

MONDAY, OCTOBER 31, 8:30 A.M.

Amelie Zirdari looked coolly at Hart, who was sitting in one of the wingback chairs across from her antique oak desk. The chair was a comfortable one, but Hart did not look comfortable, and Amelie felt that was appropriate to the occasion.

"So both the murder and the rape are solved," Amelie commented. "And that poor young woman, Angie Maitland, will likely stand trial for the killing while your star student, Tyler Jenkins, may be on trial for rape. Not a pretty picture for the law school."

Hart spread his hands deprecatingly. "But solved with the assistance of your Campus Security officers and my faculty members," he added. "Not bad, really. Tragic, of course," he added hastily as Amelie frowned.

"I understand that Angie Maitland's parents are here, and one of your colleagues, George Bush, has retained a very fine graduate of your school, an expert in criminal law, to defend her. The papers think it might have been self-defence."

"At worst, it's a form of manslaughter," Hart continued, "but I'm not expert in criminal law."

Amelie shuffled the files on her desk and opened a thick one. "On another topic entirely, I have been reviewing your only promotion and tenure case this year."

Hart looked puzzled. "But our committee hasn't met yet to review the file," he said.

Amelie smiled. "Come on, Hart. You know that my office receives copies of the entire file. It guards against zealous and sympathetic committees just omitting one or two things. And I like to look ahead. To see what's coming down the pipe."

"Absolutely," Hart replied, "although I'm not sure our committee would be entirely pleased to think you may have," he paused, "prejudged?"

"No doubt you can find a committee to recommend promotion and tenure for anyone, Hart. I understand your—loyalty—to your faculty. But it's not making a prejudgement to review the hard facts of the case before the committee speaks. And I think I have to tell you now that there's nothing like enough in this file for promotion. I don't think there's enough for tenure."

Hart looked shocked. "But, Amelie, we don't want to lose Elizabeth. She's one of our …"

"I know," Amelie interrupted. "One of your cutting-edge researchers. Except she's not. Her book—the only substantial piece of work, I might add—is really nothing more than a collection of student work with some editorial comments by her. It's not enough, Hart."

"Amelie, Elizabeth's work focuses on community activism, on nurturing students to play a role in the fight for social justice and equality. I realize that this is a controversial area to count for scholarly credit, but you must let the committee of her peers judge that. Surely …"

"Hart," Amelie looked directly at him as he shifted awkwardly in his chair, "I'm telling you that there's not enough here. Now, there are a couple of ways we can handle this. Of course, Elizabeth is within her rights to proceed through the committee. I assume there will be a positive recommendation. There always is from the law school." She held up her hand as Hart looked about to speak and continued. "But alternatively, I can offer her a six-month paid leave to consider her position—do her research—and defer her application. And, well, if she looked for another job during those six months, who would blame her?"

"But, Amelie …"

"Hart, let me be candid. This mess in the law school …"

"But, Amelie, you're not tying this to Elizabeth, are you? She had nothing to do with the rape or the murder. Not really. She was pursuing the highest calling of equality and justice. You're not …"

"Hart," Amelie interrupted sharply. "One young woman is dead, and a second—well, if her life is not destroyed, it is certainly very badly damaged. I agree that Elizabeth bears no legal responsibility. But moral? That's another story. And don't tell me that any justice has been done here. I understand from Martin that Elizabeth tried to protect Tyler."

"She didn't know he was a rapist," Hart responded.

"She didn't want to believe he was one," Amelie corrected. "She had every bit as much information on Tyler as she had on Paul Anstel. But she was willing to believe in Mr. Anstel's guilt at once."

"But she knew Tyler."

"Yes, and those who knew him knew he was capable of violent and reckless behaviour. Didn't she guess he was involved in the disruption of the mass on Saturday?"

"Perhaps. But that was for social justice."

"That again. No, Hart. I'm an educator—a researcher, yes, but I wouldn't be in administration if I didn't care about our students. I won't tolerate them being turned into sacrifices on the altar of someone's conception of social justice. And let me be blunt: I won't support Dr. Maryfield's continuation as a tenured member of this university. I suppose if her research record had been impressive, I might have had no choice. But it's not. It's weak, and we will be better off without her.

"Now, I am going to leave this up to you to handle, Hart. Naturally, you will put this in a positive light for her—a six-month paid leave—beginning at once; a chance to spend time on her research; a chance, perhaps, to make a fresh start elsewhere; and, don't forget, a chance to avoid having her tenure application denied. And a denial of tenure by us will not help her re-establish herself elsewhere. No, the leave is very much in Dr. Maryfield's interests."

And, Hart thought to himself, in the interests of a Provost who would like to avoid as much publicity as possible. But he said, "Very well, Amelie. If you are convinced that it would be a mistake for Dr. Maryfield to proceed at this time with her tenure application, then, absolutely, I will convey that to her and advise her about the leave option. She may, however, be concerned about leaving her classes partway through the term."

"I'm sure you can handle that, Hart. What is she teaching this term?" Amelie looked at the file in front of her. "I see. Legal Ethics—I know that's a compulsory course, but you can find someone else, I'm sure, to pick that up—and Introductory Contracts law—well, aren't there two sections of that? You can put them together. Graduate seminar—surely someone can pick that up too, someone who doesn't have a heavy teaching load, although I know you don't give teaching credit for that. And her Feminist Legal Studies course. Yes, well, of course, it's your call, but I would suggest changing its designation to a Pass/Fail course and awarding all her students a Pass. In light of a professor leaving midterm, with these circumstances in mind, I'm sure the Senate would approve that change."

Hart nodded, already considering with part of his mind how to discuss this with Elizabeth. But in the other part of his mind was the immediate question: And what are you planning to do about me?

Amelie smiled. "Now, you must be wondering how I'm coming along in your performance assessment, Hart, especially since you need my recommendation to be considered for a second term as Dean. This mess, of course, has not helped. But if we can avoid major public scandal, and if we can handle the Dr. Maryfield issue tactfully, well, I think your term as Dean will have scored some success, despite major obstacles. However, for your second term, I would like to see a little more practicality in the law school and a few less theory classes. The President of the local bar association, and a major donor, has expressed some concern that many of the graduates he's seeing lack basic legal knowledge. I want to see a curriculum reform based upon the current requirements of the law societies, which will give students more options for substantive legal classes and more classes in necessary skills. Can I count on your support for this program?"

Hart nodded as he said, "Yes, absolutely."

MONDAY, OCTOBER 31, 9:45 A.M.

Elizabeth left Hart's office, slamming the door after herself. Hart's second assistant later described the scene to her friends as Elizabeth emerging from the door looking like a lioness who had just missed her antelope. "If she could've roared, she would've," Nancy said. "I just ducked into the file room and hid."

Elizabeth stormed down the hall and demanded boxes from the library technician on duty at the front desk. "I need at least a dozen. And have someone bring them down to my office immediately." She turned and walked rapidly to the elevators, where she punched the button for the office floor.

Alice heard the turmoil of banging file cabinets and books hitting the floor. She stepped out of her office and noted that Elizabeth's door was open, the noises certainly coming from there. Her more prudent colleagues seemed to either all be at classes or to have decided to close their doors against the storm. But Alice's curiosity was aroused, and she knocked on the frame of the open door.

"What's up?" she asked.

"I'm leaving," Elizabeth said, pausing for a moment from pulling books from her shelves and turning toward Alice. Alice could see the signs of recent tears, but Elizabeth's voice was angry. "That bastard, Hart, has, and I quote, 'advised' that I take a six-month paid leave. And it's pretty clear he means it to be a prelude to moving along."

Alice searched for words. "I'm—surprised to hear that. Do you want to talk about it? I thought we were considering your tenure and promotion application. The committee hasn't met yet, what with all the difficulties we've had in the last week or so, but …"

"Again I quote, I'm 'deferring my application, pending the completion of my leave.' So that saves you some work, at least."

Again, Alice was uncertain what to say. "I'm … sorry," she managed.

Elizabeth put down the stack of books she had been organizing for packing and turned to Alice.

"No, you're not," she said. "You and I have never hit it off, have we? I feel women need to support each other, care for each other. But you don't get it. The fundamental inequality of our sexist, capitalist, colonialist system never seems to faze you."

"We do see the world differently," Alice agreed.

"If you, or anyone else, seriously thinks …" Elizabeth paused again as she appeared to be choking back tears. "Seriously thinks that I wanted this terrible mess to happen … for Sarah to die or for Angie … or for Tyler … Tyler!" Again she stopped, turning back to her packing.

"I feel terrible about it. You can't know how I regret what I did and how it turned out," Elizabeth added. "But all I wanted to do was to expose the hatred and violence on our campus. If we don't theorize about it, if we don't expose it, if we can't destabilize the culture, we'll never, never have true equality."

"What is the point of this 'true equality'?" Alice asked. "Doesn't it always boil down to, 'all animals are equal, but some are more equal than others'?"

"You would drag out that old trope," Elizabeth sneered. "Of course, for now, there have to be some denials of equality. We can't tolerate those who spread hate."

"Like religious people or those who don't agree with you about what's good for them?"

"Exactly," Elizabeth responded. "The old idea that there are moral rules: who did that help, and who did it hurt? Some big fairy tale daddy in the sky? Somehow, the white, heterosexual males always came out ahead. Surprise! Surprise!"

"Elizabeth," Alice asked seriously, "don't you think that what happened—isn't the culture we are now producing on this campus at the root of a lot of suffering?"

Elizabeth turned back toward Alice. "What does suffering matter if future generations are free?"

"Free for what?" Alice asked.

"Free to be themselves. To define their own lives. Free from oppression and hate."

"There seems to be a lot of hate going around on this campus," Alice observed. "I don't see Tyler as exactly an icon of love and tolerance."

"Tyler was trying, in his own way, to bring about justice."

Alice exploded. "You cannot possibly defend what he did!"

"He was trying to destabilize the campus community. That phase always requires some sacrifices."

Alice looked in astonishment. "We really don't see the world at all the same way," she repeated. "It seems to me that your vaunted equality and justice are nothing but slavery to some other manipulative system, and one that produces more unhappiness and less true freedom than many religions do."

"You," Elizabeth said with emphasis, "are simply a dupe. You don't see how once we've brought down these institutions that serve white, male privilege, we will all be better. You and the rest of the sexist, homophobic right can keep on burying your heads in the sand. But we will win."

Elizabeth shrugged and continued, "In fact, we have won. Other institutions have more progressive leadership. I'll be looking for the right spot while I'm away. And I won't take any offer that doesn't come with tenure. I don't care about this backwater; let it rot. Simply because my students genuinely tried to tackle inequality and oppression. Well, this is my reward, I suppose."

"I suppose so," Alice said, turning away.

MONDAY, OCTOBER 31, 10:00 A.M.

Hart had drawn a long breath when Elizabeth finally left his office. It had not been a pleasant interview. She had a wide vocabulary of insulting names, and she had found many of them appropriate for him. However, he thought to himself, he had stood firm, and this was definitely for the best. Eventually, she had accepted that her choices were either acquiescence with the Provost's generous offer or embarrassment once her tenure and promotion application reached higher levels. She had threatened a fight from the union, but Hart, having expected that, had countered with the information that with negotiations for a new salary structure underway, the union was likely unwilling to take on a new case. Finally, he had played the academic card: Whatever the politics of the union or the administration, the fact was that compared to the publication record of other faculty who were up for tenure and promotion, hers was weak. She was unlikely to find an arbitrator who would disagree.

"Because I've spent all my time nurturing students and involved in community activism," she replied. But Hart had shrugged and responded, "I realize the standards are outdated, Elizabeth. Far be it from me to deny that. But they are still the current standards under our collective agreement, and, whatever the bias they express ... well, it is absolutely the case that your kinds of contribution are just not weighted very heavily."

Now Hart was prepared to have another meeting. And this one, he proposed to enjoy. An opportunity to put that pompous and self-righteous twit, George Bush, in his place was one he would seize with pleasure.

"Sit down, George, please," Hart smiled as he gestured to the chairs by his small boardroom table. "Thank you so much for sparing me a few minutes. It goes without saying how grateful I am to you and Alice for helping Martin discover what really happened to Sarah."

George took a chair. "Glad to help," he said. "But I do have a 10:30 class."

"Oh, I won't keep you that long. There's just been a development. Well, Elizabeth has decided to take a six-month leave to pursue her research. Well-deserved, of course, absolutely necessary for her to advance her thinking and have time to write."

George raised an eyebrow but nodded encouragingly.

"So," Hart continued, "she will be out of her classes, beginning today. And since you teach the other section of Introductory Contracts, I'm afraid we will have to roll the two sections together. Now," Hart held up his hand, "don't worry about the extra workload. Your Contract Drafting seminar next term can easily be cancelled at this point—the student enrolment is marginal, anyway—and I don't mind your having a light load next term to make up for the extra work of the double section." Hart smiled as if the satisfactory nature of this arrangement deserved congratulations.

"But, Hart," George protested, "I've been promised a small seminar class this year. I love teaching Contract Drafting, and it's one of the few skills courses we offer now …"

"I understand," Hart interrupted, "but I think you'll agree that we are in a bit of a crunch here, losing Elizabeth like this, so …"

"So, of course, I'll help," George sighed, "but next year …"

"Absolutely," Hart replied. "Absolutely next year."

George, who had fixed his eyes on the table while sacrificing his favourite part of his work, now looked directly at Hart.

"If Elizabeth is leaving, you'll need someone to take up her Legal Ethics class. I'm developing an interest in ethical issues, and …"

"No, no," Hart interrupted again, "you needn't worry about that. I've decided to pick up that class myself. I think a strong, progressive influence in ethical matters is essential for our students. I'll hope to carry on Elizabeth's work."

George found himself at a loss for words. The humour of the situation lightened his own disappointment. Sometimes the best one could hope for was not to take oneself too seriously.

"I see," George replied, unable to resist the temptation, "carrying on Elizabeth's work. Absolutely."

MONDAY, OCTOBER 31, 8:00 P.M.

George and Alice sat at their favourite table in their favourite pub. George had his draft beer, Alice her glass of red wine, and both had just placed an order for steak sandwiches and fries with the server, who was wearing black cat ears. It was Hallowe'en, after all. "To hell with the calories," George had summed up.

Alice provided George with a description of her meeting with Elizabeth. "So she's leaving," Alice concluded. "I think she's genuinely sorry for what happened, and maybe even a bit shocked at the results of what she started. But, in the end, she just stuffed that regret down and went back to her defence of Tyler. Mind you, there's no doubt that she really believes in what she's doing."

"No doubt," George replied. "It's one of the great fallacies of our age that what you believe in doesn't matter as long as you're sincere and authentic. Crap."

Alice nodded. "I'm beginning to think you're right. But things don't always turn out well for religious believers either, do they?"

"No, they don't. We are all fallible, and we all have times when we pursue our beliefs in the wrong way. But Elizabeth doesn't think there is a wrong way. That's part of what she believes, and that's a problem."

He continued, "Elizabeth's departure has had some fallout. Hart called me to his office today …" George repeated his conversation with the Dean.

Alice sipped her wine. "But, George, I'm furious!" she exclaimed. "How could you let yourself be treated like that? And Hart—teaching Legal Ethics!" Her voice rose louder. "He wouldn't recognize an ethic if it bit him!"

"Absolutely," George replied. "And don't forget he's going to be looking for someone to pick up Elizabeth's graduate seminar in research methods. There's no teaching credit given for that. Guess who I'll bet he has in mind, as a reward, of course, for your help!"

"How can you take this so lightly?"

"Because there's no point in arguing with him. And I'm not saying I wasn't deeply disappointed, but the humour of the scene couldn't help but strike me. I'm sure he enjoyed it, and for very different reasons, so did I. I'll keep pushing for next year, and maybe by then I'll have enough students that he won't have any excuse to cancel it. I have some ideas … but right now, I'm more concerned about making sure Angie gets competent help. Her mother and stepfather are being a wonderful support, and Fr. Mark is helping them. Angie's legal counsel tells me that the prosecutor isn't too keen on the case.

"They've finally got a statement from Angie, although it had to be under some sedation, since without it, she either sobs or lies staring at the ceiling. But with some patience, a young woman lawyer from her counsel's firm was able to support her in describing the scene. Since the statement is exculpatory, they've shared it with the police.

"Angie says that she intercepted Sarah just outside the library and asked to talk to her privately. They went into the carrel, and Sarah closed the door. Sarah had been drinking heavily—the coroner confirms that—and Angie says when she tried to explain to Sarah that

Elizabeth wanted to patch things up and go on with their important work, Sarah began to cry and flail about, pushing her and hitting at her. Angie was trying to back out of the carrel when Sarah picked up the meat hammer, swung it, and in the close quarters, narrowly missed Angie. Angie pulled it away from her but then stumbled over the chair leg, flung her arm out, and … well, it was all over in a couple of seconds.

"Angie was so distressed, the only thing she could think of was getting out of there. She threw the hammer into her sack and left. She says she didn't realize she'd locked the carrel door, although it's possible she didn't, and that Sarah might have pushed the lock button on it when they went in. Anyway, given no other evidence—and the forensic investigation is consistent with Angie's story, although it would also be consistent with other scenarios—Angie might plead to a lesser charge, and she might even be able to receive some form of probation. Right now, there's no question of her being released from hospital, and until that happens, the Crown is leaving her be."

"But she was so despondent at losing what she wanted so badly."

"I don't think graduate school is really what Angie is cut out for," George said. "I've looked at her record, and she's no star academically. And from a spiritual perspective, what she really wanted was to escape the life she was living here. She feels no one respects her and that she doesn't deserve respect. She's going to need a lot of help, whatever happens. Right now, I'm hoping that she'll recover enough to go home for a time, and perhaps someday, when whatever happens to her through the justice system is over, come back to law school—somewhere else, if not here—and finish her studies."

"As Sarah had hoped to do," Alice said sadly.

"Yes, and that tragedy can't be remedied."

They both sat silently for a time.

"And what about Tyler?" George asked Alice.

"From what I've heard, he's out on bail. Whatever happened to Angie that night is still a mystery. He claims there was consensual sex and nothing else, but that in the morning Angie fell apart after he had made some innocent comment about Sarah's murder, and she rushed from his apartment in tears."

"He didn't seem concerned enough about that to try to stop her," George said drily.

"No, but he says they were up half the night with drinking and sex and that he fell back asleep. Melissa's reported the key issue, and, to give her credit, Elizabeth did tell the police that Angie had accused Tyler of rape. I think she believes he did both rapes all right, but she is somehow managing to justify it as furthering the destabilizing of the society that has to come before reform. The police have arrested him and found Sarah's key in his apartment. But he says that he and Sarah were having a 'thing,' and that's why he had the key. He says he did have sex with her that night, and she was willing, so that accounts for the DNA. With Sarah dead, and unless Angie recovers enough and decides to tell her story, I'm not sure the cases will go very far."

"That story is full of holes," George said. "Why would Sarah be so terrified she needed a hammer for protection if she wasn't raped? Why would she accuse Paul if she knew she'd had sex with Tyler?"

"True," Alice replied. "Maybe the prosecutor will decide it's worth a try. Maybe Angie will decide to tell what really happened. I can't understand how Elizabeth can still think he's dedicated to social justice. Surely, if he raped Sarah and Angie to destabilize the campus, he'd admit it and take his penalty?"

"Not necessarily," George replied. "You're thinking of classic civil disobedience in which accepting the punishment is part of the moral statement. If, and it's a big 'if,' Tyler was acting as a dedicated revolutionary for progressive causes, it's the effect of his action he was seeking, not a moral statement, which he would have despised anyway as Western colonialism. I really can't say whether Tyler is a true believer or not. I'd bet not, but who knows? Worse things have been done in the name of revolution."

"But, still," Alice continued, changing the subject, "Hart had no right to treat you like that. If the Provost knew … what I hear from Martin is that the Provost is plenty annoyed at the lack of practical courses in the law school and the emphasis on theory courses that only push one approach."

"What does Martin have to do with that?"

"You know Martin and I used to be … close … after my divorce, and …" Alice paused, and George nodded. "Anyway, we still are friends to some extent, and after helping him with this case, he told me yesterday that he and Amelie Zirdari have been dating. So I think Martin's a pretty reliable source. Maybe I should tell him that Hart's idea of a practical course is to let you teach over one hundred students in one section and cancel one of the few practical courses we offer!

"At the moment, Martin says the Provost is likely to support Hart for another term as Dean." Alice paused as George took a large swig of his beer and rolled his eyes. "Exactly," she continued. "Maybe we should try to do something about that."

"Let me think about that," George replied. "Now, Hart's beliefs are mainly about what will be best for Hart. At least we can figure him out. And the next person our progressive colleagues dig up could well be worse. How's Paul doing now that this is over?"

"Pretty well," Alice replied. "He's moving into his new apartment this evening, and he thinks the privacy and peace will be wonderful after residence life. He's got a remarkable amount accomplished on his dissertation. I do think he'll be ready to defend next fall, or maybe even this summer. It's good progress. But do you think he'll throw it all up for the priesthood?"

George smiled. "Not if he thinks of it as 'throwing it all up.' But I don't have any insights there. Anyway, in the meantime, here are our dinners."

After the server had put down their meals and they had both sampled the fries, Alice began cautiously. "George, there is one thing I'd like to talk about … a personal matter." George looked up, his expression indicating she should continue.

"It's about us. This … relationship. I don't mean I don't value our time together. I do. And I don't mean I don't appreciate you far more than before this whole thing began, because that's true too. I have come to see you as a very kind, intelligent, and sensitive man who has far more to him than I had ever imagined. And I don't mean I want in any way to spend less time with you, but I wonder … I don't want …"

George picked up her sentence. "You don't want to be a substitute in my life for love and marriage," he said. "By your thinking, a poor substitute."

"That's not quite fair. I'm not thinking that I'm being used. But … I admit that I'm confused by this. I mean, surely the natural thing is to be looking for a relationship that involves …"

"Sex?"

"Well, yes."

George put down his fork. "Alice, one of the great difficulties I think we all share today is our inability to see love except in one form. Not that long ago, only a few generations back, love could take many forms. I don't mean to drag in religion, but the love of God and love of one's neighbour involved feelings and decisions that didn't involve sex."

"But 'love of one's neighbour' surely just means looking out for others. It's not 'love' in the real sense."

"I think past generations would disagree and say that there are a number of kinds of real 'love,' and that while all love has an emotional component, not all loves are the same: affection, friendship, erotic love, and love of God. C.S. Lewis called them 'the four loves.' And the love I think we share is friendship: a love that's very much neglected now, but can be very real. It's not a substitute for other kinds of love, but a real love in itself."

"I'm sorry, George. I'm afraid I'm too much affected by the modern context. But I apologize if I seemed to be belittling something that's important to you and that you've thought about so carefully."

"No, it's good to talk about this and to be honest with each other, as friends should be. I may be lacking in erotic love, now and maybe always, but affection, friendship, and the love of God are truly open to me, maybe in a way they wouldn't be if I were in a romantic relationship. And I want them to be important in my life because I believe they are truly as important as romantic or erotic love. And I want to be thankful for the gifts God has given me because He truly has given me much."

MONDAY, OCTOBER 31, 9:05 P.M.

Tyler sat in his apartment with a glass of his expensive scotch. There were Hallowe'en parties, but he was not in the mood. He'd called Suze Lu earlier, but she had hung up on him. The story that he was suspected of sexual assault had quickly spread. He told himself that he was not worried. His father had already hired an expensive Vancouver lawyer. Sarah was dead and could not be a witness; Angie, at least at the moment, was still in hospital and, so far as he could see, had said nothing. In any event, it would be his word against hers. She had killed Sarah. Who would believe anything she said about him? He had guessed she was the guilty one. He knew she had been trying to talk to Sarah, and her silence on whether she had done so made him suspicious. When he had told her in the morning that he was not a murderer, her reaction had confirmed it. She was in enough trouble now. And, he repeated to himself, who is more valuable: me or Angie?

He turned his mind to other things. Perhaps doing a clerkship with the court was not his best option. There was bound to be some suspicion about him even if, as he expected, the case closed and the charges were dropped. He had been arrested, and he would be asked about that. The judiciary was currently very sensitive about matters of sexual assault, having been frequently attacked for giving too little weight to women's reports. He could go to graduate school. Unlike Angie, he had the grades, and in the tough subjects as well as the seminar classes. Nothing wrong with being a professor, Tyler thought, although the pay was not as good as he would have expected in a big firm where he would naturally have gone after being a clerk in the court. But the work was easier, and there were plenty of sexy students as well as young faculty. One day, he could be a Dean, or maybe even a university President. Law Deans also sometimes received judicial appointments. By then, this would be long forgotten.

If graduate school was his goal, he would need faculty recommendations. Immediately, he wondered what Elizabeth Maryfield was doing tonight. He had received an email from the Dean that afternoon, informing all her students that she would be taking a research leave, effective immediately. Feminist Legal Studies students were advised that their course would be designated Pass/Fail, and that upon submission of a two-thousand-word essay summarizing their learning in the class to date, they would receive a Pass grade in the course. He was annoyed because Elizabeth would have been good for an A+, but he had already knocked off half the essay requirement. Again, he wondered what she was doing tonight. Possibly with Hart; rumour had certainly linked their names. But possibly not. She was a little old for his taste, but still …

He picked up his cellphone.

TUESDAY, NOVEMBER 1, 6:15 A.M.

Paul was awake in an instant. For a moment, he could not remember where he was. Then, in the dim ambient light through the venetian blinds of his bedroom, he remembered that he was in his new quarters. Because the apartment was empty, the previous tenant having left half-way through the month, the landlord had agreed to his move in on the last day of the month rather than waiting for the first, and without additional rent. Being happy to put the Dogwood Blooms motel and its memories behind him, Paul had completed his move in the early evening and had set up his bed before opening a beer and toasting his new living arrangement. Boxes still littered the living room, he knew. He wondered, briefly, what had woken him but could only hear the sound of his hot-air heater blowing into the room.

He remembered too that today was All Saints, and he had planned to attend an early mass. He prayed briefly as he lay in bed for Sarah's soul. Now that he was freed from suspicion, he would send a letter to her parents. He had not tried to contact them when they had come to take her home. He too had received the email informing students of Dr. Maryfield's leave, and he had been told to contact the Dean's office later in the week to confirm who would be taking over the seminar in Advanced Research Methods. He hoped it might be Professor Gordon.

His mind ranged from topic to topic as he tried to summon the energy to get up. One by one, he prayed for those in his thoughts: his parents, Sarah's parents, Professor Gordon, Professor Bush, Fr. Mark. He paused as his former roommate's name floated into consciousness. The meeting with Richard yesterday afternoon had been difficult. There was no avoiding it because Paul needed to retrieve his few larger possessions from Richard's living space, and Paul had no keys. He had borrowed Fr. Mark's car to pick up the bulk of his books, the rest of his clothes, some pictures he had left behind, and a small antique desk that his father had given him when he left home for university.

Richard had opened the door and stood awkwardly to one side as Paul entered. "Thanks for arranging the time," Paul had said.

"That's okay," Richard replied. "I should say ... I mean, I ought to tell you ... I'm glad to hear you're now in the clear. I know maybe I should have offered to have you move back, but ..."

"But we didn't get on that well, anyway," Paul added. "Don't worry about it. I've got a good place that I'm moving into, and I'm very happy with it. I think I can get some part-time work to cover some of the extra cost. There is one thing, though, that I'd like to ask."

Richard nodded.

"Why were you so certain I had raped Sarah?"

Richard looked away. "Hell, I don't know, except you were always so weird. And really unbelievable about your sex life. Did you really expect the rest of us to think you weren't having any? This is the twenty-first century. We don't have the hang-ups our parents had. We don't have to have babies, and we don't have to spin some fantasy about true love. It's just good fun—I mean, assuming everyone agrees. Either you were lying about women, or you liked men but lied about that too, or you had such a perverted mind, you could have done anything. I guess I should say I'm sorry. And I am sorry I misjudged you. But I can't take your moral prejudices; frankly, you're a bigot. And that's dangerous."

"Why am I a bigot? I don't think I ever tried to force you to agree with my sexual morality."

"Hey, it's pretty clear you don't approve of me or my friends. And your blatant adoption of a religion, which even you can't deny is homophobic, transphobic and racist … I mean, of course you're entitled to your private beliefs, but, man, it scares me to think of people like you influencing the law. Anyway, I was wrong on this one. But I'm not going to pretend I'm sorry you're moving out."

Paul had then gone into his former room with his boxes and, in an hour, was moving them into Fr. Mark's car. They had exchanged no further conversation.

After thinking over the scene and wondering whether he could have said anything that would have made a difference, Paul reluctantly prayed for Richard as well. After all, God had brought his name to mind; therefore, it was Paul's responsibility, at least, to pray.

Half an hour later, Paul was showered and unpacking boxes. He had found his coffee maker and his coffee. Breakfast would have to be eaten at the McDonalds down the street. He heard a knock on his door. Opening it, he saw Fr. Mark carrying take-out bags.

"Egg McMuffins," Fr. Mark said. "Got anywhere to put them?"

"Thanks, I was just thinking about breakfast."

"I thought you'd likely be up unpacking, so I took a chance. I've had breakfast, and I'm off to the campus office shortly, but I thought you might want to borrow my car later today for a major grocery shop. You can't live on McDonald's for long. I should be back here to do some paperwork around 4:00 p.m."

"Thanks again, Fr. Mark. I'm going to unpack for a couple of hours, catch the noon mass at St. Athanasius', and then go up to campus to meet Professor Gordon and check in about who's picking up the graduate seminar. But I'd also like some advice."

Fr. Mark perched on the nearest box. "Okay. What's up?"

"I'm not sure what I should do now. This … this whole thing has been a terrible strain. Looking back, I can see that I didn't pray when I should have; I didn't trust God when I needed to; I didn't exactly lose my faith, but I could see how I might. When things go, well … funny, everyone assumes that it's when things go terribly that people believe. But for me, it's when things are okay. I think the truth is that when things are bad, I have a hard time believing that God is there."

"You're not alone in that, Paul," Fr. Mark replied. "In fact, while it may be true that 'there are no atheists in foxholes,' that just means that desperate people try to bargain with any power that may be for their lives. It's not real, deep, and abiding faith. It may mature into that, but the kind of desperate pleading that phrase refers to is a natural reaction to fear. True faith is much more complicated.

"I know you're still thinking about a vocation," Fr. Mark continued, "so you put your faith under a microscope and blame yourself if it doesn't come across without flaws. But faith requires real, hard work. You must be prepared to believe, as St. Paul says in Romans 8:28, that 'all things work together for good for those who love God, who are called according to his purpose.' You need to abandon yourself to God, knowing that in the end, even if the end isn't in this life, the right and the true will win.

"And how, exactly, do you accomplish that? By God's grace and by giving thanks. St. Paul says to the believers in 1 Thessalonians 5:18 that they must 'give thanks in all circumstances; for this is the will of God in Christ Jesus for you.' I know you're thinking: This time, I escaped, but next time ... and you're right. Next time some crisis strikes, you may not escape. Not with your reputation, or your happiness, or your life. But keep giving thanks. And I know you're thinking: My faith is too weak. And you're right. But moaning about its weakness makes it weaker.

"My advice to you, Paul, is first to finish your PhD. Give thanks. Keep trying to learn to give thanks. Give thanks that you have faith in something that can help you seek the truly good. Think of those in this tragedy who only have faith in power and destruction. If you can learn that lesson, some good will have been wrought already. And in heaven, we can trust the one who suffered for us and suffers with us to make all things right again."

Paul heard Fr. Mark in silence. It was not the message he had hoped to hear. There was no blinding light on the road. There was no sense that the world had changed for him in that instant or that anything was clarified or settled. There was only recognition of a long and difficult path ahead to be travelled step by step, mistake by mistake, small victory by small victory, if he was lucky. Only a small piece of advice. Only a small voice in his soul that assented to that advice. For the first time since that morning when Richard had shouted him awake, Paul put his head in his hands and wept.

I know Paul wept because he told me. He wept for Sarah and the life she had lost, and he wept in acceptance of the burdens of daily life that those behind still had to carry. He visited me, of course. I say "of course" because it's the Christian thing to do, to extend forgiveness so that you can be forgiven.

George visited me too, as did Alice, every week or two for those long months I spent in prison. As might have been expected, I plea-bargained out. The prosecutor was not sure of being able to convince a jury that I had not acted in self-defence but was unwilling to settle for less than a sentence with jail time. We compromised on just over two years, but, as is usual, I did not serve nearly that long. Not that it was that bad: minimum security, maybe closer to a college dorm than a place for repentance and punishment. George and Alice became my friends. George started a blog discussing his ideas on culture and faith. It acquired a huge following, and eventually it was the basis for a book that has also been a best seller. Alice says it gives her hope. As I write this, they have remained close friends, and both, although in their seventies now, continue to teach at the law school part-time.

I never did go back to law school, as is likely obvious already. I think George may have been disappointed, but Alice understood. I didn't love the law. I certainly didn't love the law conceived of as a power struggle to mould society to one's beliefs. No, I wanted no more to do with that. And I didn't love the law the way Alice did: as a beautiful, technical artifact of a great tradition. It wasn't my thing at all. By the time I was really ready to think about my future, I was taking a course in creative writing through the prison, and my professor was helping me edit my stories for a collection. It was published two months after I "graduated" back into freedom. It sold well, as did my next book, and my next.

Alice says that this is good. Although Sarah's death was a tragedy, I was able to bring some good out of it. I tell her that's a lofty way to think about being a best-selling writer. It seems like trivializing Sarah's death, as if being a successful writer could in any way equate. But I suppose, had I decided to give up, I would simply have compounded the tragedy. I didn't. And that's the best I think I can look for.

My cottage is comfortable, and I live in it alone. After the horror with Tyler, I have never wanted a man in my life. But don't feel sorry for me. As George has said, erotic love is only one kind of love. There are others, and I have been blessed by them all. And I have the painful, ecstatic, boring, and glorious hours when all I see is my computer and the words I struggle to place on the page.

Tyler was not convicted, by the way. In fact, he didn't even have to face a trial. Sarah was dead, and without the complainant, the prosecutor wasn't willing to try. He did become a professor, but he didn't stick with it long. His father died a year after he got his first academic appointment and left him enough money that he didn't need a job anymore. He dropped out of sight. I suppose he's creating chaos somewhere half-way around the world. I never told the whole story of that night—never until now. No woman deserves rape. I wonder, however, if I believed that at the time. I wonder if I might have gotten away from Tyler if I had not been so overwhelmed with the need to be punished for my actions. When I realized he knew I must be the killer, I believed only my death could make reparation. Did he know that? Count on it? Perhaps.

Hart was reappointed as Dean, and as I have said, Alice and George survived his second term, although they tell me that it was only with the assistance of the scotch that George kept in his bottom desk drawer. He did become a judge, as he had wanted. Alice says his judgements are distinguished only for their political correctness. So far, he has not been elevated to the Court of Appeal. Elizabeth Maryfield accepted an appointment as an Associate Professor with tenure at a progressive American university only four months into her leave. As far as I know, she has still only published one book, the one that was in press when she was at the Ataskin law school. But her institution is dedicated to social justice, and therefore doesn't care about all that traditional stuff like publishing. She was promoted to the rank of professor last year.

Of course, Hart and Elizabeth are two of the reasons why this story will not be published for many years to come, not until all the major players, including me, are dead. Although I have not used anyone's real name, if I were to publish this now, it would be easy enough to look back ten years to 2017 and find out who was who. The dead cannot sue or be sued for libel, and anyway, why would I want to damage anyone further? No, I have done enough of that. And I have written this story primarily for me, although my writer's vanity hopes perhaps that someday there will be readers of it, if only to set the historical record straight.

Now that the story is told, truly told, even if still in secret, will I be able to write still? A prestigious university has offered me a post for a year as a writer-in-residence, teaching a seminar on the popular novel. I could still, with my roller bag, get on that airplane and sit in an office behind ivy-covered walls. It would be a break from writing. And I would have what I once wanted: respect without effort. But now I certainly could not fit into that small bag all I want to take with me from the life I have. I think I will say no.

Writing has been a way to stop the tragedy from spreading, and it has also been my punishment; strange that redemption and repentance, reparation and retribution should somehow all be present in the same act. And I think that cycle will continue, continue for my life long. I will keep telling this story under many guises and many veils, but it will not be the same story anymore. As I have written and lived through the past, I hope I have grown. And because every day, whatever I write, I know that I push back the dark a little further, and I struggle a little closer to the boundary of the country of the blind. One day, I will reach that border where the light is, and I will see.

Angie Maitland, Victoria, B.C., November 1, 2027.

Lightning Source UK Ltd.
Milton Keynes UK
UKHW011853060721
386748UK00007B/298/J